3 8538 00006 7418

W9-BMI-896

RIEFE, Barbara
Against all odds

S DATE DUE

35044

STOCKTON
Township Public Library
Stockton, IL

Books may be drawn for two weeks and renewed once.
A fine of five cents a library day shall be paid for each
book kept overtime

Borrower's card must be presented whenever a book
is taken. If card is lost a new one will be given for
payment of 25 cents

Each borrower must pay for damage to books

KEEP YOUR CARD IN THIS POCKET DEMCO

AGAINST ALL ODDS

The Lucy Scott Mitchum Story

Forge Books by Barbara Riefe

Against All Odds: The Lucy Scott Mitchum Story

THE IROQUOIS SERIES
The Woman Who Fell from the Sky
For Love of Two Eagles
Mohawk Woman

AGAINST ALL ODDS

The Lucy Scott Mitchum Story

BARBARA RIEFE

A Tom Doherty Associates Book /New York

AGAINST ALL ODDS: THE LUCY SCOTT
MITCHUM STORY

Copyright © 1997 by Barbara Riefe

This book is printed on acid-free paper.

A Forge Book
Published by Tom Doherty Associates, Inc.
175 Fifth Avenue
New York, NY 10010

Forge® is a registered trademark of Tom Doherty Associates, Inc.

Library of Congress Cataloging-in-Publication Data

Riefe, Barbara
    Against all odds : the Lucy Scott Mitchum story / by
Barbara Riefe.
        p.   cm.
    "A Tom Doherty Associates book."
    ISBN 0-312-86075-7
    1. Frontier and pioneer life—West (U.S.)—Fiction.
2. Overland journeys to the Pacific—Fiction. 3.
California—Gold discoveries—Fiction. 4. Women
pioneers—West (U.S.)—Fiction. I. Title.
PS3563.I3633A7   1997
813'.54—dc20   96-30589
                                                    CIP

First Edition: January 1997

Printed in the United States of America

0 9 8 7 6 5 4 3 2 1

This book is dedicated to
Rachel Dawson Riefe

And stepping westward seemed to be
A kind of heavenly destiny.

—William Wordsworth
Stepping Westward

1849

ONE

Lucy Scott Mitchum inspected the prairie schooner with a frown, a critical eye and no few misgivings. Renowned for their sturdiness, prairie schooners were the most popular vehicles selected by prospective emigrants crossing the Great Plains to Oregon, California and the Southwest. Such wagons sold for between sixty and ninety dollars. This one had cost Noah seventy dollars, his grin confirming his satisfaction with both purchase and price when he told her. Skeptical by nature, Lucy decided that only time would tell how reliable it would be. But it did look rickety.

Now, while Noah lay on his back inspecting the rear axle assembly and four-year-old Lynette sat playing with her doll on the hard, dry ground, Lucy ran a hand over the canvas bonnet painted with a combination of beeswax and linseed oil to waterproof it as she wondered how Noah, of all people, had gotten such a bargain. He had no gift for haggling; selling their house back in Baltimore to the first interested prospect, for at least four hundred dollars less than it was worth, proved that. Impulsive by nature, impatient with lengthy discourse over anything he was buying or selling, he had jumped at the wagon's price of seventy dollars when it was offered.

Why did it go so cheaply? Lucy poked, jiggled and

squinted closely at every part, every bolt. What was wrong
with it that couldn't be seen? The staging area at Council
Bluffs, Iowa, two-and-a-half miles east of the Missouri
River and opposite Omaha, displayed two other prairie
schooners, all that were left for sale, it being late in the year
to start the two-thousand-odd mile trek west. But this was
Noah's choice, his contribution to their comfort en route,
purchased without so much as a "what do you think?"

Of course she hadn't been around when he bought it,
being occupied with selling some of their furniture to get
the wagon load weight down to the advised twenty-five
hundred pound limit. The wagon wasn't old, wasn't new,
didn't threaten breakdown looking at it, but finding nothing
wrong failed to eliminate one suspicion: with so many emigrants departing from Council Bluffs since winter's end,
so many wagons purchased, why had this one been passed
up until Noah? Reaching the rear of the wagon, examining
the grease bucket hanging from the hook under the tailgate, she straightened and looked across the way. Herman
Schwimmer, wagon master of their train, returned her
wave. He started toward her, patting Lynette on the head as
he passed. About forty, heavyset, carrying an old man's
paunch, he was handsome in a rough-hewn way. He spoke
with a slight, purring-soft German accent, but was no foreigner. He had been to California twice, and knew the trails
and travails of the journey better than any of the other men
in the train.

Lucy lowered her voice when Schwimmer came up.
Lynette continued talking to her doll; Noah had moved to
the far side of the wagon, kneeling to check an iron tire. It
was his second inspection, he'd gone over every inch of the
wagon before handing the money over to the elderly previ-

ous owner, who, it turned out, owned most of the wagons that had been sold.

Schwimmer tipped his disreputable-looking hat. "Beautiful day, Missus Mitchum."

"Mmmmm, let's hope the rain holds off at least till we're across the river."

She beckoned Schwimmer closer to the wagon, lowering her head conspiratorially. "Herman, look over this wagon, tell me what you think. Your honest opinion, don't hold back."

Stepping back, he surveyed the wagon from grease bucket to tongue, then bent grunting over his belly to check the underside. He shook a wheel, kicked it, shook the reach and hounds under the middle of the wagon bed to test them for tightness, and stood up, red-faced with the effort. Noah came around; he and Schwimmer exchanged friendly nods.

"You mind my asking, Noah, how much she cost you?"

"Seventy dollars."

Lucy saw Schwimmer's reaction; he was impressed.

"You done yourself proud, Mister."

"I think so." Noah looked Lucy's way.

"She ain't new but she's tight. No cracks, good quality metal. Just be careful you don't overload her. What you getting to pull her?"

"I haven't decided yet," said Noah. "Not horses, of course. They're asking up to ninety dollars apiece for mules."

"You don't want mules."

"Why not?"

Schwimmer shook his too hairy head and bunched his chin in disapproval. "Get yourself oxen. They're slow as molasses in January, but they can take it, and won't stampede on you like mules or horses. And the Injuns don't generally steal oxen. Also, if you find yourselves up against it out in the desert they can be cut up for beef."

"How much?" Noah asked. Lucy could see him tense slightly; the savings they'd brought with them from Baltimore were dwindling; they certainly couldn't leave the jumping-off place flat broke.

"I wouldn't pay no more than fifty bucks a head," said Schwimmer. "You'll also need gear, yokes and suchlike, o' course. But that won't set you back much. If I was you I'd buy four yoke, although some folks get by on three. But be prepared to lose at least one yoke, likely two, before you get to where you're going. Your lead yoke is always the first to go."

"Why?" Noah asked. "They don't pull any harder than the others."

"It ain't the work, it's the alkali dust. The lead yoke protects the yokes behind, but it's them what gets the trail dust up their noses day in, day out. In a good blow, when the dust is really up, they can suffocate easy."

"I have extra muslin," said Lucy, "couldn't we cover their noses?"

Schwimmer laughed. "Make 'em look like Mex banditos? It's been tried, Missus, but they don't like their noses covered, poor dumb beasts; they'll shake it or snort it off." He looked over at the family equipage neatly collected with the canvas that covered it in bad weather folded on the ground near a chest of drawers. There were tools and extra parts for the wagon, including a spare wagon tongue, a wheel, two tires, heavy rope, chains, kingbolts and linchpins. Schwimmer walked over and began checking through the various items. He concentrated on the winches and pulleys. Then turned.

"You'll be needing extra oxshoes."

There was food in wooden boxes; flour, coffee, baking soda and the like in bags. Cooking utensils, tent supplies, weapons: among them a double-barreled, percussion-lock shotgun which Noah had yet to fire. He'd confessed that he'd never fired any type of gun. Lucy wondered: would his first target be an animal or an Indian?

In a battered oxhide-covered trunk were handy articles: liniments, bandages, a campstool, a chamber pot, a wash-bowl, three different types of lanterns, candle molds, a quantity of tallow and articles for sewing.

A large, deep box with a square of canvas in lieu of a lid tied around the top contained luxuries: canned foods, Noah's books, a few plant cuttings Lucy insisted on bring-ing, Lynette's dolls, the family album, Lucy's three pieces of jewelry and other things. The butter churn was huge. Schwimmer eyed it skeptically.

"One half the size would do just as good. And you sure got a lot of chests o' drawers."

"All our clothing, bedding, linens, extra blankets," said Lucy.

Schwimmer scratched his grizzled chin, made a face of apology and sighed. "You got more'n twenty-five hundred pounds; I mean counting you two at least a couple hundred over."

"What's a couple hundred?" said Noah.

"Them's famous last words, Noah. Even thirty pounds overweight can bust an axle. You best think about lighten-ing."

"We've already sold a perfectly good dining room table with matching chairs for a pittance of their worth," said Lucy, "and other things."

Schwimmer pointed. "How's about that big chest?"

"That's an armoire," said Lucy, "it's packed full."

"It'll take up half the wagon bed. Can't you unpack it, put everything in the nooks and crannies in the wagon? Get rid of all that wood weight. You two met the Willoughbys yet? Anson and Ruth from western New York. He brung along seven sheeted iron stoves. Seven. Each one weighing well over a hundred pounds. He had to sell six to get his load weight down. I can't tell you what to dump, I realize all this stuff is near and dear to your hearts else you wouldn't have lugged it all this way, but if I was you two I'd think serious about selling off that . . ."

"Armoire," said husband and wife.

"Whatever. Noah, what say we go look at oxen?"

Noah looked at Lucy as if asking permission. The two men walked off. Abigail Havers, a farmer's wife from Indiana, came over smiling a greeting.

"So you and Noah finally got yourselves a wagon. Looks sound and sturdy to me, though I know as much about wagons as I do about the moon."

Her pigeon gray hair was done up in a bun so tightly it seemed to Lucy to draw her face upward. Vigorous, sure-striding and eternally cheerful, Abigail had read every book, pamphlet and magazine article written about the westward trek; and was able to separate fact from fiction, reality from journalistic fantasy. As a wedge into discussion of the armoire Lucy mentioned Anson Willoughby's by now famous sheeted iron stoves.

"I saw him peddling them day before yesterday," said Abigail. "Poor man had tears in his eyes. How can anybody feel that way about a stove, for pity's sake? If he was a black-smith and they were anvils would he hug them all good-bye? He kept one; one too many if you ask me." She laughed. "Which nobody has."

"It'll come in handy, won't it?"

"Not on the trail. Out on the prairie the wind can blow the bark off a tree. A body can't keep any kind of stove lit."

"How do you cook?"

"Best way is a fire pit, a plain old hole scooped out of the ground, lined with buffalo chips."

"With what?"

"Dried droppings."

Lucy blanched slightly. Abigail tittered.

"When in Rome, dear heart. They burn better than any wood and they're all over the plains. There's stretches where wood is as scarce as hens' teeth. I see you don't have a stove."

"We had a first line Merit Sunshine with nickel trim," said Lucy wistfully. "We had to sell it and the icebox with the house."

Abigail picked up Lynette, talking baby-talk to her, getting little-girl talk in response. She put her back down with her doll. Abigail was childless; Lucy concluded that she couldn't bear children, for she obviously loved them enough to bring them into the world if she were able to. She cocked her head and hawkeyed Lucy.

"You're not exactly drowning in enthusiasm for this, are you? Not like Noah." Lucy shrugged. "Menfolk get fired up so easy."

"With Noah it was more like he was bitten."

"The gold bug, I know." She laid a friendly hand on Lucy's shoulder. "But not you. It's not easy, I know, dropping your life like an armful of kindling, your family and friends, packing up and moving clear across the country. I know women who refuse to do it. They put their foot down and it stays down."

"He's my husband, Abby."

Even as she heard her own words Lucy knew it was more than loyalty that made her agree to go west. Her father was a minister, and she'd been brought up imbued with a much stronger-than-average sense of duty. She could not persuade herself that Noah was a failure. Perhaps if she could all of this would be easier for her. Failure in one place is reason enough to move and start over in another. Failure or not, he was a good man and was entitled to change his direction in life. Baltimore had been a grinding struggle. She remembered the day he came home from work as excited as a small boy introduced to his first puppy. He'd come bursting into the parlor. She was finishing a cup of tea and reading to Lynette.

"Lucy, Lucy, look at this!"

He thrust a newspaper in front of her. The one-word headline covered the full width of the page.

"California?" Lucy frowned, puzzled.

"Ten letters that spell gold, my love. Gold! Lying around on the ground just waiting to be picked up."

"Like chestnuts."

"Read about it."

"Later, Noah, first let's talk."

He folded the paper, tossed it on the divan and cleared his throat, unable to conceal the sudden onset of nervousness.

"Let me start," she went on. "You want to go running out there."

"No, no, no, I want to talk, discuss it. I mean the possibility . . . the advisability of . . . of selling everything and . . ."

"Oh dear . . ."

"Please don't."

"What?"

"Start out throwing cold water. Be fair, it's not like deciding what to cook for supper. It's very involved, all sorts of aspects and angles, positives and negatives to be considered. We should discuss it."

"What's to discuss? What do I know about California?"

"What do I? I mean apart from what's in this article. What I do know is that thousands of people are leaving the East every day. Hundreds from Baltimore."

He sat beside her pouring tea into her cup. She had gotten up, gotten him his cup and saucer out of the corner cabinet. She poured his tea. He began stirring in sugar, stirring, stirring . . .

"Put California to one side, for the moment," he said. "Think about here, what we have, where we're heading, what the future holds . . ."

"We have security, stability, family, friends."

She stopped his stirring.

"Very well," he said, "let's take one thing at a time. What security? My job in the office at Eureka Printing? The rut I'm stuck in that's gotten so deep it's up around my ears?"

"You earn a steady salary. You put food on the table, clothes on our backs."

"All the while hating my job. I hate it, my darling."

"Noah."

"With a passion." She set down her cup and stared. He avoided looking directly at her. "I know, you had no idea. But it's the truth, I've always hated it. I never said anything, never brought how I feel home with me."

That was true, which only served to make this revelation quite a surprise.

"The only reason I'm telling you now is because for the first time I can see a chance to escape."

"You make Eureka sound like prison."

"It's my prison. I know, don't be so melodramatic. All right then, call it a dead end. And this . . ." He poked the newspaper. "This is a door at the side that leads out. You talk about security, stability, when have we ever had either here?"

"But we do."

"*If* we do, they're tenuous at best. Twelve years ago the depression hit and we're still feeling the effects. For years Eureka's been on the verge of closing its doors. One more fact of life I didn't bring home." He held up thumb and forefinger a quarter inch apart. "We've been that close a score of times. Why do you think I haven't gotten a raise in God knows how long? And there's Lynette—what's best for her. To bring her up in this pesthole risking typhoid fever, tuberculosis, God knows what. Breathing this foul air, drinking this sewage that passes for water. Out West the air is pure, you can actually see the sun, feel its warmth. There's so much soot and smoke here you can barely see the sky."

"Aren't you overlooking family? Friends?"

"We wouldn't be leaving the country. We can write; when we strike it rich we can come back for a visit; the folks can visit us. As for friends, we'll make new ones. Ask yourself this, how can ten thousand emigrants be wrong?"

"They may not be, but what they're looking for may not be for us."

"How will we know if we hold back? If we don't get up the gumption to try it?"

On he rambled; it began to sound as if he were trying as hard to convince himself as he was her. Still, she should keep an open mind, and it was neither easy nor would it be fair of her to dismiss the possible advantages of leaving: what they'd be getting away from, "escaping," he kept saying, as much as what they'd find upon arriving in California. He painted the future with uniformly beautiful colors and the present in varying shades of gray. She never knew him to be so persuasive about anything; of course he'd never before had inspiration quite so glowing, so promising. At least in his estimation. How she'd love to march down to that newspaper and give the whole staff what for!

"Please listen," he said. He went down on his knees in front of her, his hair tousled, his eyes widening by the minute, seizing her hands in her lap. He looked ready to propose. "I can go out first, scout the territory, get us a place, get established, prepare everything. Then come back for you two."

"No, dear."

"Why not?"

"If we go. If. It'll be the three of us. There'll be no sep-arating. That could be for years."

"It wouldn't."

"You don't know that, and what if, God forbid, some-thing should happen to you? Before you even reach there?"

"What could?"

"What couldn't? Wild Indians, highwaymen; everybody knows the riffraff of the country is rushing out there: thieves, escaped convicts, murderers."

"You think I'd fall in with anybody like that?"

"They could easily find you."

"You're making me sound like a wide-eyed gull with money sticking out of every pocket."

"Hardly."

"I'm just naive, is that it?" He sighed in exasperation.

"Are we going to start arguing? Look, why don't we just put it aside for now. Regroup and have at it again later. Give me time to think about it; at the moment I'm feeling bowled over."

"I know, I know, but you know me; I get an idea and out it jumps."

Lucy patted his cheek, nodded, sipped and while he ran on about gold and California and a future as rosy as dawn over Chesapeake Bay she looked around the parlor at the few treasured acquisitions of married life. And thought of the house surrounding them. It wasn't regal, it wasn't much. But it was home.

She walked with Abigail and Lynette thinking about the armoire, how she'd have to give it up, having already part-ed with the table and chairs. How many more pieces of the past would have to be sacrificed in order to fit what remained into the ten-by-four wagon bed?

"If men only knew how hard this is on a woman," said Abigail. "They change their lives as easy as they change shirts; to a woman it's like changing her skin."

An accurate analogy. Only why was that? Because women never did catch the fire of enthusiasm? Because men were pulled west?

"Women have to be pushed," murmured Lucy.

"What?" Abigail asked.

"Nothing. Nothing important."

"You seem a little homesick already."

"I miss my parents, my sister, my friends, but I don't lie awake nights brooding about it. I'm really trying to keep my eyes on the horizon."

"That's the spirit."

"At the risk of sounding smug and self-satisfied, I don't worry about myself."

"Or Lynette, I'm sure."

"Noah's a fine man, Abby: a good husband and father, not lazy or shiftless. He's honest, I respect him for a dozen traits of character. But all this is so different from anything he's every attempted that it worries me. It's not his game."

" 'Game'?"

"He's not cut out for it. I look at your husband, Herman Schwimmer, Anson Willoughby, they seem so adaptable to emigrating. Handy, resourceful, they know which end the ox's head is on. And practical. Noah's the furthest thing from practical; he's almost wildly imaginative, head in the clouds, impetuous, absolutely brilliant out of any book. But that's not what's needed, and what is he's woefully short on. You know, when the wagon bogs down in a torrential downpour, a wheel breaks, an ox dies or Indians come whooping out of the trees, he'll be lost. We've a gun he hasn't even fired yet. He's never fired *any* kind of gun."

"How does he know the one he bought works?"

"The man who sold it to him in Baltimore said it does." Lucy laughed mirthlessly. "I must sound terrible: disloyal, complaining, cowardly. I don't mean to . . . "

"You don't think he'll be up to protecting you two out there."

"Oh Noah's no coward, he'll do his best, he always does. But honest effort and good intentions don't always get the horse shod."

"Ah . . ." Abigail put her arm around Lucy and hugged her. "That's where the wagon train comes in. Everybody helps out everybody else. Just you watch, one way or another he'll contribute. Who knows? He may turn out to have a way with oxen like Saint Francis of Assisi had with all God's creatures."

"Maybe. He at least deserves the benefit of doubt."

"Don't doubt, Lucy, keep an open mind. We're all in this together, we'll all come out of it bright and shining together."

"That's another thing, all of you are going on to Oregon; we're going over the mountains to California. We'll reach a point where we'll have to split up."

"At a place called Pacific Springs, I hear."

"How far from here?"

"I'd have to ask Mr. Havers. I'd guess a little over half-way. Why don't you ask Herman Schwimmer."

"Where's not important, just that eventually we'll be parting company. Putting us on our own."

"Ah, but by then you'll be seasoned travelers. You'll have met your first Indians, run from your first buffalo stampede and enjoyed dozens of other novel experiences."

" 'Novel,' I like that."

"Cheer up, dear heart, by early October you'll be home."

" 'Home.' "

They could see Noah and Herman Schwimmer coming back leading three pair of oxen and carrying yokes, rope and a whip. Lynette ran to her father. Noah and Schwimmer were talking spiritedly and laughing; Noah looked to be enjoying himself in another man's company . . . a rarity. Lucy's conscience twinged as she watched the two of them. *Was* she shortchanging him? If that was how she actually felt about the situation she would have to hide it from the others. To them it would look terrible. She could think of no worse humiliation for Noah.

But would it all turn out too much for him to handle? Or would he grow into this new shirt of his?

TWO

Rain fell heavily throughout the night. Before dawn the staging area had been reduced to a quagmire. The downpour tested the wagon bonnet, but the leaks that showed were mercifully few in number; when the rain finally stopped Lucy sewed up the holes and, at Abigail's suggestion, sewed four pockets, two on each side, for extra storage space. Fortunately, everything the Mitchums owned fit into the wagon and was loaded before the rain struck.

Everything fit except the armoire.

Lucy sat looking out the rear of the wagon while Noah and Lynette slept on piles of bedding transferred from the armoire before it was sold, for about a third of its value. A disheartening thought came to Lucy, that at some point ahead, in a desert or in mountains when the oxen weakened to a point where a night's sleep failed to restore their energy, other possessions, maybe even more furniture, would have to be jettisoned. So much left behind already, so many pieces of their lives, so little retained with which to start a new life once arrived. She set a hand on a small barrel snugged in a corner against the tailgate. Filled with cornmeal, it was packed with eggs; as the eggs were used up the meal would be used to make bread. This would help lessen weight and increase the amount of open space when bad weather forced them to sleep inside the wagon.

She watched until the rain let up and the sky began brightening, then loosened the bonnet pucker rope letting in the day. She got down from the wagon, slipping and sliding in the mud, and looked about. There'd be no finding a dry spot to build a breakfast fire. The only dirt that wasn't mud was under the wagon, and without the oxen yoked up there was no way she could move the vehicle forward or backward. This once they'd have to do without coffee to start the day, although back home Noah hated walking out the door without at least one cup to warm his breakfast. At that, was it missing his coffee or going to work that made him grouchy?

Father and daughter woke up at the same time. Five wagons were to comprise the train; a small train, considering that previous trains fifty and sixty wagons long had left from this very jumping-off place. But that was weeks before. Everybody knew that they were starting late, but it didn't seem to worry the men. The Havers, the Willoughbys and others were up and about. Herman Schwimmer helped Noah yoke the oxen while Lucy prepared breakfast, invited by Marcia Talley to share the fire she'd managed to build. Marcia was a young schoolteacher from Boston who was traveling with the Coombs. Sarah Coombs had three children, one of them a few months younger than Lynette. Lucy had met and spoken with Sarah only briefly two days before; and come away with the impression that she was quite neurotic, perhaps even unstable, with a "tendency toward shrieky," as her mother would have described it. Sarah's husband was a farmer and lay preacher; they were from Ohio.

Breakfast for the Mitchums was eggs, a small portion of their precious bacon, milk for Lynette from the Willoughby's cow and coffee.

"Enjoy the coffee while you can," advised Abigail, who stopped by the fire to chat. "Once we're out on the plains the water'll taste so bitter from alkali your coffee'll likely crack your teeth before you can get it down your gullet."

The sun had cleared the horizon when the train started out, with the Schwimmer wagon in the lead and the

Coombs' wagon in the rear. Noah and Lucy's wagon and worldly goods took the next to the last place in line. By the time the train had covered the less than three miles to the Missouri River, with Omaha rising on the opposite bank, the sun had vanished, the skies assumed a leaden look and the rain resumed. A deluge. In the midst of it the wheels had to be removed from the wagons and the wagons themselves carried across the river on two flatboats. A battle every foot of the way against the turbulent water. The flatboats were attached by pulleys to ropes stretched across the river to prevent their being carried downstream, but even with the men and the flatboat workers poling with all their strength both boats landed far down the opposite bank. Ropes were tied to the horns of the oxen to help them cross against the current; it was touch and go until the last beast scrambled up the other side.

Hammered by the rain, the men worked feverishly to refit the wheels to the wagons. The dismal weather and the backbreaking labor failed to discourage Noah. The wheels in place, he mounted the seat above the jockey box, picked up the reins, slapped the rear oxens' rumps and grinned broadly as the rain dripped off the brim of his hat and plopped in his lap. Proud of him and telling him so, Lucy joined him on the seat as off they rolled, starting the gradual ascent to the elevated river terrace on which Omaha perched.

"Sacramento Valley here we come, love!"

Lucy leaned forward, sticking her head out from under the bonnet to scan the skies; and got a face full of wind-tossed rain for her daring. He laughed as she wiped her face.

"And will we be able to unpack before we have to start picking up the gold?"

"O ye of little faith . . ."

She laughed gaily. The quote from Matthew prompted her to try and recall where she'd packed the Bible. Everything they owned had been moved around so since Baltimore that finding anything specific threatened to take hours.

And so it would be for the next four-and-a-half to five months.

═══════════════ THREE ═══════════════

Crossed the Missouri in a downpour like a barrel tipped upside down. The first test of our mettle? Noah's enthusiasm shows no signs of flagging. More power to him; I've never seen him slave so, and all the while still learning the ropes of westering. Lynette seems to be enjoying the journey. Still I worry; she's not a robust child, and very fair, she'll need constant protection from the sun, if it ever comes out. We're told it can be brutal. Will she be up to the rigors ahead? What do we do for a doctor if she takes ill? Abby Havers, a dear, sweet woman, seems to know as much if not more of what we'll be in for as does Herman Schwimmer. She doesn't harp on the dangers any more than he does, but dangers there are, lurking like phantoms around every turn.

The rain, fierce as it was, does keep down the dust, which, according to Abby, can be savage. The oxen are out of their yokes and have been fed and watered. They seem to be bearing up well. As for our companions, we seem to have a fine group. Sarah Coombs worries us, she seems to drift in and out of clarity. Sometimes

makes no sense whatsoever. Noah saw her babbling to
her oldest boy about the stars, of all things. He just
stood listening as if used to it. Will Sarah be able to
stand it when the going gets really rugged? I get the
impression, just one slender thread is all that's left for
her to hang onto sanity.

Getting to know Marcia Talley, who came and rode
in our wagon until nightfall. She's a schoolteacher and
as I, too, aspired to teach at one time we've a good deal
to talk about. She's riding with the Coombs and is very
worried about Sarah. Marcia's fun, vivacious, outgoing;
by the time we part company, we'll be the best of
friends, I'm sure. I wish we could go on to Oregon, but
I'd never suggest it to Noah. The stars would go out of
his eyes quick as a wink.

Marcia can't wait to get to Oregon. Teachers are
badly needed there as they are all over the West. She's
not short on gumption, I mean to move so far from home
all by herself.

After supper tonight I tried to wash clothes in the
Platte River, but it was much too muddy. One could
almost wish for the rains to resume. I'd lay our dirty
clothes on top of the bonnet. The land on both sides of
the Platte is covered with short grass but no trees; unre-
lieved barrenness. As I write this the wagons have been
drawn up in a circle, what Mr. Schwimmer calls a cor-
ral. They will be every night, with the animals inside; a
tight fit; with only five wagons, the circle being quite
small. It's protection against Indians, as we are starting
across their hunting grounds. We're between the war-
like Pawnees to the north and the Cheyennes to the
south. No one seems particularly worried. Until some-

body pipes up with a horror story about stealing, scalp-
ing and worse.

Lucy yawned, stuck her pencil in her hair and closed her diary. Climbing down from the wagon, she joined Noah and Lynette in their tent. She fell asleep almost immediately, despite the screaming, half-naked Indians brandishing tomahawks and shooting arrows running through her head.

The train moved south of the Platte toward Fort Kearny, some two hundred miles distant. There they would be stopping to rest and provision for the much longer leg to Fort Laramie, in Wyoming Territory. Lucy had taken to living in a hoopless, straight-skirted cotton dress, apron and kerchief, disdaining the slat bonnet worn by Abigail Havers, Ruth Willoughby and the other women, save for Marcia Talley. As yet they had seen neither Indians nor buffalo, nothing but endless barrenness clear to the horizon and the shallow, eternally silty, slowly moving river, its waters of no use for washing, drinking or cooking, thanks to its high alkali content in addition to the mud.

The slow pace of travel, the tension mounting daily in every heart, as the emigrants kept their eyes out for Indians, encouraged nervous exhaustion that added to physical exhaustion and made the onset of darkness, tent and blankets most welcome. So tired did Lucy become she had to force herself to write in her diary.

On the seventh day since departing Council Bluffs Lynette awoke coughing and feverish. An onion mashed in sugar proved efficacious as cough syrup and prevented sore throat; but Lucy didn't know what to do about her fever. Abigail Havers came to the rescue with a homemade liniment, a combination of goose grease and turpentine which she liberally rubbed on Lynette's throat, chest and stomach.

The concoction smelled foul and the odor filled the back of the wagon, but the dosage eventually brought down the patient's fever. Lucy ordered Lynette to nap as they rolled along, but the trail was badly rutted and the wagon bounced and jolted so it was impossible for her to fall asleep.

Graves, some marked by weather-beaten boards, others mere mounds, still others displaying skeletal remains in open holes, were continually seen on both sides of the way.

"It's like traveling through the world's longest cemetery," commented Lucy. "It makes you wonder if anybody gets to where they're going."

"Most have," said Noah. "They're streaming into California."

"Getting there first, picking up your gold."

He laughed good-naturedly. Marcia Talley was back riding with the Coombs for the day. Noah and Lucy rode on in silence for a time. Then she noticed his worried look.

"What's the matter?"

"Anson Willoughby. One of his oxen's gone lame; it happened while you were back inside tending to Lynette. Anson had to free it from the yoke along with its healthy partner. He tethered both behind. He rubbed the limb with horse liniment but it doesn't seem to help. What the ox really needs is rest, but we have to keep going."

"He certainly can't leave the poor creature."

"He doesn't intend to. It'll just have to limp along until it's healed."

Other problems cropped up. The next day, the second Saturday since departing Council Bluffs, threatened another deluge when it began thundering just after sunup. The skies turned black and the wind began gusting but no rain fell, although the thunder persisted. Late in the day the wind came up in earnest, blowing so hard no one could get

a fire going for supper. It was impossible to pitch a tent and
wagons shuddered and shook, threatening to topple. Every
pucker rope was secured as tightly as possible to keep loose
articles from blowing out of the wagons. Sarah Coombs'
oldest boy lost his hat in the river.

On Sunday morning Olin Coombs assembled the emigrants and conducted worship service with the wind howling so he could scarcely make himself heard. The train set
out, the oxen all but blinded by the swirling sand, lowing
continuously in protest. The landscape continued uniformly barren, studded with creosote bushes and sagebrush. Too
weary to write in her diary the night before, Lucy opened it
and read what she'd written two nights ago. She and
Lynette sat with their backs to Noah; he had covered his
face with a bandana against the swirling sand. Lynette was
much improved. Lucy wrote.

*Why we keep going under such conditions is a mystery
to me. The oxen don't want to, nor do any of the other
animals. Out here Sunday is no day of rest; it's so late
in the year we'd be foolhardy to waste it in such fashion, according to Herman Schwimmer. It may sound
irreverent to some, but they're not here. First and fore-
most in everyone's mind is keep moving, keep moving.*

*Schwimmer wonders why we haven't seen any
Indians as yet. I can't help feeling they're seeing us,
watching us. We're still in Pawnee territory, and,
according to Schwimmer, and Abby agrees from what
she's read, the tribe is as bloodthirsty as any in the
West. As I noted before we're continually passing graves
of poor souls who tried and failed to make it across the
Great Plains, but whether they died of illness, as
Schwimmer contends is likely, or at the hands of sav-*

ages, is impossible to know. The Pawnees are tradition-
al enemies of the Sioux to the north. Lord help us if the
two decide to battle each other while we're passing
through!

It wasn't until late Sunday afternoon before the wind died
to a breeze and the oxen, delivered of their discomfort,
ceased lowing. Anson Willoughby's injured ox was still
limping; as a result his two healthy yoke had to work that
much harder to keep up with the other wagons. Fortunately,
it was level going for miles on end. When the train stopped
for the day Lucy got down and walked forward to the
Havers' wagon to thank Abigail for bringing Lynette's fever
down.

Abigail greeted her as she got down from the driver's
seat. And stepped on a snake. It hissed, coiled and reared,
showing its hideous fangs. Lucy screamed; but before it
could strike a pistol sounded, killing it. Herman
Schwimmer came up blowing the smoke from the muzzle of
his weapon. Abigail leaned against the wheel clutching her
heart and gasping, her eyes protruding.

"Best look before you come down, Missus Havers," said
Schwimmer quietly and continued walking down the line of
wagons.

"Thank you, thank you, bless my soul." Abigail managed a weak grin. "Now there's something I don't remember reading about in any magazine or newspaper."

Screaming was heard coming from the Coombs' wagon
at the end of the train; Lucy and Abigail ran back with the
others. Nancy, the Coombs' seven-year-old, had fallen out
of the wagon. She lay on the ground writhing in pain and
bawling loudly. She'd broken an arm. Together Lucy and
Abigail managed to set, splint and bandage it, while the

child's mother fell apart completely. She carried on so she visibly embarrassed Olin; mumbling apology, he hurried her back inside the wagon and tried to calm her.

That evening Marcia Talley confided to Lucy that she felt ill.

"Inflammation of the bowels . . . I don't think it's serious, just painful."

Lucy found Abigail, who produced a small bottle from among scores of others in a nail-studded oak box.

"It's homemade from Solomon's Seal. You're to take one teaspoonful three times a day in a glass of something, preferably wine."

Marcia grinned. "I'm afraid I didn't have room to bring my wine cellar."

"Water'll do," said Abigail.

"Lucy," said Marcia, "would you mind if I ride with you and Noah?"

"Mind? We'd love the company."

"It must sound cowardly of me but I can't help feeling . . ."

"It's being so close to Sarah, isn't it?" said Abigail.

Marcia nodded. "The poor thing is getting worse by the hour. Babbling to herself, deaf to everyone. I'm afraid what just happened to Nancy will cause her to snap completely. I'm just in the way back there. I try to talk to her and she looks right through me. And her eyes are scary."

"I don't understand Olin," snapped Abigail. "How can he put her through this in her condition? What possessed him to start out? She should be in a hospital!"

"Shhhh," whispered Lucy. "I'll go back and see how she's doing."

"Marcia just told you 'how she's doing'!" Abigail sighed. "I'm sorry, Lucy, I don't mean to snap. It's just that that man riles me so. I'll go back and talk to her. Let's just pray that Nancy's accident has the reverse effect."

"What do you mean?" Marcia asked.

"That it turns out good for Sarah, not bad. The child needs her mother's care and attention; maybe concentrating on nursing Nancy will get Sarah out of herself."

Marcia's eyes told Lucy that this was a far-fetched hope. Lucy agreed. Her aunt Lillian, Daddy's oldest sister, had carried on much the same way before going insane; she'd thrown herself off a roof. Abigail put her hands together in an attitude of prayer, shook her head grimly and set out for the Coombs' wagon. She spent a full hour with Sarah, but came back shaking her head.

"It's like talking to a stump," she said to Lucy and Marcia.

The oxen were showing signs of tiring. Schwimmer blamed the prolonged storm, or "sandstorm," as he called it.

"They should all recover, but until they do we'll have to slow the pace." He had summoned the emigrants together, with only Olin and Sarah Coombs absent. "Up to now we've been covering twenty to twenty-five miles a day. We'll have to cut it down to fifteen at best. Luckily, Fort Kearny is just up the way."

A cheer went up; he silenced his listeners.

"Barring bad weather, redskins or the need to detour, we should reach there sometime late day after tomorrow. The plan is to lay over at least one full day. Give the beasts a good rest. And us."

Another cheer; Maynard Havers got out his harmonica and played "Open Thy Lattice, Love." The emigrants immediately seized the spirit of the occasion. The music, singing and dancing went on until most were unable to keep their eyes open.

Lucy thought it was beautiful to see this little knot of brave souls out in the middle of nowhere striving to find enjoyment and relaxation in the midst of the most arduous, most dangerous journey any one of them would ever undertake. For a precious hour all worry, all tension, was shrugged off and happiness reigned.

That night Lucy blinked away sleep to write a brief entry in her diary. She found it hard to concentrate; Sarah Coombs' face appeared fixed to the screen of her imagination. She felt so helpless. . . . All of them did. Sarah was doing more and more poorly with every passing day.

FOUR

Shouting woke Lucy from a sound sleep. Emerging from the tent she found everybody else staring at a wild-eyed Olin Coombs, who was running up and down the side of his wagon in his underwear. He clutched Nancy to him while her sister Melinda cried and her older brother Clarence stood staring, looking stunned.

"She's gone, she's gone!" exclaimed Olin.

Abigail came up to Lucy. "I knew it. . . ."

"Did she give any hint when you talked to her?"

"I told you I couldn't get a word out of her. Like Marcia said."

The men approached the distraught Olin, who finally got control and command of his voice.

"I woke up, she wasn't there. I looked outside the corral, you can see miles in every direction, there's no sign of her."

Abigail succeeded in getting both girls to quiet down. Tears streamed down Olin's pink-splotched cheeks. Noah put an arm around his shoulders comfortingly while Marcia took both girls aside and talked to them.

"A couple of us'll stay with them," said Abigail to Herman Schwimmer.

The wagon master organized a search; the men fanned out in all directions except north, reasoning that Sarah wouldn't attempt to cross the river. It was shallow and fordable, but the water was filthy and she was one of the cleanest individuals Lucy had ever seen. The interior of the family's wagon was spotless and neat, as were the children. She had never seen Sarah with so much as a hair out of place, despite her problems.

After upwards of two hours searching with no sign of her, the men returned.

"She must have crossed over after all," said Maynard Havers.

Others nodded. Olin stepped forward. "She didn't," he murmured. "I've thought it all out. I know what happened. She walked into the water, laid down and drowned herself deliberate."

Everyone gasped.

"You don't know that," said Schwimmer.

"I know my Sarah. Look down a ways, maybe even as far as half a mile. Sooner or later her body had to have snagged on a rock or maybe just washed ashore." He pointed downriver.

"He could be right," murmured Anson Willoughby.

He was.

Sarah lay half in the water about a quarter mile east of the camp. Olin ran up and dropped to his knees beside her body, covering his face, weeping softly. Lucy stared down at Sarah's face when they turned her over and was struck by her placid expression. In death she had found the peace that

eluded her. They carried her body back to camp.
Schwimmer proposed that the grave be dug in the middle of
the trail.

Olin protested. "There'll be no marker . . ."

"You don't want to mark it," Schwimmer said. "You've
seen. Most graves we've passed, especially around here,
have been dug up."

"A lot more ain't," muttered Havers.

"It's the redskins," Schwimmer went on. "Most graves
we've passed are no more than two or three feet deep. They
dig 'em up and steal the corpses' clothes. You sure don't
want that for your missus, Reverend."

Olin shook his head.

"Let's start to digging."

Olin delivered the eulogy. It was midmorning by the
time the train was ready to roll on. The men gathered
around Olin and his children; all were dry-eyed except
Nancy, who whimpered softly while burying her head in her
father's embrace.

"You decide what you're going to do?" Schwimmer
asked him.

"We're going on. Sarah would want us to. There's sure
nothing in Good Hope for to go back to. When we left
Ohio we promised the good Lord we'd keep going till
Oregon, whatever happened. Even this. It won't be much of
a life without Sarah and won't be easy—what with the
young-uns and all—but with the good Lord's help we'll
manage. And whatever's in front of us it's got to turn out a
better life than Good Hope."

He surveyed the gathering, his eyes misty. Lucy's heart
tugged so she had to look away. Noah squeezed her hand.

"A pity none of you good folks really got to know my
Sarah. Even you, Miss Talley, I mean before Sarah's mind

started abusing her. That woman was the salt of the earth. She give birth to all three young-uns all by herself, no doctor, no midwife, not even me around. She worked her fingers to the bone she did, to make us a happy family, poor as church mice though we was. But happy, so happy . . .

"Some of you may think it downright simpleminded of me to bring her west, it being such a hard journey, but it was her idea, what she wanted. And what she wanted I gave her, if it was in my power to. Now she lies in Abraham's bosom, my Sarah, my wife. And the four of us are alone. But if you folks don't mind we'll stick with you till Oregon. I promise we won't none of us be a burden."

There were tears in Lucy's eyes as she climbed up onto the driver's seat alongside Noah. In her heart she was certain it was the daily hardships, aggravated by Nancy's accident, that had pushed Sarah Coombs over the edge into self-destruction. A pity she didn't have a sister or some other female relative to share her problems with.

Even this early in the journey Lucy sensed she was getting a clear picture of the different way men and women approached emigration. Night compared to day was not as different. That the men looked forward while the women looked back all but went without saying. Even before Council Bluffs she could see that; she didn't need Abigail Havers to point it out. Men argued, competed, carried on boisterously, exercised their bravado, looked forward eagerly to hunting, to shooting Indians—in short engaging in all the things that allowed them to show off their manhood. Did they fear it might be questioned? Even Noah had taken on a different persona since leaving Council Bluffs. His voice sounded lower, his walk had taken on a slight swagger, he laughed a little too loud, he was constantly fussing with the oxen or the wheels or the brake or other parts of the wagon, as if to demonstrate his newly acquired trail skills for her and Marcia Talley's benefit. He had even taken to practice-shooting his shotgun. He tried to shoot a jackrabbit three days before, missing it by a wide margin, which didn't embarrass him. He insisted practice would help improve his aim and in time he'd become expert.

So the men played manly while the women, as to be expected, concerned themselves with family. Unlike the men, they did not see emigration in the clear light of expected success. Uppermost in the women's minds was survival. Less visionary, but decidedly more practical.

Noah's exaggerated optimism only diluted Lucy's expectations, although he wasn't aware of it. As to the Indians, the men saw them as enemies even before seeing them; the women saw them as helpful guides, despite their innate fear of them. To the women the most dreaded enemies of the trail were disease and accident. And unlike their men, out of the harshness of the life, out of the daily disorder of traveling, the women created and held onto order and routine as their anchors of self-possession.

"Doesn't all this just . . . just charge you with expectation?" burst Noah. "Make you want to see what's around the next bend, what's on the other side of the next hill?"

"Not really."

Lynette sat between them. Lucy had shown her how to make a cat's cradle; now Lynette's little fingers were all of a tangle with string. Lucy helped her free herself.

"It does me," asserted Noah.

"I'm sorry to disappoint you, dear, but trailblazing and adventuring just don't fire me up. That's the difference between men and women."

"Why?"

"Isn't it obvious? You men need to prove yourselves,

which is what makes all this so fascinating to you . . . the challenge."

He grunted. "That's nonsense."

"Is it? It doesn't 'fascinate' women because we're more secure with ourselves. Because we have stronger foundations."

He snickered. "I knew it."

"What?"

"One way or another you'd ring in which are more mature, men or women, right?"

"Which do you think?"

He laughed. "I'm supposed to say women, Lynette."

"Say it, Daddy."

Lucy laughed and patted her head. "Don't bother, dear heart, don't ask for the impossible."

═══ FIVE ═══

Graduating second in her class from Miss Paige's School, Lucy set her heart on a teaching career. She adored children, the younger the better, and felt comfortable with them. She had the patience and the desire, the training she would acquire. The prospect of teaching burned within her, until she met Noah Mitchum.

From the outset their marriage was a happy one peppered with few spats . . . and only one serious difference of opinion. Daddy insisted on buying the newlyweds a house, as he had for Lucy's older sister Lynette when she was married four years before. Husband and wife talked it over; Lucy could see nothing wrong with accepting her father's offer. Noah could, and even after she talked him into accepting his regret lingered. He wanted to pay his own way in everything and considered "moving into his father-in-law's charity" no way to start out.

But for her sake he shoved his pride to the back of his mind. He attacked his job at Eureka Printing; he did his best, but the work just wasn't worthy of such diligence, such singleminded dedication. It was a job and that was all it was. It didn't demand superior intelligence; in Noah's opinion any idiot could shuffle the papers he shuffled. The challenge simply wasn't there. As time went on and the rut deepened, his enjoyment for even some few aspects of the work diminished, then eventually disappeared altogether.

Unfortunately, times were rough; many men as well-educated as he, even better, were out of work, unable to find even the meanest type of manual labor. So Noah stayed at Eureka; the company repaid his loyalty by not firing him, which he alluded to too often for Lucy's liking. Life went on, Lynette arrived and now the Sacramento Valley promised to do the same, eventually.

Into her daydream he blundered. "What are you thinking about? Home, right? Wrong, it stopped being home when we sold the house."

"I disagree," she murmured.

Lynette was asleep in the tent; they strolled by the softly burbling river hand in hand, alone for a few precious minutes. Stars in abundance fired the heavens, the full moon stared blankly.

"You do have a point," she went on, "home isn't stone and wood and windows. It's . . . wherever you feel inside you belong; the best place, the right place. Right now we're in limbo."

"And when we get to California we'll make it 'the best

place, the right place,' you'll see." There was a pause. He lowered his voice before resuming. "Homesick?"

"I don't know if you'd call it homesick. It is all a bit wrenching. I was born in Baltimore, grew up there, never left except for my four years at Miss Paige's School in Ellicott City. Listen to me, I sound like a schoolgirl missing mommy and daddy, tears on my pillow every night."

"I miss our parents, yours and mine. I miss the house."

"Eureka Printing . . . "

"I miss the people; not the job, the niggling salary. The thing of it is you have to believe you were made for better than you're getting; being satisfied is giving up."

"Can anyone ever be completely satisfied with his or her lot?"

"*I* will be out there, I'm sure of it. And you'll love it, I promise. You'll wonder why we didn't leave five years ago!"

"Mmmmmm."

"Have I told you how grateful I am, Mrs. Mitchum, how happy I am you're my wife? Grateful, because I know you're doing this just for me. But once we're settled you'll see that it's as much for you and Lynette. It's not just a crazy whim, Lucy."

Oh but it was; which didn't necessarily make it wrong, ill-advised. He began repainting his favorite pictures of the future. She only half-listened, drifting back to Baltimore, to the rectory, her father's office. He was at his desk, she sat across from him. . . .

"His mind's made up?"

"With a vengeance."

"It's his job of course; if he had something better, some-

thing up to his intelligence and ability. Too bad times are no
better. He'd be more in a position to pick and choose."

"I don't know, Daddy, if it's *the* job or any. Which is aca-
demic, inasmuch as he's no longer here."

"I beg your pardon?"

"He's been in California all week; in mind, if not in
body. Already emigrated, now all that's left is to follow
through."

"He *has* been badly bitten."

"Near fatally."

Her father laughed. He had a wonderful laugh, he
would throw back his great leonine head and roar laughter;
it always gave her a good feeling, it cheered everybody who
heard it, even strangers. Sometimes he would laugh until his
face became ripe red and webbed with tear tracks. She'd
miss that laugh, that man, her mother, her sister, her
friends, Baltimore. She was suddenly about to take off her
world like a hat, and try on another. Would it fit? Would it
be right for her? Doubts returned, flying as thick and fast as
the swallows suddenly sweeping by outside. Her father laid
his huge hand over hers, squeezing it lightly.

"My instincts tell me it'll work out famously for both of
you. He'll make it work. Men love challenges and this'll be
his life's challenge. It'll be fine, Lucy, this is the East and it's
logical and normal that Americans spread west. It's right,
and now you three'll be part of it, heading out for your destiny, eh? My daughter, the pioneer. And when you get there
your mother and I'll expect a long letter, even if it takes a
year getting here." He winked. "Which I'm sure it will."

"Funny . . ."

"What's that?"

She watched while he got out his pipe, then filled and
lit it.

"You seem enamored of the idea. I'd have thought you'd hate it."

"I'll hate losing the three of you. Dear me, I'm making it sound like you're dropping off the edge of the world. But how can anyone 'hate' such courage, such enterprise. It'd be selfish of me to rail against it, to try and discourage him. I envy Noah—if I were forty years younger I might be prey to the same urge."

"I appreciate that, Daddy, you're making me feel good about it."

"You should." The clock on the wall behind him chimed five. "Let's go home. We'll stop by your place, pick up Noah."

"Mrs. Foley, the next-door neighbor, is watching Lynette."

"We'll pick her up. Only not Mrs. Foley."

Again he laughed, all but shaking the walls. . . .

"Are you listening?" Noah asked. "I said at Fort Kearny we'll both be able to take baths. I feel like I've grown a second skin: dust combined with sweat. And look at my hands." He showed his blisters.

"Oh, Noah . . ."

"They're nothing. No, they're something: badges of a sort; awarded me in honor of hard work. I haven't worked this hard since I cut down the apple tree in the backyard four years ago. Lucy, I love it! Aches, pains, exhaustion and all. Wait and see, when we get there I'll build us a house you'll be proud to call home!"

He would. She'd help, only not with the roof; she was deathly afraid of heights.

SIX

Anson Willoughby's lame ox recovered, Marcia Talley's illness ran its course, Olin Coombs began being both father and mother to his children. The cheerful music of Maynard Havers' harmonica drifted down the line of wagons. The weather continued ideal.

One afternoon, with a brilliant sun firing the heavens to their discernible limits, Herman Schwimmer halted the train. Gathering the emigrants around him, he checked the map and announced that they were only about three hours away from Fort Kearny. A cheer went up. Maynard Havers played and executed a jig accompanied by the others' clapping. The impromptu celebration stopped abruptly when Noah shouted, pointing at a cloud of dust coming toward them from the north.

"Redskins!" burst Abigail. "Pawnees for sure. Now listen up; everybody's to keep their heads. No guns, no weapons, nothing but smiles on your faces. I've dealt with 'em before; if nobody gets nervous, if nobody does nothing foolish, we'll just parlay, give 'em what they ask for and they'll be on their way. Whatever you do, if one comes up to you, say *you*, Miss Talley, and wants to feel your hair, let him. He won't harm you none."

"See here," began Noah.

"He won't, trust me. You've all heard they're like children—and they are. They'll do things spontaneous-like: like yelling too close to your ear for no reason at all and when you least expect it. Like picking at your belongings or your food and throwing 'em on the ground."

"You said to give them what they ask for," said Abigail Havers.

Schwimmer nodded. "That's right. This is their land we're trespassing on. They expect some token of hospitality. It's common courtesy; they offer gifts to strangers, they expect us to do the same. And sharing food is a special sign of friendship. The only things you don't give are money, powder and whiskey. All right, here they come."

Splashing across the river on the sorriest, the gauntest-looking ponies Lucy had ever seen came the Pawnees: naked to their waists, their upper bodies painted a vivid scarlet up to and including their scalps, fringed with hair in the back, out of which sprang horsehair and feathers. Many warriors showed painted black handprints on their chests.

"Oh oh," murmured Schwimmer.

"What?" asked three of the men standing nearest him, Noah among them.

"War paint. They paint themselves after victory in battle. The handprints are enemies they've killed hand-to-hand."

Lucy counted nearly forty Pawnees, but once they reached the near bank of the river and began milling about it was impossible to count exactly. All carried guns as well as bows and arrows and long-handled tomahawks.

"Stay back," Schwimmer cautioned the emigrants.

He approached a warrior wearing more feathers than his companions. There was an arrow through his hair, bone necklaces wound around his ears, bead and stone necklaces around his neck along with a brass medallion. His deerskin trousers were dusty and ripped, his moccasins on the verge of falling to pieces. Schwimmer and he began talking in words and sign language. Lucy cocked an ear and strained but couldn't make out a syllable. Then another Pawnee came riding up, his pony rearing, causing Schwimmer to step quickly back. The only red displayed by the intruder was on his cheeks. He wore a knee-length U.S. Army coat, long trousers with beaded decorations at the knees, and carried a tomahawk with a three-foot handle, the butt of which was festooned with feathers. Clearly, he was a chief and the leader of the party. He addressed Schwimmer in halting English. Lucy stared fascinated as the Pawnees dismounted, coming closer, bringing with them a foul body odor. Schwimmer preceded them with a smile so forced it looked like a death grin.

"Everybody just relax, you're doing nobly. Just keep calm. They want money, powder and whiskey. Cross your fingers we can get them to settle for loot."

"What sort of 'loot'?" asked Willoughby.

"I told you, trinkets and such; no family heirlooms. Needles and thread, hand mirrors, any cloth you ladies can spare, the gaudier the better. And food: eggs, biscuits, bread, anything. Whatever you do, don't hold back. If you don't hand over what they want they'll just take it."

"This is outrageous," muttered Noah.

"Shhhh." Lucy tugged his arm.

"Maybe," said Schwimmer staring at the chief. "But giving up a few doodads beats parting with your scalp."

Two warriors approached Lucy. One pointed at her necklace of inexpensive glass beads. She took it off and handed it to him. Noah glared.

"Just relax, dear," she murmured between clenched teeth. The Pawnee grinned toothlessly and slipped the necklace around his own neck. One of the others, standing close by, grabbed and pulled it, breaking the string and scattering the beads. Both threw themselves to the ground to snatch up the loose beads.

"Stupid beggars . . . " muttered Noah too loudly.

Marcia Talley sucked a breath between her teeth. The

warrior Schwimmer had addressed before the chief arrived, pushing up too close to Noah.

"Stupid beggars," he repeated, his pronunciation perfect.

The chief came over, the breeze ruffling his coattails. The Indians stood motionless as did the emigrants; all eyes had fastened on Noah and the warrior confronting him. Noah's hand went to the butt of his pistol. . . .

Schwimmer stepped between the two.

"Now, now, boys, let's just relax. Missus Mitchum, have you got a nice gift for our friend here?"

"Of course."

The crowd, red and white, remained rooted. Noah and the Indian continued staring as Lucy hurried to her wagon, dug into a pile of bedding and produced a cast-iron teakettle, holding it aloft. Then, with exaggerated ceremony, she proferred it to the Pawnee confronting Noah.

"For you, Chief."

"Chief?" exclaimed the Indian with the red face paint. "He is warrior, not chief. I am chief. Chief Yellow Sky."

"I'm Lucy Mitchum."

Yellow Sky addressed the recipient of the gift who glared at Noah and backed off. Noah sighed visibly and it was Lucy's turn to glare.

"I'm sorry," he murmured sheepishly. She said nothing. "It just slipped out. But it's the principle of the thing."

"Darling, kindly put your principles in your pocket and keep it buttoned."

Abigail Havers standing within earshot laughed, more to relieve nervous tension than in amusement. It brought a towering brave up to her. His shadow covered her completely. Maynard took a step toward them clenching his fists, but stopped when Schwimmer touched his arm.

Abigail stared up at the Pawnee, blanching and fighting to swallow.

The Pawnee pointed to her belt; it bore an attractive silver buckle in the shape of a shield, somewhat similar to the medallion he wore. Without hesitation, she undid it, whipped off the belt and gave it to him. But another Pawnee came striding up and snatched it away; the first brave snatched it back. The chief intervened, whipping out his knife and waving it between their chests. Both went rigid. He took away the belt, looked from one to the other and handed it back to Abigail.

The "visitors" were treated with the utmost hospitality. Gifts were graciously offered and exchanged. The emigrants were quick to hand things over, mainly trinkets and food, before the Pawnees could pilfer whatever might catch their eye. About nine dollars in silver was given to the chief along with a small quantity of powder. But no whiskey, although everyone knew that Olin Coombs kept four jugs of sour mash whiskey wrapped in a comforter under the seat of his wagon.

After a tense hour, the chief assembled his men and they rode splashing back across the river. Leaving eleven badly shaken emigrants watching their dust thin and finally disappear altogether in the direction of the distant Sand Hills.

Schwimmer came up to Noah and told him, loudly enough for all to hear, "Mister, you come scary close to getting a tomahawk square between your eyes. I hope you learned your lesson."

"Amen," said Lucy.

When husband and wife had gotten back on the driver's seat and the train started out, Noah couldn't contain himself.

"I am sorry, Lucy, it was stupid."

"You did surprise me."

"You thought I had more sense. I told you, it just——"

"Slipped out." She patted his hand. "I know. Our first Indians."

"Nearly our last, thanks to my big mouth."

Both laughed but there was no humor in either effort.

SEVEN

Fort Kearny had been built many miles from the nearest available supply of timber—no installation in all of Nebraska had timber at hand. When Kearny was put up a sawmill was constructed first, then wood was brought in from as far away as Missouri and processed and sawed and hammered providing lumber for a number of low buildings. Upon completion of the fort a twenty-eight-hundred-foot stockade fence was erected around it. Buffalo chips, of which there was an abundant supply in the vicinity, served as fuel in winter.

The stockade fence, three hundred seasoned soldiers and six howitzers combined to discourage the local Indians from attacking. The Pawnees, however, could assemble and mount at least fifteen hundred warriors, so the threat of attack was never far from Commandant Royce Hamblin's thoughts. The government supplied Kearny with provisions for distribution to passing wagon trains; Congress encouraged emigration and willingly voted funds to assist in populating the West.

Many trains started out even farther from California and

Oregon than Council Bluffs, although those forming in
Independence, Missouri, and other southerly jumping-off
places, generally headed southwest over the Santa Fe Trail
rather than northwest to cross Nebraska.

Herman Schwimmer introduced the emigrants to
Colonel Hamblin and his staff and everyone was invited to
dinner that night in the mess hall. The main course was
turkey awash in gravy, accompanied by a variety of fresh
vegetables which had been grown by the enlisted men.
There was a choice of coffee, tea, cider or lemonade. Olin
Coombs turned up his nose at all four, left before dessert—
his three children in the care of Marcia Talley—and
returned to his wagon and one of the jugs under the driver's
seat.

The children were well behaved and the colonel's aide,
Lieutenant Palmieri, a dashing young Pennsylvanian, fed
them and Lynette Mitchum sugar cookies and taffy until
both Marcia and Lucy called a halt, fearing stomachaches in
the dead of night.

Wheels and axles greased, tires checked, other necessary
preparations attended to, the wagon train set out at noon
the next day in a light drizzle. Lucy noticed Marcia Talley
intently watching Lieutenant Palmieri wave good-bye until
he became a speck against the front gate. Fort Laramie,
Wyoming, the next stopping-off place, lay about 330 miles
to the northwest. To reach it the train would have to pass
through what remained of the widespread hunting grounds
of the Pawnees, and then trespass those of their neighbors
and blood enemies, the Cheyenne.

It threatened to be the single most dangerous stretch of
the migration.

EIGHT

Olin Coombs' mourning for his Sarah took the form of drinking. He was beginning to look bleary-eyed and his speech was slurred. One of his four jugs was emptied and discarded.

"Three to go," said Noah to Lucy.

Marcia Talley had joined them more or less permanently, welcomed by both Mitchums. Lynette minded not at all giving up her place on the driver's seat; she was content playing with her dolls behind the three adults.

"I worry about the children," said Marcia. "I should go back and ride with him, at least until dark. Until they're asleep."

"He's not getting surly drunk," said Noah. "I doubt he will, he knows his responsibilities."

Lucy nodded. "He won't risk having to give them up because he can't control himself. He'd be humiliated."

"He *is* in mourning," said Noah. "Women mourn without display, quietly, to themselves. Men reach for liquor, but Olin won't go overboard."

"He's a good father," said Marcia. "He adored Sarah. You'd think he was a Yankee." Both Mitchums looked at her questioningly. "Back where I come from Yankees have a reputation for being great good family men. Good husbands; I know, my father certainly was, and both my uncles. Oh, I'm not saying husbands from anywhere else are bad."

"You are in a way," said Lucy grinning.

"No no, they're just not like Yankee men."

"And how are 'Yankee men' different?"

"For one thing they're more devoted, closer to their wives. More considerate, more . . . gentle. Lots of husbands

I've seen don't lift a finger to help their wives; they get stuck
with all the heavy-duty work besides cooking, washing, caring for the children. They have to get the wood—out here
collect the buffalo chips—fetch all the water, make the
campfires, unpack at night, pack up in the morning."

Lucy was grinning at Noah. "While the men sit around
bragging and smoking with their feet up."

"Don't look at me, I help."

"He does; if I didn't know better I'd think you were a
Yankee, dear."

"They're the best husbands," said Marcia determinedly.

"Miz Talley . . ."

It was Clarence, the Coombs' oldest boy, running alongside the wagon with a worried look on his old-man face.

"What is it, Clare?"

"Paw. He keeps falling asleep. I'm afraid he'll fall off the
seat and bust his neck. Can you? . . . "

Noah handed the whip to Lucy. "I'll take it, Marcia."

He went back with Clarence to the Coombs' wagon at
the rear. Olin was awake but bleary-eyed and bobbing from
side to side. Noah and Clarence climbed up on either side
of him; Noah took the whip. Just in time, as Olin began
snoring and fell backward.

His son caught him, pinching him awake.

"Go back inside and sleep it off, Olin," said Noah. "I'll
see to the oxen."

Olin needed no further encouragement. In seconds he
was snoring loudly. Relief spread over Clarence's face like
sunshine.

"He'll be fine, son, just a tad too much wet corn."

"I'm going to throw those jugs in the ditch!"

"I wouldn't. Right now they're his salvation, they're
what'll get him through the worst of it, just as long as he

doesn't overdo it. He's not getting roaring drunk, is he?"

"No, but . . ."

"Tell you what, when he wakes up I'll talk to him."

"Would you, Mr. Mitchum, please? He's dreadful sad about Maw; he can't even talk about her without tears filling his eyes."

"He loved her very much."

"We all miss her something fierce." Tears glistened in his eyes and he passed the back of his hand under his nose.

Olin awoke two hours later.

"Clare," said Noah, "take the whip. Snap it every now and then. Keep them from lagging. Can you handle it?"

"Yes, sir."

Noah joined Olin in the back of the wagon. "How are you doing, Olin?"

"My mouth feels like I've been chewing rotten leather. Sorry to put you to all this trouble."

"No trouble." Noah eyed the three jugs and then one at a time picked them up, weighing each in his hand. One was almost empty, the other two full.

"I feel downright ashamed, Noah."

"No reason to."

"I drink 'cause I'm a weakling. Some fine example to set for the young-uns, eh? I held off drinking long as I could, honest. After dark I'd take all four jugs out, set them in a row and just stare at them. Never opened nary a one until the night before the Injuns showed up. I opened one, sniffed it and took a slug. It burned the inside of my mouth it's been so long since I tasted any. Sarah frowned on drinking—her daddy died of it. I had to sneak the jugs onboard behind her back. She died never knowing they were there. They're comfort, Noah, that's all they are."

"I know. And I've no right to advise you."

"I should toss all three into the ditch, right? I know that'd be right and proper but I just can't. The stuff is comfort. . . . I said that, didn't I? My main trouble is I just can't take being without her. It gets harder and harder. Losing her like that was like my heart was torn plumb out of my chest. I can't sleep worth a hoot; the whiskey helps there, too."

Noah interrupted quickly. "I can't see anything wrong with taking a drink now and then, but—and I'm sorry to say it—you seem to be drinking more every day. If it was just you . . ."

"It's the young-uns, I know. You're right, they deserve better than a weakling for a father."

"You're both father *and* mother now." He grinned and laid his hand on Olin's shoulder. "You think both of you should be drinking?"

Olin managed a weary smile. "That's a good joke, a serious joke. Will you do something for me?"

"Name it."

"Go? And take these three jugs with you?"

Again Noah grinned. "I'm not partial to sour mash whiskey."

"Maybe the ditch has a taste for it. Take them. From this day forward you're looking at the Reverend Olin Mortsen Coombs, teetotaler!"

NINE

After Fort Kearny they entered buffalo country, a continuous alkali-whitened, parched and desolate plain. The fine dust kept a cloud around the wagon train, so thick at times the driver of one wagon could barely make out the vehicle ahead, although less than thirty feet separated them. The dust penetrated nostrils and eyes, ears, mouth, hair and clothing. And traveling in it were sand gnats by the thousands, so small they could barely be seen, but carrying a bite so powerful it could bring tears to the eyes of a fully grown man.

Olin Coombs had suffered his deprival for two harrowing days and nights, but he showed no resentment toward Noah and gradually his system became accustomed to chronic sobriety. It was late in the afternoon, the sky overhead a slowly darkening blue, the sun suspended like a copper coin above the horizon, firing the clouds near it in varying shades of orange. Distant thunder sounded, just barely audible; but no lightning lanced the sky. And the thunder had an unusual sound to it, not like immense boulders crashing against each other, more an even and continuous rumble.

Then the wagons began to shake, set trembling by the trail beneath the wheels. Schwimmer halted the train and quickly got down. The emigrants ran as he called them together.

"Buffalo! A stampede!"

"I don't see any buffalo," said Noah.

Schwimmer pointed behind them. Close to the ground rolled a pure white cloud, widening even as they stared at it. Coming straight for them. Gradually, as everyone stared transfixed, the white cloud began to slowly darken, at length turning solidly black. To Lucy it took on the appearance of a mountain on the move. The shaking increased.

"Hurry!" shouted Schwimmer. "Get your wagons off the trail sharp left! Move!"

"Why left?" bawled Havers.

"Just do it! Hurry, we got less than a minute!"

The men leaped onto their seats and pulled their wagons off the trail as instructed. Looking back at the oncoming herd, Lucy could see that the order made sense. The herd was moving in a perfectly straight line; anything remaining in its path would be crushed. Still she stood rooted, hypnotized by the sight, as did Marcia Talley.

"Everybody!" shouted Schwimmer, barely able to make himself heard above the awesome noise. He had parked his wagon and hurried toward Lucy and Marcia. "Over to the wagons, you two; the far side and keep back well clear o' the wheels!"

Lucy and Marcia quickly joined the emigrants collected on the far side of the wagon line. The men and children bellied down to watch the herd pass, while the women timorously peered over the backs of the still-yoked oxen, who were standing obediently, their huge, dull eyes filled with fear.

The ground, the wagons, the oxen, the emigrants shook uncontrollably as the herd drew closer.

"What if they turn?" shouted Ruth Willoughby.

"Just stay were you are, Missus," shouted Schwimmer, then got down on his belly in the dust, his hat off as a chin rest.

The front of the herd drew closer and for the first time Lucy could see individual animals. They began passing, running very fast with wild snorting, noses almost touching the whitened ground, tails flying. The bulls stood at least six feet tall and weighed upwards of a ton. A great mass of blackish brown hair covered the head, neck and forepart of the body. The thunder of their passing became deafening, so loud the two Coombs girls began screaming; Lynette heard and joined them.

Then, breaking through the thunder came the crack of a rifle. A second shot and a bull stumbled, fell and rolled on its side. The animals following it swung around it; one tried to leap over the prostrate form, stumbled and fell on it. Quickly, before Schwimmer could get another shot off, it righted itself and went galloping on.

All the emigrants looked over at Schwimmer. He pulled back his rifle, smoke still issuing from the muzzle.

"A ghost buffalo," murmured Noah as he, Lucy and the others crowded around the dust-whitened buffalo.

"One tasty ghost," said Schwimmer.

He was right. That night everyone gorged on buffalo steak. Schwimmer showed the women how to prepare the meat. Fat was rendered in a hot skillet; the steak was seared on both sides and then, at a lower heat, it was cooked just like beefsteak. Gravy was made by adding a tablespoon of flour to the pan drippings and cooking it until it browned. Stirring constantly, a cup of milk was added and brought to a boil.

"The redskins eat the liver, the tongue, just about every part," explained Schwimmer.

"It's built like a locomotive," said Lucy. "However did you kill it with only two shots?"

"Just lucky, Missus." Schwimmer cut a piece of steak and stuffed it into his grinning mouth. "At least one shot hit just behind the last rib; punctured its diaphragm and collapsed its lungs."

The steak was delicious and a most welcome respite from the dry food everyone was back to eating since the turkey at Fort Kearny. Lucy saw one irony in the occasion, however. She mentioned it to Noah in bed that night.

"We cook the meat of one buffalo with a fire made from the chips of another."

"You think it's possible they were related?" He smirked.

"Go to sleep."

TEN

The next evening Lucy got to talking with Ruth Willoughby; it was the first time they'd exchanged more than pleasantries since Abigail Havers introduced them back in Council Bluffs. There was no coolness between Lucy and Ruth—they hardly knew each other—on the trail their paths just never seemed to cross. Lucy found out that Ruth was a Canadian and like her biblical namesake, the Moabite and great-grandmother of David, she had married a "foreigner"; from below the border.

Lucy already knew that Ruth was almost slavishly devoted to Anson. Ruth made no attempt to disguise her near reverence for him. Lucy recalled Marcia Talley's views of husbands, her respect for Yankees, in particular. Anson was no Yankee; from what Lucy had seen he took decidedly unfair advantage of his wife's high regard for him, going out of his way to put all the work he could on her. He appeared to think it a privilege for her to wait on him hand and foot in addition to her daily chores. Ruth even yoked, unyoked, fed and watered their oxen.

When Lucy looked back on it, about the only labor Anson had performed since leaving Iowa was to rub liniment on his ox's lame ankle. The Havers shared the work as had the Coombs before Sarah's tragic death. Nor did Noah drop all the chores in Lucy's lap.

Not the case with the Willoughbys, and yet in fairness to Anson Lucy had never seen him order Ruth about; she jumped at whatever the job like a newly hired maid in a wealthy household, running about like a puppy, in her eagerness to please her lord and master.

The biblical Ruth was renowned for her faithfulness, but she wasn't obsequious. The glaring imbalance of the couple's relationship annoyed Lucy, but she held off discussing her feelings with others, even Noah and Marcia. She was no gossip, the Willoughbys were none of her business.

But the mere idea of one partner putting the other upon a pedestal nettled her strong sense of fairness. If Anson had been a unique physical specimen, strikingly handsome or blessed with extraordinary intelligence, there might be reason for Ruth to look up to him; but he was none of these things. On the contrary, Lucy thought him depressingly ordinary.

"He can't even play the harmonica," she muttered.

Marcia Talley was riding with Lucy, Noah was back keeping Olin Coombs company, which had become a daily routine. He insisted that it was to boost the Ohioan's morale, help him through his mourning. Lucy didn't object. It was, after all, temporary; Olin desperately needed a receptive and sympathetic ear, somebody had to supply it.

"What did you say?" Marcia asked.

"Nothing. What's the matter with that ox. The one on the left in the middle team?"

Lucy didn't wait for Marcia's answer, getting down, running up to and stopping the lead team. Olin's oxen behind them also stopped, as did the three wagons ahead. Herman Schwimmer came back as Noah and Olin joined Lucy.

"There's something wrong with that ox," she said, indicating the one that had drawn her attention.

"Has it gone lame?" asked Noah.

Schwimmer was stooping and examining the creature's hooves, one by one. He straightened. "It's lost its left rear shoe. The right front one is working loose, too. Have you ever shoed an ox, Noah?"

"No."

"A horse?"

"No."

"All shoeing's pretty much the same. Any of you other fellows haven't had the pleasure, gather around. I'll take you through it, Noah, but you'll have to do the actual shoeing."

Lucy could see the wisdom of that: if any shoes loosened or were lost beyond Pacific Springs, after the other four wagons had turned northwest to follow the Oregon Trail, the job would fall to Noah.

Noah called to her. "Lucy, would you please go back along the trail, try and find the shoe?"

"Don't bother," said Schwimmer, "no sense refitting a worn shoe. Best replace it with a new one. And, while you're at it, that other loose one, as well." The wagon master smiled at Lucy. "You can go find the old one to keep for luck, if you want, although I don't know if oxshoes bring luck the way horseshoes do."

Noah got out his can of shoe nails and a hammer and pliers from the jockey box. Herman Schwimmer cleared his throat.

"Pay attention, fellows; front horses' hooves take six

nails, rear ones, eight. But an oxshoe takes eight, front and rear. As you can see, the shoes are bigger, heavier and generally last longer than horseshoes, but they're not permanent. On a trek like this they should be replaced every month, sooner is even better. Noah, step over here, please."

Noah bent over and slowly lifted the ox's leg as Schwimmer prepared to instruct him step by step.

"An ox is not as skittish as a horse but you still got to be careful, gentle, and no sudden moves. A kick from a horse, mule, ox, anything, can snap a shinbone easy as busting a yardstick over your knee. Look close and you can see that hoof's in good shape.

"Now there's hot shoeing and cold, but cold'll do just fine, seeing as we got no blacksmith with us. Set the shoe squarely, make the fit perfect. Drive your first two nails at the heel calk, the third one at the toe calk. Then the other five. All the while holding the hoof good and steady, Noah."

He replaced both shoes with no difficulty, earning spirited applause. He removed his hat and bowed low.

"Good job," said Schwimmer, "you can shoe my beasts any time. One last thing, fellows, the surface we been traveling over ain't too hard on shoes, but later on when we get into rocky country they'll wear out like they was butter. You saw both hooves looked healthy; the flaking is normal wear, nothing to worry about. But cracks and splits mean trouble. And sand cracks are the worst. A sand crack is a split in the hoof at the top of the horny wall that spreads downward.

"All sorts of ailments can afflict a critter's hoof: corns— not like yours and mine—bruises on the sole; sidebone, ringbone, navicular disease, thrush, shrunk heels and on and on. One thing you got to remember: don't ever replace a shoe without checking the condition of the hoof. That's all, let's get moving."

Lucy ruefully watched Noah walk back to Olin Coombs'
wagon and climb up onto the seat alongside the new wid-
ower. Marcia watched, also.

"Why don't I go back and sit with Olin so you and Noah
can be together?"

"No, thanks just the same. That would force Noah to
come back. I'm not that spoiled; besides, I enjoy your company."

He returned when the train stopped for the night. As he
approached, Lucy, even before he spoke, could see that his
conscience was troubling him; the way he averted his eyes
made it obvious.

"How is he?" she asked, striving to avoid making it
sound sarcastic.

She had already made the supper fire with buffalo chips
left over from that morning. She was in the midst of making buffalo jerky, slicing the meat along the grain into thin
strips two to three inches in length. They would be hung on
a rack in a pan and baked until thoroughly dry. Until they
were ready to eat, fried cakes, the last of the string beans
they'd acquired at Fort Kearny and the last two pieces of
dried apple pie would comprise supper.

"Man's improving by the hour," said Noah. "The best
part of it is his opinion of himself is rising like a bird. I'm . . .
sorry, Lucy."

"Sorry?"

"For neglecting you so the past four days."

She grinned. "Five."

His own grin in response was sheepish. "I've been his
sponge, I let him talk and talk and I take it all in. His conscience has got him in a corner and is flailing away. He
admits he wasn't much of a husband. He was a disaster."

"How so?"

"Abusive, nasty to her for no reason, neglectful; he'd go off on three-day drunks leaving her to fend for herself. The way he put it she'd need four more arms there was so much work."

"He wasn't like that here, not that I could see."

"No, this was back on the farm in Good Hope. Some 'good hope' poor Sarah had. All his sins, all his crimes, just pour out of him. Would you believe, I haven't asked him a single question? What little money they had he squandered on liquor. We always heard how dirt poor they were back then. He was the reason; the farm did all right, with her tending to everything day in, day out."

"How did he abuse her?"

"Beat her."

"The snake . . ." The word came hissing out.

"Mercilessly, at times, he admits it. Oh, he's paying for it now."

Lucy scoffed, suddenly seething, her arms folded tightly in front of her, eyes stabbing him. "Don't be naive, there's no 'paying' for wife beating. Somebody ought to take a horsewhip to him. I'd love to!"

"I know, I know. If it helps any, right now he's suffering blue demons. And probably will continue to until the grave."

"Which can't be too soon. Poor Sarah; poor, poor woman."

"He insists he's the one drove her crazy."

"I'm sure he did."

"I don't think so. And believe me, I'm not defending him. The wonder is why she didn't turn on him and break his neck with a shovel."

"She's half his size for God's sake!"

"That's true. But you should hear him, he's spouted

more truth these past few days than in all his years up to now. It just pours out of him."

"For all the good it does her. And he calls himself a man of God!"

"Lay preacher."

"Heartless bastard!"

"Lucy! You're getting all worked up. . . ."

"How can you even sit beside him? He's filth, an animal!"

"He's lost his wife."

"His victim, you mean."

"He may be everything you say, but he's still a human being."

"I knew he beat her. You can tell, it's in their eyes, the way they look at their victim. Like a wolf at a chicken. His poor children. . . ."

"Oh, I'm sure he doesn't abuse them."

"Bully for him!"

"I'm famished."

"Will you be riding with your new dear friend again tomorrow?"

"Not if you don't want me to."

"I'll not stop you."

"These fried cakes are delicious."

"They taste like wood, not enough salt!"

Lynette had taken to sleeping in the wagon, burying herself in a pile of bedding. Since the tent was pitched every night within a couple feet of the tailgate Lucy saw no harm in permitting her to sleep there.

"I like the privacy for a change," said Noah as he lay back.

"How dare he beat her!"

"Darling, please . . ."

He turned on his side and lay his arm across her chest under her breasts, Testing, she decided. Her mood of the moment couldn't be more foul. Still, why take her anger with Coombs out on him? How could she fault him for playing Good Samaritan? Only now it turned out Olin was about as deserving of Noah's attention and kindliness as Samson was of the razor. She kissed Noah's cheek. Rising on one elbow, he kissed her on the mouth. She responded eagerly, her heart quickening.

In an instant she wanted him inside her. Since the Pawnees, they had rarely even embraced. Everyone's nervousness had intensified since the Indians' "visit." Unseen savages were everywhere, invisible arrows came whirring from every direction and fear magnified at night, despite Schwimmer's repeated assurances that Indians never attacked after dark.

All of which fled Lucy's thoughts.

"Make love to me, darling," she whispered.

His response was a soulful groan. In seconds, their nightclothes were above their hips, their bodies interlocked, kissing passionately. His erection throbbed against her thigh; reaching down she grasped it. Now he was poised above her, his organ finding her lips and slowly parting them, penetrating. She seized his buttocks but he resisted hurrying, driving deeper, continuing his slow entry, tantalizing her so she began moaning.

He entered her full length. She gasped, going momentarily limp, her eyes rounding huge; her thoughts whirled and fled. The animals in them joined in wild abandon. She moaned and moaned, reveling in him, consuming him, her hands ascending his back to his head, pulling it to her and devouring his mouth.

They climaxed as one, the world exploding, showering down like a sky rocket. Drenched, they lay back gasping, utterly spent. Her body was melting, bones liquefying, she felt as if in the next instant she would begin slowly dissolving. It began raining, pattering softly down on the canvas. They lay in silence gazing upward for a time, then rolled on their sides back into an embrace. His breath deliciously warm against her throat, he spoke.

"I love you so, Lucy Scott, I'm the luckiest man who ever lived."

"I'm the lucky one." She pressed a finger against his lips, kissed one lightly, then the other. "And here we are, my darling, two against the world on our great voyage into the unknown."

"You're wondering will we make it to port. . . ."

"We will."

"You can bet your soul we will. How many others have, why not us, eh? The day'll come we'll drive down the mountainside into the beautiful, beautiful valley, into the Promised Land. We'll find ourselves a plot, build a house and settle down."

"And off you'll go to the goldfields."

"Not for long. You come, too. . . ."

"And Lynette? No, that's your dream. All yours: private, personal. Go out and find it, make it come true, then come home to us to stay."

"With golden bells on, as rich as Croesus of Lydia."

"Or as poor as Job." She tittered. "Just not as patient." There was a pause. "Noah?"

"Mmmmmm?" He began pecking lightly all over her face.

"I don't care two pins about the gold, you can come

home with your pockets empty, with holes in them; just see
that you do come home."

"If I have to crawl on my belly."

She kissed him hungrily.

They made love.

Marcia Talley rode with Olin Coombs the next day and
would from then on. Late in the morning the train came
upon five Indians: two men, a woman and two boys. One
was about ten, the other younger, Lucy guessed. All of their
clothing was ragged and dirty, with not so much as a plain
stone necklace around any of the adults' necks. From the
way they were dressed it was impossible to tell their tribe.
Wherever they had come from, they looked to be outcasts,
and when Lucy and Noah drew closer they could see why.
All five were stricken with smallpox, the adults hideously
disfigured and in the advanced stages of the disease. When
they ventured close to Anson Willoughby's oxen he shouted and gestured them back. More in fear of contagion than
annoyance, Lucy decided.

Coming closer to them, Lucy could see that most of the
scabs on their faces produced by the dried pustules had fall-
en off leaving reddish brown spots among permanent pits.
Hands outstretched, they begged for food. Abigail Havers
and Ruth Willoughby gave them bread and buffalo meat.
Lucy gave them some of her jerky, the remaining fried cakes
and water. When they emptied the jug and moved to return
it, Noah gestured for them to throw it away.

The train rolled on. Lucy stood up on the seat, looked
around the bonnet, then gasped.

"What's the matter?" Noah asked.

"The woman's fallen, the others are bending over her."

"Doing what?"

"Nothing, just gawking at her."

On they trundled, jiggling and jouncing as the wheels passed over a series of lateral ruts.

"Oh my God," murmured Lucy.

"What now?"

"They're going on, leaving her there."

"She's dead."

"Maybe not, maybe just collapsed. They can't just leave her to the buzzards, it's inhuman."

"What else can they do?"

"They can't! Noah, stop. . . ."

"Lucy . . ."

"Stop, I'm going back."

"No you're not!"

"I have to, I have to see."

"And when you get back there, then what? Be reasonable, dear, what can you possibly do for her? You can't even touch her. That's be all we'd need—you stricken with smallpox. Lucy, get hold of yourself; be sensible; you can't do a blessed thing for her, don't go back."

He was right. She turned and sat slowly, so upset she was trembling. She tented her fingers against her mouth.

"It just seems so cruel."

"Life is cruel. For her, them, Sarah Coombs, all of us sooner or later. Please, don't look back there anymore."

But she couldn't resist one last peek. She stood up, turning around, holding onto a bow through the canvas. Only they'd come too far; all she could make out were black dots against the azure sky; imperfections in the dusty landscape. As she squinted at them out from under her free hand, they merged into a single blot.

ELEVEN

The incident badgered Lucy's thoughts the remainder of the day and all through supper, although she spared Noah conversation about it. She took it to bed with her. While he snored contentedly she thought about the outcasts of Israel in the Old Testament. Noah was probably right, the woman had collapsed and died then and there. If she were still breathing, the men would have at least moved her to the side of the trail. They were already infected themselves, there'd be no danger in their touching her.

How long would the others survive? Virtually everybody she'd ever heard of who'd contracted smallpox eventually died. No disease she knew of was more contagious—but how did Indians catch it? She recalled reading about an epidemic ten years earlier that had ravaged the tribes of the upper Missouri, the gift of infected white traders who doggedly refused to let the disease interfere with business. Had white men given these Indians their smallpox? Who else?

The poor woman. Lucy found herself speculating on how much better off the Indians would be if the white man had never set foot across the Mississippi.

Lynette woke up the next morning crying loudly enough to wake the oxen. She was suffering from toothache. Abigail dosed her with chamomile tea but it failed to help. Lynette cried louder and louder in Lucy's arms.

"Let me take a look," said Noah.

He got Lynette to open her mouth, but when he took hold of the tooth with thumb and forefinger to test its firmness she screamed deafeningly and bit him.

He roared and danced on one foot holding his finger. Concerned with Lynette, Lucy took little notice of his discomfort.

"Is it loose?"

"I don't know, I never got that far."

"Stand back, Noah. Sweetheart, mother's going to see if your tooth is loose, okay?"

"It hurts! It hurts!"

"I'm sure, but I want you to be brave and let me see how loose it is. It may hurt a little but promise you won't bite."

"I won't, I won't. Ooooooo!"

Again she bit, but knowing it was coming Lucy got her fingers out of the way just in time. The tooth was firmly set, but down near the gum line a cavity could be seen.

"It could be much bigger below the gum line," murmured Lucy. "I'm afraid we'll have to . . ."

She paused, smiled sympathetically at Lynette, put her down and pulled Noah out of range of her hearing.

"Yank it," said Noah.

"Please. Don't use that word on your daughter, Noah Mitchum."

"All right, pull it."

"That's better."

"It's the same thing."

"Just not as primitive."

Lynette resumed crying, bringing both running back.

"Let me," said Noah, "there's a set of mill-jawed pliers in the jockey box."

"Wait."

"What now?"

"The last time you used them was to pull loose nails out of the oxshoe."

"I'll clean them . . ."

Out of Lynette's view the pliers were heated in the breakfast fire, then plunged into water to cool. Father and mother approached slowly, Noah holding the pliers behind his back. Lynette looked suspiciously from one to the other.

"Lynette, sweetheart," began Lucy, "Daddy's going to pull that horrible, painful thing out of your mouth. All you have to do is hold still. Can you do that for mother?"

The other emigrants had long since gathered to watch. Marcia Talley's pretty face creased with sympathy, as did Abigail's and Ruth Willoughby's.

"Have you ever done this?" Lucy asked Noah.

"It can't be that hard."

"You haven't. I once pulled one of my own baby teeth."

"Really?"

"It was so wobbly it was on the verge of falling out. Would you rather I did it?"

"No, no, no . . ."

His expression contradicted his self-assurance. Lucy took the pliers from him; he made no protest.

"Open wide, sweetheart."

Her dexterity surprised her—in went the pliers, out came the tooth ushered by a spine-chilling scream.

"There," said Noah, "that wasn't so bad was it?"

Lucy lowered her head, staring at him out from under her upper lids. Then handed back the pliers. Picking up Lynette, she patted her back as Abigail applied a poultice of savory to the hole. Mercifully, it brought speedy relief.

TWELVE

The two oxen leading Herman Schwimmer's team at the head of the train inhaled too much alkali dust and suffocated. They died less than two minutes apart. He unhitched them and with Maynard Havers' help butchered them on the spot, leaving him with only three pair.

"I can pick me up another yoke up the line. The bright side is we'll be eating fresh beef from here to Fort Hall, at least."

"He just shrugs it off," said Lucy to Noah out of Schwimmer's hearing. "The poor creatures."

"He did warn us it could happen."

Lucy frowned. "I worry about us, I mean beyond Salt Lake City when we get out into the Great Basin. All by our lonesome."

"We'll be fine, we'll just make sure we have plenty of water, plenty of forage."

At the point where Schwimmer's oxen had died the wagon master estimated that the train had come 460 miles since crossing the Missouri River. Over the entire distance they had yet to venture from within sight of the Platte. Now they could see the confluence of the Platte's north and south forks. At this point it would be necessary to ford the south fork. Halting the train for the night, Schwimmer called the emigrants together.

"In case it ain't crossed your minds, folks, today is July the ninth. We been on the trail exactly one month. Let's talk about the river. As shallow as it looks it can fool you and be mighty dangerous. You may not have noticed but the south fork gets narrow and widens again and again. It can be anywhere from a half mile to a mile wide, and crossing her's not exactly stepping across a puddle. No flatboats out here, nobody to give us a hand. At high water you can take off your wheels and turn your wagon boxes over, make 'em into flat-bottomed boats that can be floated across. Only if they leak you could be in for a peck o' trouble out in midstream."

"My wagon's tarred every crack, every seam," said Anson Willoughby. "Tell them how you did it, Ruth."

Schwimmer scratched his grizzled chin and shook his head. "You might think it is, Mister, but if you get it out in deep water it could turn out to be no more waterproof than your hat. If it goes down then where are you? All your goods'll be riding on it, you'll lose everything.

"One way to waterproof wagon boxes is to tack buffalo skins over 'em. Of course first you got to catch the buffalo."

"So how do we get across?" Noah asked.

"At the narrowest point—which looks to be right about yonder." He indicated.

"How deep?" asked Maynard Havers.

"That's something else. The distance ain't bad, not much of a current, but how deep depends on the holes at the bottom. There ain't no shortage of same—which is how cattle drown, people, too. I advise you to keep your wheels on."

"Any other ideas?" Noah asked.

"We'll just have to do like others have before us. We double team the wagons. Hitch two sets of oxen up to one wagon. Also raise your boxes six or eight inches higher by sticking blocks under 'em. Drive into the river, get across fast as you can move your teams, land high and dry, bring the oxen back and hitch up the next wagon."

"Sounds like it'll work," said Maynard Havers, trying his best not to sound worried.

"Cross your fingers," said Schwimmer. "Just remember,

if your wagon sinks into a hole you could lose everything you got in the world."

"While we're on the subject, how about if one of us walks across first?" suggested Noah. "Feel along the bottom, find a route that's level underfoot."

"It's been tried," said Schwimmer. "It could help, but it don't always work. You volunteering?"

Noah was an excellent swimmer, Lucy knew, but this would be no leisurely exercise. He'd have to dive and feel with his hands as well as his feet. As she expected, the challenge appealed to him. It was his chance to prove himself in front of the other men. The new Noah continued to emerge.

"Was it necessary to volunteer?" she asked him in a whisper.

"We want to get across without drowning everything, don't we?"

Before sunup the next morning Lucy was awakened by hammering. Noah was driving two stakes into the sandy soil near the riverbank. He had stripped to the waist. He was placing the stakes about eight feet apart and had two identical stakes that he would tie around his waist. The other emigrants appeared yawning and stretching. The sky was rosying in the east.

"These two'll be driven in on the other side," Noah explained. "We'll just follow the path across."

Easily said, not quite as easy to accomplish. It took him almost an hour to find a route across with a level bottom. He drove the stakes in opposite, bowed to his fellow emigrants' applause and swam back.

It took most of the morning to move all five wagons across, but it was done without any significant mishap. The trail on the south side started out running sharply uphill.

One by one the wagons were slowly pulled by the teams and pushed by the emigrants up to the crest. At the top, Schwimmer came up to Lucy.

"On the other side of those trees it goes on for more'n twenty mile straight as string across a high tableland. With not a drop o' water anywhere to be found."

"Then what?"

"At the far end it drops suddenlike toward the Valley of the North Platte."

The slope at their feet was steep—at least forty-five degrees; chains had to be gotten out and the wagon wheels locked to the wagon boxes. To prevent possible injury to the oxen they were removed from the tongues and men and women laid hold of each wagon tongue in turn. The wheels immobilized, one by one each wagon was skidded down the slope. The first four vehicles made it to the bottom without accident, but by the time everyone grouped around Olin Coombs' wagon tongue and started his wagon down all were exhausted. Two-thirds of the way down, the wagon began picking up speed. Schwimmer shouted.

"Let her go, let her go!"

Men and women jumped clear, the wagon careened, sliding at an angle faster and faster, finally toppling over, smashing its bows and dumping everything in the bed into the cover, ripping it in half a dozen places. Down the hill everyone raced. Luckily, Clarence Coombs' father had forbidden him to ride down on the driver's seat, in spite of Clarence's pleading; which as things turned out, unquestionably saved the boy's life. Damage to the contents of the wagon was limited to broken china, two lamps and a broom handle that had snapped in two. But the bonnet was ripped in a number of places and all five bows were badly splintered. Inspection confirmed that they were beyond repair.

Schwimmer pointed out a thick stand of trees.

"It couldn't have happened in a better place, Reverend. That there's Ash Hollow. You can cut boughs in there, scrape off the bark, shape 'em into temporary bows. Make sure you save your nails. And them holes in the canvas can be sewed."

Abigail and Ruth volunteered to repair the damaged cover. Lucy felt as if she should help with repairs, but couldn't bring herself to do so. It may have been petty, but in the last few days she'd taken an intense dislike to Olin. When the Coombs' wagon was righted it was discovered that the left rear wheel had lost its tire. It was found, a fire started, the metal heated, the tire restored, cooling and shrinking securely onto the wheel.

"You're lucky you didn't bust a wheel," said Schwimmer. "Not packing a spare you'd have to make one out of that walnut table or some furniture. Wouldn't be the first time a wagon rolled on what used to be the dining table."

They moved on to Ash Hollow, a grove that was to provide the first shade in a month of travel. Entering it, finding herself surrounded by trees, Lucy gasped. It was a marvel of nature, a misplaced Eden, temporary protection from the relentless and cruel July sun. Cool and dark, the thick woods had sprung up around a spring. An Eden indeed, an oasis of coolness, of beauty; a refuge from wind and sand as well as the heat.

"This is even more beautiful than Druid Hill Park in Baltimore," murmured Lucy to Marcia.

Carrying every conceivable type of container, from cup to cask, everyone converged on the spring. The water was ambrosia, a welcome relief from the water long since become tepid and tasteless brought from Council Bluffs.

While Lynette picked wildflowers, Lucy and Marcia sat under a tree taking in their surroundings.

"Exquisite," murmured Marcia.

The sun sent slender golden shafts through the foliage gilding the ground; birds sang and wildflowers abounded. Like ladies in ballgowns, pink and white wild roses displayed their velvety loveliness. Blue lupines crowded the base of a tree. Yellow lupines circled a tree close by, and a galaxy of albescent stars danced on the ends of saxifrage stems in the breeze playing among the trees. From where Lucy sat she could see yellow orchids blossoming in profusion.

Herman Schwimmer came up to them smiling apologetically. "All the casks and bottles are filled. The reverend's got the wood he'll need for his bonnet bows. I'm afraid it's time to move on."

"Can't we stay just a little longer?" Marcia asked.

"Not more'n a few minutes. We still got practically the whole afternoon ahead of us. I purely hate to waste it."

Lucy hated leaving, but dawdling at Ash Hollow would be an indulgence the train could ill afford. She speculated on what lay ahead. Schwimmer had told Noah that the train was entering Cheyenne territory and the danger of attack would greatly increase. If they could reach Fort Laramie without incident, however, travel from that point on would be less risky. But the fort was upwards of a week's journey away.

"This is no sightseeing trip," said Marcia to the wagon master as she took Lynette's hand and started toward where the wagons were parked.

Lucy laughed. "It's sure not a pleasure trip."

All five wagons were readied. Out of Ash Hollow the

trail would parallel the sandy banks of the North Platte for two-and-a-half days. The land would rise continuously, but the grade was nothing like the hill they had skidded down earlier.

They started out, Lucy looking back around the bonnet for a final glimpse of Ash Hollow. They made excellent time that afternoon, nearly fifteen miles by Schwimmer's calculation. Over the next two days, as the altitude rose, the nights grew colder. Far ahead, faintly visible through the dissolving mist of early morning, rose the snow-mottled Laramie Mountains, the steps to the Rockies.

"Our first mountains," said Noah, "and the far side of the last ones will take us down into the Sacramento Valley.

Lucy acknowledged this observation with a grunt.

"What are you thinking about?" he asked.

"Ash Hollow."

"Taste it," he said, handing her a water bottle.

THIRTEEN

Herman Schwimmer seems more and more worried about Indians, although as far as I know he's said nothing beyond voicing his concern to Noah and the men back before Ash Hollow. He just looks worried, and what else could be on his mind? Purportedly, the Cheyenne are even fiercer than the Pawnees. The territory we're coming into is that of the northern Cheyenne. They pick on wagon trains and don't hesitate to attack forts, which makes Fort Laramie vulnerable to their depradations. And Abigail says Laramie is not an army post but only a fur trappers' trading post, which comes as a disappointment. It's also the only fort around for hundreds of miles in every direction.

On the bright side, we did get through Pawnee territory with only the one encounter and no bloodshed. I pray we do as well on this leg of the journey; whoever runs it, Fort Laramie will certainly be a sight for sore and anxious eyes.

Spoke with Abigail Havers today, which is where I got my information on the Indians; she agrees that the Cheyenne are to be avoided at all costs; only in this wide-open country how do we stay out of their sight? She says that Maynard (she always calls him Mr. Havers) persists in his optimism—that we'll come through with flying colors and not a hair harmed on anybody's head. Of course he hasn't read what Abigail's read.

Olin Coombs seems all but fully restored. His bonnet bows to occupy him have turned out a blessing in disguise, according to Noah, who, incidentally, is no longer riding with Olin. It's back to the Three Musketeers. Noah and I got a surprise from Marcia; it turns out that she was once married to a Frenchman who'd come over and was planning to become an American citizen. He eventually did but left Marcia after two years of "constant squabbling." The experience soured her on marriage, which I find sad. It's one of the reasons she left Boston for a fresh start in Oregon. She should be married, she's meant to be; some girls aren't, some would simply never be asked, but not her. I see the way she looks at Lynette, the way she talks to her. She'd love a child of her own; too bad the husband pickings in Oregon are so slim.

I see the way she looks at Noah, too; if I wasn't

*around she'd set her cap for him in a minute. But she's
not the type to be interested in a friend's husband, she
has too much integrity. And we have become friends.
I'll miss her dreadfully when we leave the train. We've
already promised faithfully we'll keep in touch, which
may prove a little hard since neither of us knows exactly where we'll land. The Sacramento Valley is huge and
Oregon even bigger.*

*Marcia seems determined to get me into teaching;
she raves about it at every opportunity. I can't deny I'd
be teaching today if I hadn't met Noah. But everybody
has roads they start out on and never reach the end of.
I know if Noah had a choice of careers he would have
gone into politics.*

*As difficult and demanding as this journey is it's
done wonders for him. It's gotten him out of himself;
he's made friends with all the men, he's become amaz-
ingly self-reliant, he takes excellent care of the wagon.
He's even taught himself how to use his gun; at least
now he can hit the broad side of a barn. (His words.) I
love him so, he's so good-hearted; all by himself he res-
cued Olin Coombs from the slough of despondency.
And his enthusiasm for California hasn't diminished
one whit; if anything, the fire burns hotter than ever.*

*Yet I can't help worrying about his running off to the
goldfields when we get there. From all I've read and
heard life is cheap and dangerous in the grand quest.
The gold seekers are an army of strangers, and it's said
that lifelong friends, even brothers, shed each other's
blood and worse over a tiny nugget or a few flakes
panned from a stream bottom. I just wish Noah wasn't
going out alone.*

He's asleep, as is Lynette in the wagon.

Everybody's asleep except Olin working on his new bonnet bows and good-hearted Abigail up sewing, repairing holes in same. Tomorrow morning we'll be passing a formation called Court House Rock. From there on to Fort Laramie is about a hundred miles; so at Court House Rock we'll be one-third of the way through Cheyenne territory.

That's five or six, at the most seven days.

FOURTEEN

Cheyenne Dog Soldiers had moved out of the Black Hills in force and were heading south toward the Platte River. The first night on the trail they camped near a thick stand of willows. The lodge hides were spread, the tripod main support frames raised and anchored, the additional poles set in place and the cover applied and pinned above the entrance. Twilight shadowed the campsite; the sun was half a copper coin depositing itself in the crest of the Rockies. To the east the Green Bottom River, its clear, cool waters fed by springs and melted winter snows, coursed indolently through the land. High bluffs sentineling the river bends sent down cascades of rose vines wearing myriad delicate pink blossoms. In the slate-colored hills two bighorns appeared, stepping surefootedly down from the rim, their preposterous and at the same time magnificent rounded horns framing their white-muzzled faces. Brown creepers, horned larks and western tanagers trafficked the clear air heralding the bighorns' appearance and a red-tailed hawk soared high overhead.

Black Fox, chief of the Cheyenne Dog Soldier warrior

society, entered the lodge and sat cross-legged opposite Chief Dawn Hawk and Chief Many Bows, the Ancient One. Half a moon earlier eight Dog Soldiers had been murdered in their sleep by a party of drunken fur traders and the chiefs were unanimous in vowing revenge. Black Fox in particular was determined to take ten white lives for the death of each single Dog Soldier under his command; among the traders' victims was his younger brother.

The Ancient One drew his gnarled and wrinkled finger in the dirt by one knee.

"We move down to here where Rawhide Creek rises from the hidden springs. Cross the creek here and move toward the setting sun."

"And approach the fort out of the shadow of the mountains," said Black Fox. "From there is where they will least expect attack."

"But," said Dawn Hawk, "the walls of the fort are made of adobe and higher than the smokehole of a lodge. And smooth, hard to climb."

Black Fox grunted disdainfully. Dawn Hawk was envious, and his pessimism was well known among the tribal leaders; rarely did he hesitate to voice his doubts about any venture undertaken by the Dog Soldiers.

"The walls do not worry me," said Black Fox. "There is no need to climb over them." His two listeners crinkled their brows in puzzlement. "Better we force the traders out."

"How?" asked Many Bows.

Black Fox smirked, his fingertip found his temple. "My plan is here. You will know it when you see it work."

The Ancient One raised the finger he had used to draw with in the dirt. "All the white ones inside must die and their bodies burnt. Only then will our dead be avenged."

Black Fox nodded. "The fort will be left a burnt-out husk, a warning to all whites that tribal lands are sacred and they do not belong here."

"How long before we get there?" asked Dawn Hawk.

Black Fox held up four fingers. "This many sleeps and you will see it. Every Dog Soldier heart will sing of the destruction of our enemies."

The Ancient One's furrowed face cracked into a smile. "And the night before we get there we hold the Dog Dance."

Black Fox nodded, his dark eyes gleaming and widening. "And when the sun begins painting the new day on the sky, we attack!"

"Four sleeps," repeated Many Bows. "To vengeance."

FIFTEEN

Court House Rock rose four hundred feet in tiers, a massive pile of volcanic ash and clay that, to some eyes, resembled a municipal building in St. Louis. No one in the train had ever seen the Court House in St. Louis, so there could be no argument. To Lucy, though, Court House Rock looked more like an outsized Egyptian temple in ruins.

Noah took one look and snickered. "Maybe the real thing in St. Louis is in even worse shape."

Ahead of them stood an even more dramatic natural edifice. Another barren, interminably dry and dusty fourteen miles led to Chimney Rock. It rose more than five hundred feet into the sweltering air, its base surrounded by huge piles of debris, the chippings of eons of wind and weather sculpturing.

Twenty additional miles up the trail came Scott's Bluff, a collection of towers and parapets, gulches and ravines. The bluff itself turned out to be a freestanding cliff towering some eight hundred feet above the treeless plain near the Wyoming line.

Arriving at Scott's Bluff brought the train to within two days of Fort Laramie. The emigrants stopped for the night. As Maynard Havers got out his harmonica and serenaded the gathering with "Bonny Barbara Allan," the supper fires were started and food brought out for preparation. Noah approached Herman Schwimmer.

"How far have we come, Herman?"

"Exactly's hard to tell, I mean from Council Bluffs. It's a knowed fact that from Independence, Missouri, to the fort is six hundred forty mile. Take away about seventy mile from that for us leaving from Council Bluffs and you got what?"

"Five-seventy."

"Five hundred seventy mile. Which is roughly one-third of the way to the Willamette Valley."

"Oregon . . ."

"Oregon."

"We're heading for the Sacramento Valley."

"I know that." Schwimmer raised his hands in a gesture of helplessness. "I couldn't begin to guess how much farther that is. I only know that them that are taking the Oregon Trail will need to cross the Great Basin and the desert from the Humboldt Sink to the Carson River. And then climb the Sierra Nevadas middle o' October. Noah, you ever hear o' the Donner party?"

"Who hasn't?"

"They're the best example I know o' bad timing. You and your missus got to make certain sure you get to Salt

Lake City by the end of August at the latest. Carve that fact in your mind."

"Why then?"

"On account you . . ." He poked Noah in the chest. "You don't want to be high up in the mountains come the middle o' October. In case nobody's told you, it snows early and heavy up there. It's the last place on earth you want to be when the heavens open up white. You could ask George Donner; if he hadn't starved and froze to death up there by Alder Creek he could tell you."

"I'll keep him in mind, Herman."

"It's more'n four hundred mile from Fort Laramie to Salt Lake City. You can figure for yourself how many wagon days that is."

"How far from Fort Laramie to Fort Bridger?"

"A tiring good haul; you'll be stopping there but not us. On past Fort Laramie the next bit o' Nature's folly is Independence Rock, where everybody stops to scratch their name. A bit less than eighty mile west of there is what they calls the Ice Slough."

"Surely there's no ice in midsummer."

"There's ice all year 'round; we'll be seven thousand feet up in the Wind River Mountains, the crest o' the trail."

"Go on. . . ."

"Next comes South Pass. At the western end o' South Pass is a spot called Pacific Springs. That'll be where you and us part company. You'll head for Fort Bridger, we take the Sublette Cutoff on up to Soda Springs. It'll be all mountains for a time for both of us, the Wasatches. Then comes Salt Lake City for you. If I was you I'd change oxen at Fort Bridger. Get yourself fresh muscle, you'll be needing it. Oh will you ever. . . ."

SIXTEEN

That night Lucy lay awake thinking of Ash Hollow, again comparing the Hollow with Druid Hill Park. Thoughts of Baltimore and home came—the parsonage. She had come home for Christmas vacation; the following June she would be graduating from Miss Paige's School. She had planned to continue her education at Greenville Women's College in Greenville, South Carolina, but she had met Noah Mitchum the previous summer and from then on her interest in her education and a career teaching began to wane; love having blossomed, marriage took first priority. He proposed, she accepted.

Daddy had given his consent, though somewhat reluctantly; Mother made no effort to hide her disapproval. Both Daddy and she liked Noah and were not averse to their daughter's marrying, but both thought she was rushing into it.

It was the week before Christmas, and the Scotts were looking forward enthusiastically to the holidays. Eight inches of snow blanketed the city from Bare Hills to Curtis Bay, the tree was up and painstakingly decorated, heaps of gifts surrounded the stand, an enormous wreath, the gift of one of Daddy's parishioners, decorated the front door, dwarfing the window wreaths. The three of them sat in the living room enjoying Daddy's eggnog. He had sprinkled too much nutmeg on his and was trying to spoon off the excess, much to Mother's amusement. Then her smile darkened into a martyred expression.

"If you could only put it off for four short years," she said. "Finish your education and then be married, providing you'll still want to."

The fire crackled merrily in the grate, snow lined the outside windowsills like glair fur; Lucy set down her eggnog.

"What you mean, Mother, is if Noah and I postpone it eventually one of us or both will lose interest."

"That, dear, never entered my mind."

"Didn't it?"

Daddy had finished spooning his nutmeg; he cleared his throat and began shifting about in his chair as if it was no longer comfortable. The conversation seemed to be making him as uneasy as it was his daughter. He let Mother repeat her litany of objections to the marriage, but, as he put it, he didn't think it fair for two people to push one into a corner.

"Surely you'll agree that the relationship that can stand firm while putting marriage off has proven itself a strong one."

"Our relationship is the Rock of Gibraltar, Mother."

"How do you know if you don't test it?"

Her mother's tenacity resembled a trap. Once sprung the king's army couldn't free you.

"Understand, Lucy, your father and I don't disapprove of Noah. Not at all, we're fond of him."

"Very," added Daddy, his lone contribution to the discussion so far. Lucy eyed the ormolu clock on the mantel; the discussion—really more of a speech by Mother—was approaching the end of the first half hour.

"Does Noah know how terrifically important completing your education and going into teaching is to you? Have you told him in so many words? Oh, it's not that marriage would prevent your teaching, but without college you'll never be qualified. Not to teach in Baltimore schools."

"Mother . . ."

"On the other hand, if you do get married and down the

road decide you want to teach—I'm speaking in terms of years later—how can you possibly attend college out of the city and care for your husband and children at the same time?"

"I . . ."

"You do intend to have children, don't you? My point is, dear, if you take time off now instead of continuing, won't it be that much harder to resume?"

"Mother, you ask questions and don't give me a chance to answer."

"Do you? Intend having children?"

"Of course."

"There you are then."

"You're confusing me, where am I?"

"It's quite simple, once you've started your little family you'll never go on to college. Your whole world will change, your focus, your aim. Education and a teaching career will be swept under the rug in the house; you'll be dusting and mopping every day. My dear, the point is, if you two love each other—and I expect you do, at least think you do—you should be prepared to wait the four years." The martyred look intensified, Lucy could almost see tears glistening. Daddy was still trying to find a comfortable position in his chair. "When I think of how hard you worked at Miss Paige's, how well you did . . . to throw it all away. What does Noah say? Surely he has an opinion."

"We haven't discussed it, not in any great detail."

Mother's jaw sagged; disbelief narrowed her eyes. "Lucy . . ."

"It's true. Because it's really all up to me, wouldn't you say? My life, my decision. I don't need his opinion; he obviously doesn't feel he should offer it."

"Perhaps I should talk to him."

Daddy had turned to shifting his legs one over the other; changing, changing. He paused. "I wouldn't if I were you, Emily."

Lucy's heart thanked him. In touchy situations (and what could be touchier than this?) he reined his emotions and invariably gravitated to what was sensible. While Mother, bless her heart, always seemed to sail off in six directions at once.

But Lucy couldn't bring herself to resent her attitude; she was concerned for all the right reasons. At least Mother thought so. As she got older she seemed to add new dimensions to the term well-meaning.

"It just seems tragic that you should lose out on your education."

" 'Tragic'?" murmured Daddy and rolled his eyes.

It earned him a reproachful frown.

"Mother, you may think it's a mistake," said Lucy. "I don't happen to. I see it as a choice. Not easy, I didn't think about it for only ten seconds and decide. It's been weeks and weeks; now I've decided, it's what I want to do. . . ."

"So you'll do it," said her mother, her tone offended. "Everett, aren't you going to say anything?"

"My dear, you've said it all."

"There's no cause to be frivolous."

"I wasn't aware I was being 'frivolous.' The girl's in love, she wants to marry the boy. For the life of me I can't see that as tragic."

Mother rose to her feet and looked off as if at another world (one where good judgment reigned?). "I'm going to bed."

Off she rustled. Daddy sighed and shook his head.

"If she's trying to make me feel guilty," said Lucy, "she's succeeded."

"You've no reason to, my dear. May I ask an impertinent question?" Lucy nodded. *"Would* Noah wait the four years?"

"What you mean is does he love me enough to, isn't that it?"

"You're answering a question with a question."

"I don't think love is by degrees; he either loves me or not. I think he does, I think he'd wait."

"That says a good deal about his character."

"I'd worry about me, not him."

"You?"

"I mean four years is so long; anything could happen. Before I finish and graduate I could meet someone else."

"And leave him high and dry? Isn't that stretching it? I saw you two together all last summer. I could see how deeply you care about each other. As much the understanding and harmony as love. In marriage people must make sacrifices. No two lives fit together as neatly as mortise and tenon. Husbands and wives have to make . . . modifications. In their behavior, habits, many areas. You have to change your plans, right? Adjusting, cooperating, is what keeps a relationship on track."

"Exactly."

"Another 'impertinent' question. What's he doing to adapt to you?"

"A great deal, beginning with taking a job he probably wouldn't dream of taking were it not for me."

"Eureka Printing."

"He's better than that, Daddy."

"It's a start. These are hard times; any job has to be the right one for most young fellows."

"He's always wanted to go into politics."

Her father chuckled. "Dear me, I'm sure he's better than 'that.' "

"Seriously, only it's a relief to know he won't be. Only don't ever tell him I said it. I simply can't see him as a politician. He's too ethical, he has scruples, integrity."

"He certainly seems to."

"He does. But getting back to this: we love each other. Why should I risk losing him? Running off to South Carolina for four years I could. It's just too long to wait. So there you are. Daddy?"

"Yes?"

"We have your permission, do we have your blessing?"

"Need you ask? You have your mother's, too. For all her picking around the edges and histrionics. She's being a mother, my dear, it's not only her prerogative it's her responsibility. Parents, mothers especially, can't resist plotting out their children's future for them, usually without consulting the child. When something unforeseen arises it's disruptive to them. It's mothers who think that mothers know best. She's only doing her duty as she sees it. Listen to me, I've no right being so judgmental."

"Except I agree with everything you say."

He winked, grinned and waved a finger. "Because it's what you want to hear. More eggnog?"

"No thanks, I've got to get to bed. Are you going up?"

"In a bit." Another wink. "Give your mother a chance to get to sleep. And I'd like to sit for a few minutes, maybe come up with an idea for this Sunday's sermon."

She squeezed his hand affectionately, kissed his forehead and went up to bed thanking the Lord for her father's support. Would Mother resent their ganging up on her? Probably. But this, too, shall pass.

It did. That night turned out to be the last time Mother talked about college and a teaching career. Capitulation was complete; from then on and through their wedding, the seas were calm, the sailing smooth.

Lucy leaned over and kissed the sleeping Noah, causing him to stir in his sleep. She pulled the blanket up more snugly under his chin, at the same time wondering what her life would be without his love. Too lonely, too empty, too unrewarding to be believed.

SEVENTEEN

As she did every day, Lucy awoke before dawn, with the other women and Olin Coombs, to start the fire, boil water and see to preparing breakfast. The day arrived muffled with cloud cover, the air heavy and threatening rain; and everybody in the train was out of humor to varying extents. Before breakfast the rain came, falling heavily, drowning the fires, limiting the meal to crackers and raw bacon.

This sat not at all well with Lynette, who awoke cranky, her disposition deteriorating as the downpour increased. Her resentment fired Noah's impatience and his scolding irritated Lucy. Only the oxen seemed able to take the dismal day in stride. Even Herman Schwimmer, usually the soul of forbearance, seemed incapable of reining his temper. A bedraggled-looking Marcia Talley was invited into the Mitchums' wagon by Lucy.

"It's not the rain," Marcia said, peering out at the drear and empty landscape, "it's the travel; everybody's worn to a frazzle, it's finally getting to us, and we're not even halfway there."

Noah grunted. "And everybody's supplies are about half-used up, and the oxen are getting weaker and slower by the hour."

He was right about the oxen, Lucy had noticed. And ahead, beyond Fort Laramie, the mountains would begin. At long range the previous afternoon, when the skies were so clear one could see for a hundred miles in every direction, the slopes of the Laramies looked like green meadows, but, Schwimmer warned them, up close they would turn out to be dry sand and rocks, studded with stunted clumps of sagebrush and greasewood.

The rain stopped around noon, but clear weather, even the belated appearance of the sun, failed to pick up the emigrants' spirits. Benumbed by boredom, drudging their way through the dull daily routine, men and women alike sank progressively deeper into their personal doldrums, from which only the sight of their destination would extricate them. Fort Laramie's appearance would pick them up, Schwimmer assured everyone; fresh meat and other provisions would be available. Prized beyond all else would be the precious full day's respite from jiggling and jouncing, battling mud or dust, rain or the blazing sun and enjoying the sweet silence of motionless wheels.

Black Fox had led his Dog Soldiers, Dawn Hawk, Many Bows and their escorts to within a few miles of their objective, situated at the junction of the North Platte and Laramie Rivers. Before sunrise the next day Fort Laramie would come into view to the east. When the sun parted the horizon they would attack.

"How many men inside do you think?" the Ancient One asked Black Fox.

"Not any bluebacks, if that is what worries you. Maybe fifty traders, maybe not so many. All with aching heads from tonight's whiskey. And even not drunk not good fighters like the bluebacks; they have no one to lead them, to organize *che-ga-wa-to.*"

"Resistance," murmured Dawn Hawk.

Envy gleamed in his eyes, reflected Black Fox; of him, of his leadership and the loyalty of his followers. Envy that Dawn Hawk could no more rid himself of than could he take off his skin; it fed his heart as antelope meat fed his belly.

"In the old days," said Many Bows, "that fort was a stockade; easy to burn down from outside."

"Inside the walls is much that is wood," said Black Fox. "Fire will be our friend in vengeance." He stood up waving his arms, calling his followers to him. When they had assembled he spoke.

"It will still be dark when we come within sight of the fort," he said. "Even at night you can see it against the sky. But before we get close enough to see it you will gather switches, grass, whatever and prepare as many torches as you can carry. Torches and fire arrows will turn the inside of the fort into one big flame. In seconds, the traders will be fighting each other trying to get out."

Many Bows chuckled. "And how high do you think the pile of corpses will reach outside the gate?"

"Better you ask how many will survive to shoot at our warriors," muttered Dawn Hawk. "They have guns."

"So do we, Dawn Hawk," said Black Fox, "look around you."

"Too few. And they will have iron logs that spit fire and noise and death."

Black Fox snickered derisively. "Only we will not give

them time to load them. When our fire comes raining down their only thought will be to get out. And those that can will run straight into our arrows and bullets." Evil darkened and twisted his features. "I hope there are more than fifty, more than a hundred. I hate traders as much as bluebacks . . . all are the same, all rapists and killers of our children. Enough, gather your switches and grass and when you are done we will hold the Dog Dance."

The Ancient One's voice cracked as he whooped. Those closest to him laughed good-naturedly, picking up his shout as he repeated it.

"We should get to the fort by sunrise tomorrow," announced Schwimmer that evening. "If you folks are willing to skip breakfast tomorrow and move out two hours before."

To this the emigrants agreed unanimously.

"Can we swap our oxen there?" asked Anson Willoughby.

Everyone had gathered around the Willoughby's fire; even the three Coombs children and Lynette.

"No," said Schwimmer, responding to Willoughby. "Not till Salt Lake City. And since that's off the Oregon Trail, only the Mitchums'll be passing through there. The rest of us'll have to wait until Fort Hall to do any swapping."

"How far to Fort Hall?" asked Maynard Havers.

"From the far end o' South Pass only about two hundred mile."

"Only, he says." Havers threw up his hands.

"You've been good travelers, all of you," said Schwimmer. "Taking everything that comes, working through it; you're patient and for the most part uncomplaining, up to standing the gaff where others I've traveled with just give up and go back. You've reason to be proud o' yourselves, all o' you. But—and I hate to have to tell you this, as if you didn't know already—the hardest part's ahead of us."

"The mountains," said Abigail.

"They're like no mountains you've ever seen back East. I'm not saying it to discourage you, just to impress upon you that after Fort Laramie you got to spare your oxen. You have so far, but you're going to have to even more. You'll have to lighten your loads even more, the lighter the better.

"There'll be no more twenty to twenty-five mile a day. Some days we'll be lucky to cover a hundred yards. Climbing will be as tough on your wagons as on your beasts. You can depend on busting at least one wheel, and consider yourselves lucky if you don't lose your whole rig down a ravine. Every day one of us'll go ahead to scout the trail."

"I don't understand," said Anson Willoughby, "I thought you knew the trail."

"I do. But mountains are funny; wind and weather can change 'em. Streams change their courses, freezing and thawing breaks rocks, pieces fall, strike other rocks and can end up blocking the trail with a wall ten foot high. It's either remove it stone by stone or go around it. And when you got a ditch a mile deep either side, you'll need wings getting around it."

"You said before we'll have to lighten our loads," said Abigail. "How light, how many pounds?"

"That I can't predict. You'll find out when the time comes. If you come to a grade so steep the oxen pulling and you pushing can't get up it, you got no choice but to lighten your load. And not just for that grade, I mean permanent. You're going to see enough goods thrown out on both sides of the trail from South Pass to Soda Springs—which is a little more'n fifty mile south o' Fort Hall, to fill every store in New York City and half in Boston. There's just no way of getting out o' paying a high price to get to where you're going. But folks don't hesitate to pay it."

"How far is it from Fort Hall to the Willamette Valley?" asked Ruth Willoughby.

Everyone's eyes save the Mitchums repeated the question. Schwimmer stared at Ruth for a few seconds and toed the ground with his boot. The others held their breaths.

"I wish you hadn't asked that, Missus, I've already discouraged you enough for one day."

EIGHTEEN

The skies over the distant Missouri were lightening into fireweed pink when Schwimmer halted the train. They skipped breakfast, as planned, in order to reach Fort Laramie that much sooner. But as the train rounded a bend, the emigrants gasped as one. Flames and billowing black smoke issued from the fort. Faint screaming and war whoops could be heard and Indians surrounded the walls. The emigrants began getting down from their wagons to move forward for a better look.

Schwimmer shouted. "Everybody back up and get off the trail. Left or right, find yourselves cover. If you can't, just keep driving, get out o' their line o' sight fast as you can!"

"Not that fast," said Noah glumly, looking down at his oxen. He got out his whip, steering the oxen sharp right toward a stand of willows by the North Platte. Maynard

Havers followed him. Reaching the trees, the four adults assembled, leaving Lynette in the wagon peering out the front with frightened eyes.

"My God . . . " murmured Lucy.

The traders inside the fort were pouring through the gate only to be met by a fusillade of arrows and scattered gunfire. At that distance the guns didn't sound like guns, but like corks popping. As the emigrants stood watching in horror, one after another trader fell dead, bodies collecting like cordwood, none more than a few steps from the entrance.

"It's a massacre," murmured Noah.

"Five minutes later and we would have been up near the gate smack in the thick of it," said Abigail.

Lucy swallowed her fright again and again. "Don't look, sweetheart, stay back in the wagon."

"Mind your mother," snapped Noah.

The attack ended in under a minute. From all appearances, not one trader had survived. Those who failed to make it outside to be shot and killed had to have perished in the flames. Now the Indians were going about methodically scalping their victims. Fewer than a dozen chiefs and braves had gotten back on their horses. They sat watching the grisly work.

"Are they Pawnees?" Noah asked Maynard.

"Not in Wyoming."

"They could be Cheyenne or Sioux," said Abigail. "Or any one of a dozen other tribes. It's all covered in Reverend Littleton's book."

They continued watching, mesmerized by the grim spectacle. Twenty minutes later by Noah's watch, all the Indians were back up on their horses and riding off to the north. The Mitchums and Havers waited another fifteen minutes before driving back to the trail. One at a time the other wagons reappeared. Before starting out Schwimmer spoke.

"What you're going to see up close won't be a pretty sight. Reverend Coombs, Noah, if I was you I'd keep the youngsters inside. And maybe some o' you ladies rather not look."

He misjudged them, none of the women hid their eyes. Lucy counted thirty-eight corpses outside the gate; most of them had been scalped.

"We just can't go on and leave them like this," she murmured. "We have to bury them."

"That'd take at least three days," said Noah.

Schwimmer, Havers and Willoughby came up.

"They should be buried," said Lucy.

Schwimmer shook his head. "Can't do that."

"Why not?"

"It's just not done."

"I find that hard to believe, we must have seen two thousand graves up to this point, not even counting those hidden in the middle of the trail."

"One or two killed or died at a time, Missus, not this many."

"It'd be un-Christian to leave them to the buzzards."

"She's right," said Havers.

"I can't argue that," said Schwimmer, "only, in this sun they'll start to stink in no time. Once they do none o' you'll want to go near 'em. But there's better reasons to leave 'em and go on. It's un-Christian, it's heartless, but this ain't the East. There's lots o' things you do as a matter o' course back there just can't be done out here. These poor souls can't be buried properlike. I wish we could do it but we can't. Look around you, we can't get any feed for the oxen here and our Ash Hollow water is getting down. Your animals can drink the river water but we can't. Most of the springs we've passed are poisoned, the nearest decent water is in the Sweetwater River and farther on there'll be springs in the mountains. But there's nothing here. Don't blame me, blame the redskins. Forage is just as important. We got to find decent grass, it's either that or you start busting up your mattresses to feed your critters.

"I can't order you to go on, all I can do is advise. Only Missus Mitchum, delaying ourselves to bury these poor souls is wrong six ways from breakfast. It's never done, never."

"He's right," said Noah quietly.

Lucy nodded reluctantly. Before leaving they looked inside the fort. It looked as if a single enormous blanket of black ash had been laid over the interior and snugged in place at the corners. Even the adobe walls were blackened inside.

By the time they were ready to move on, Lucy had to moisten her hanky in order to breathe. And the queasiness lodged in the pit of her stomach was beginning to spread upward. If she wasn't up to helping bury the dead, how could she expect others to be?

NINETEEN

The Indians destroying Fort Laramie promises the first of many "last straws." As confusing as that may sound. Only Abigail Havers is right: it could have been much worse for us, we could have driven up to the gate to be suddenly surrounded by them and all of us dead in two shakes of a lamb's tail.

They were as thorough as fire can be. Picking

through the ashes would have been a waste of time, nothing could have been salvaged. The men even saw blackened rifle barrels twisted like corkscrews, so intense was the heat. What stock the traders had the Indians took with them when they rode out.

The question is why did they attack? If they were Cheyenne—which seems likely—why wait until now to destroy the fort? According to Schwimmer, it's been in operation for fifteen years. Are the traders and the tribe at "war"? We wouldn't hear about it if they are, but that's hard to believe. If they are, wouldn't the fort have been better prepared? Sentries sent out to watch the trails coming from the north, where most of the Cheyenne villages are? Guards posted? The cannon placed, ready to repel attackers? I don't know a thing about strategy, but staying on the alert has to help in defending yourself.

Farther ahead is Fort Bridger, after South Pass. At the far end of South Pass is Pacific Springs, where we separate from the others. That won't be for at least two weeks from now, as once we begin climbing into the mountains we'll slow to a snail's pace. We're told there'll be plenty of grass for fodder and fresh water from the Sweetwater River, so we can stock up before we turn off for Fort Bridger. But our poor oxen, already tired out from getting us this far, will have to work doubly hard climbing through the mountains. What if one of our pairs dies? What if we lose two pair? We'd be marooned up there bag and baggage. It's so late in the season—there are no wagon trains behind us and no expectation of catching up with any ahead. We'd have to leave everything, including the surviving oxen, and walk to Fort Bridger.

And what if we reached there only to find the Indians have destroyed it, too? They told us back in Council Bluffs that the hardest part of getting to Oregon or California is the problems that are impossible to foresee: everything from freakish weather to man-made catastrophe. Only every day seems to bring a calamity of some sort; taken together, week in, week out, they begin wearing one down. Where are all the pleasant surprises? In the Sacramento Valley, according to Noah, the eternal optimist. How I wish some of his rosy outlook would rub off on me. Only—one of us has to be pragmatic!

Lynette didn't see the corpses outside the fort up close, thank the Lord; only as Noah says, there'll be no way to protect her from now on. Sarah Coombs was the first dead person she's ever seen. How does one protect a child from the primitiveness, the cruelty and bloodshed of the frontier? Blindfold her? Bury her in bedclothes from morn till night?

Keeping one's femininity intact en route is near impossible. Women who don't care how they look, how they dress, have no problem. Marcia was complaining about that very thing the other day, she takes such pride in how she looks. Anything you put on out here is covered with dust in half an hour, or spattered with mud. Your skin gets as hard as a man's; your hands get as rough as a lumberjack's. I miss so many little comforts that barely registered in mind back in Baltimore, one and all taken for granted. Clean sheets, a comfortable bed, rugs, carpets with lovely designs to walk on. I miss toilet water, easy chairs, wall mirrors, wallpaper. I miss windows looking out at lovely trees, at the garden. I miss church and Daddy's sermons. I miss a thou-

sand things, all small sacrifices and easy to put up with separately, but taken together they make for a wrenching change. It's like my life has been hollowed out and all the pretty things, the comforts, the luxuries, helpful devices and contrivances spilled out.

Now we can look forward to walking over the Rocky Mountains. A year ago, if anyone told me I'd be climbing the highest mountains in the country while pushing the back wheel of a wagon I'd have laughed in his face.

The good side is that none of this is forever. However difficult and exhausting, it's only a means to an end. A worthwhile end—at least Noah thinks so. And all of us in the wagon train get along, a rarity when strangers are thrown together under such difficulties and such trying circumstances, according to Schwimmer.

And best of all, our little family is together. I could never have tolerated Noah's coming out here by himself, getting settled and sending for us. If it has to be done, this is the only way to do it. I'm grateful, too, that I'm not pregnant. I hear that traveling overland while pregnant can be a nightmare.

The weather is brutally extreme and defies predicting; most of the scenery is as barren as an empty barrel, but some is breathtakingly beautiful; and the sunsets can be glorious. So the good may be outweighed by the bad by a wide margin, but good there is, and, as Noah keeps insisting, reaching the Sacramento Valley will be well worth the struggle. For his sake even more than mine I hope he's right. His judgment deserves affirmation, it'll do his ego good.

*I just wish that when we do get there he didn't have
to go running off to the goldfields.*

"Considering everything, what I miss most is a bathtub,"
said Marcia.

Lucy nodded emphatically. "That's high on my list,
too." Noah chuckled. "It is. A bathtub's so much more than
soap and hot water. You step into a tub and you're in sort of
a warm heaven. Walled in, protected, the heat envelops
you, relaxes you; in seconds you feel deliciously soft and
limber."

"Deliciously, no less." Noah grinned.

"She's right," said Marcia. "There's nothing a woman
can do for herself to compare with lounging in a tub; you go
limp as old lettuce, let your mind drift off, you doze. There's
so much more to a bath than just scrubbing off the day. It
does for your body what . . ."

"Fishing does for your nerves," said Noah.

"Oh, much more, there's all the difference in the world;
and once you're done washing and rinsing you could stay in
your tub forever. No interruptions, nothing to see or do but
relax, and it's all for you. Only for you. It's pampering at its
most glorious."

"The warmth, the sweet fragrance of the soap, the
peaceful surroundings," said Lucy, "it really is like taking
time in heaven." Marcia nodded, her eyes dreamy.

"The door locked, the knowing you don't have to talk to
anyone except yourself. You can sing if you like without
anyone looking at you strangely. Your problems rise up with
the waves of heat and vanish for a precious little while. You
relax, feel all the strain and tension go out of your neck,
your shoulders, every part of you."

"You do remember to wash," said Noah.

"We're talking about after you're done," said Lucy. "When you can lounge."

The three of them shared the driver's seat; the Laramies were drawing closer, this would be the last day riding. Starting up into the mountains everyone except the youngest children would begin walking. And pushing and pulling when it was needed.

"The very first thing I buy when I get to Oregon will be a bathtub," announced Marcia. "Even before food. A copper plunge bath, the biggest I can find."

Noah laughed. "If you can find one."

"Even heavy tin will do, japanned, blue inside."

"You'll need necessities before you can think about luxuries," he went on.

"Whoever told you a bathtub is a luxury?" Lucy frowned. "Not to a woman. A man can wash in a laundry tub. You'd be satisfied with a bucket, Noah Mitchum."

Marcia laughed. "You don't know what you're missing."

"I bathe to get clean, Miss Talley, lying in a tub all day verges on the sinful. What a waste of time."

"He hasn't been listening," said Lucy.

"Lounging in a bathtub is pampering oneself on the grandest of grand scales," said Marcia. "And the beauty of it is that it doesn't cost a fortune. Try it sometime; keep adding hot water and lounge for half an hour."

"Oh, an hour at least," said Lucy.

"However long you can spare. I recommend it highly for divesting oneself of an especially bad day. You wash it away and lounge till you're so relaxed you hover between wakefulness and sleep. It's sublime."

"There's nothing to compare with it," said Lucy.

"You get to between wakefulness and sleep and you feel transported. That's why it's so important to lock the door so no one can disturb you."

"Abigail Havers brought along her bathtub," said Lucy. "I've seen it."

"Maynard must have been looking the other way when she loaded it." Noah laughed.

The wagons trundled on into the sunset; the mountain crest sent down shadows that broadened as they came sweeping toward them and the sky began assuming a coppery tint. Only two small cloud wisps could be seen; fair weather ahead. Lucy studied the clouds as they hung motionless and wondered: *how long*.

══════ TWENTY ══════

Walking through the rugged Laramie Mountains introduced the emigrants to blisters, bruises and severely aching feet. Nightfall of the second day found them suffering, sighing and soaking their feet in Epsom salt in warm water at day's end. The mountains continuing to rise ahead presented a formidable and rapidly discouraging challenge. Schwimmer tried his best to keep up morale; the emigrants paid little attention. Lucy and Marcia shared a washtub half-filled with water into which half a pound of Epsom salt had been poured. Marcia winced as she dried her feet before gingerly rubbing on a liberal application of Dr. Small's Arnicated Carbolic Salve.

Lucy examined the raw places on her own feet. "They feel like every bone is broken all the way up to my knees."

"I once had a cousin who could walk a whole city block

on his hands." Marcia managed a grin. "I may try it for a few days."

"I won't make it to sunset tomorrow." Lucy glanced upward at the towering black wall ahead. It seemed set into place solely to prevent their going any farther, as if the Far West were an enormous club room permitting entry to members only. Late in arriving, she, Noah and the others were barred from admission. "The closer we get the higher the mountains," she murmured. "Would that we could fly over them and land in South Pass."

"I'd like to fly all the way to the Willamette Valley. How high up is this South Pass?"

"Over seven thousand feet, according to Abby. More rocks all the way though, I'm sure. And still more for Noah and me till we reach the notorious Great Basin."

Marcia looked grim. "Abby isn't looking well lately, have you noticed?"

"She looks terrible, all she does is cough."

"Is it serious do you think?"

"She doesn't say, I don't ask. How old do you think Abby is, Marcia?"

"Late sixties?"

"At least. I'm getting worried. Up to Fort Laramie she was so vigorous, bursting with energy from morning till night. Now she drags about. I heard her arguing with Maynard; he was insisting she ride in the wagon. She wouldn't hear of it, you know Abby. Did I tell you Nancy Coombs' fracture is healed? Her father took off the bandage and splints this morning."

"About Abby . . ." began Marcia.

"Will she make it?" Lucy shrugged and shook her head disconsolately. Marcia looked away sighing. Lucy followed her glance to a split rock barely visible in the darkness. It was on the far side of Noah's wagon. The split ran a consistent six inches wide from the bonnet to the top of the rock, at least forty feet high. All the rocks around them seemed to be coming apart. "I think Abby's biggest problem is in her head. She's always been so active, so tireless; people like that have the hardest time giving in to illness. They refuse to, I suppose because they see it as a sign of weakness, which they can't stand. To them slowing down is a mortal sin."

A shadowy figure appeared up the trail walking toward them. In the darkened enclosure of the surrounding rocks it was impossible to make out who it was until a sharp, dry coughing broke the stillness.

Abby joined them, smiling a greeting that fled her face as she coughed. She had brought down a pot of tea.

"It's Lalla Rookh. Delicious. Mr. Havers and I have had our fill, I thought you two might like a cup."

Lucy got out cups, Abigail refusing the one offered her. Her cough persisted. It embarrassed her; in vain she tried to push it down her throat to where it wouldn't be so loud, while muffling it with her fist. A strange cough: hollow, at the same time sharp; and unproductive.

"How do you feel?" Marcia asked.

"I'm all right."

Lucy studied her, her large, bony hands planted on her knees, shoulders as wide as a man's, ramrod posture, chiseled chin high and proud. Only her normally swarthy skin was taking on a waxen look. "Are you taking anything for that cough?"

"Hammond's Remedy. And gallons of tea. It's my lungs, I was born with weak lungs, though you'd never know it to look at me, I'm such a horse." She laughed gaily, which started her coughing again. "For years I've done everything

I can to build them up; nothing helps. I don't get colds, I get hacking coughs that just won't quit."

On more careful inspection her waxen complexion was beginning to look a sickly white to Lucy; her lips were unusually red and around her eyes was red. Whatever was wrong with her lungs, it didn't affect her breathing, which was deep and measured. But clearly she was very ill.

"You should stay in the wagon," said Marcia.

"How can I? I weigh a hundred and forty pounds. The cattle can't be pulling that much extra weight, to say nothing of Mr. Havers losing out on my pushing."

"You can't think about that," said Marcia. "Besides, it may be for just a day or two."

Lucy nodded. "What's wrong with you could go away as fast as it came."

Abby grunted. "I know. Mr. Havers insists I ride, only how can I?"

"You'd rather walk and risk serious complications," rasped Lucy.

Abigail's head jerked sharply; by the light of the fire she suddenly looked deeply offended.

"What she means is . . ." began Marcia.

"I heard. If my condition upsets you, Lucy, I'm sorry. But it's still *my* problem; I'll thank you to keep your opinions to yourself." She coughed, and for fully ten seconds couldn't stop. "This is embarrassing."

Lucy spoke. "Why don't you ride in our wagon? Noah won't mind, he and I push together; you could keep Lynette company."

"No thank you," said Abigail. "Mr. Havers needs my strength, what's left of it. And you and Noah have enough weight without adding mine."

"Abby . . ."

"Let's not argue, please, I'm not up to it. I'd best get back before one of us says something she'll regret. Good night."

She left coughing.

"Listen to her, she'll be dead in a week," snapped Lucy.

"Lucy!"

"I'm sorry, martyrs make me sick. It's so stupid, when you know what to do and don't do it out of sheer obstinacy. She'd deliberately risk her life so as not to be a burden. What 'burden' will it be for him if she dies? She makes me furious!"

"Why harp on it, she won't budge."

"Maybe I'm talking to the wrong Havers."

Noah had come over; his expression said that he could feel the tension. Marcia told him about Abigail; Lucy continued to be angry.

"Stubborn mule! You've got to help, Noah."

"Me?"

"Talk to Maynard. Tell him how worried we are. Tell him we're . . . we're mortally afraid for her. Doesn't he know how sick she is? Can't he see?"

"I'm sure he knows. She's very forceful, very determined. And proud. She refuses to let Maynard do all the work. It's intolerable to her."

Lucy scowled at him. "Good God, he's as bad as Abby," she said to Marcia.

"Lucy . . ."

She was on her feet, standing too close to him. "Can't you see she's killing herself pushing that stupid wagon? She is, she might as well be swallowing poison drop by drop. She should be flat on her back. Rest would cure that cough, she could be good as new in a few days."

"She could," said Marcia.

"I can't argue that," said Noah, "I just hate sticking my nose into something so sensitive, so personal."

"You didn't hesitate to stick it into the wife beater's sorry business."

"The what?" asked Marcia.

"Nothing."

"Who's the 'wife beater'?"

"Olin," murmured Noah, and explained.

Shock flowed slowly down Marcia's face; she gasped. "Olin Coombs. To hear him talk he worshiped her. . . ."

"Never mind him," said Lucy. "Sarah's in a better place. Free of him. That's all water over the dam. Noah, this is getting more and more desperate by the hour. You can save her, you've got to convince Maynard how serious it is."

"What makes you think he doesn't know already?"

"If he did wouldn't he put his foot down?"

"Maybe he's tried and can't get through to her. The more he complains the tighter she closes her ears."

"*I'll* talk to him," snapped Lucy.

Noah shook his head. "I wouldn't if I were you."

"The two of us'll go to him," suggested Marcia.

Noah winced. "Abby would love that."

Lucy glared. "Who cares? Better to lose her friendship than her. Right, Marcia?"

Noah sighed. "All right, all right, I'll talk to him."

Lucy drew a breath in sharply. "Whoever approaches him she'll blame me. I don't care. This ridiculous wild-goose chase has already taken Sarah Coombs, I'll be damned if Abby has to die, too!"

Noah sighed. "Somehow I knew the trek would be the culprit."

"Oh who cares? She's what's important. It's hardly the time to get touchy about choices."

"I think the three of us should talk to Maynard," said Marcia.

Lucy nodded. "Good idea, go get him, Noah."

Noah threw up his hands and started up the trail. Lucy and Marcia finished their second cup of tea. They were rinsing out the cups when Noah returned with Maynard. Lucy and Marcia took turns elaborating on their concern about Abigail. Maynard nodded repeatedly but said nothing until they had finished.

"Something's got to be done," added Noah, as if feeling obligated to contribute.

"You're more'n welcome to try," murmured Maynard. "You got my blessing. I've worn out my throat talking, all she does is set her lips like she does, shake her head and cough some more. She knows her lungs are failing, knows what could happen. She doses herself with pills and powders, teas and roots and leaves; but she refuses the best thing she can do for herself: quit working. I even fixed a bed for her in the wagon. Comfortable as can be, fit for Queen Cleopatra herself, but she refuses to get into it. I been tempted to knock her over the head and pile her in but she'd only wake up and climb back out. When she's not pushing from behind she's pushing on a wheel or pulling the oxen. I can't get her off her feet, can't stop her from helping. Is this crazy or what? She's like a machine you can't turn off." Tears came sliding down, tracing gleaming courses down his cheeks into his beard. "You think I can't see she's killing herself? Heading for the grave like Lazarus the beggar, him that was laid at the rich man's gate, full of sores. Long before Independence Rock and

the Sweetwater I'll be piling stones on her corpse, oh mer-
ciful God in heaven!"

He caught himself. " 'Cause her mind's made up that's
how she wants it."

"I don't believe it," said Lucy.

"Believe what you like, Lucy, we're talking about Abigail
here. There's folks that'll put on their Sunday best, take to
their bed and wait for Death. Not her, she's got to be
doing—cooking, fetching, helping some neighbor or pushing the wagon—she'll be doing it when Death lays his cold
hand on her shoulder. The sickness in her lungs got nothing to do with it, *she plumb can't stop doing*. She's like an old
clock, you wind it up and it keeps going till it stops. Only
nothing can stop it before the spring gives out. Now, if
you'll excuse me, I'll thank you all for your caring and your
concern but I got to go back. Not that she needs me; I can't
do anything, I just watch. Good night, all."

"I'll talk to her in the morning," said Noah, "I promise."

"No you won't," murmured Lucy.

Marcia agreed with a shake of her head.

TWENTY-ONE

Down from the heights the wagon train came to a rough
and desolate stretch of land, not a drop of water, not a spear
of grass to be seen; only a rumpled landscape of bare hills,
no rocks, no sand, no dust. The temperature rose to 104
degrees. Descending the slopes, Lucy had joined Abby
walking at the rear of the Havers' wagon. As Lucy joined his
wife, Maynard moved up to the front.

"I'm not pushing," said Abby.

"You're not getting into the wagon."

"Has everyone elected you to work on me, or is it strict-ly your idea?"

"I didn't leave a perfectly uncomfortable driver's seat to come up here and argue. You look frightful."

Abigail coughed as if to underscore the opinion. "Thank you."

"He's begged you to get to bed in the wagon."

"I'm afraid if I do he'll sneak up on me and tie me fast."

"It's not funny, Abby. Look at Olin Coombs."

"What's he got to do with anything?"

"You've seen, he's helpless without Sarah."

"I hear he can blame himself for that."

"That's not the point, he really is as helpless as a four-year-old. He's lucky to have his son and the two girls. How do you think Maynard would do without you? Be honest."

"I wouldn't know."

"That's not honest. He'd be lost, and you know it. Noah would be lost, too, without me. Maynard doesn't need you to push and pull, he needs a wife, not an extra ox."

"What he really doesn't need is extra baggage; which is what *I'd* be riding. If we were to lose even just one ox because of extra weight I'd never forgive myself."

"You mean his oxen are more important to him than you. You're a lovely person, Abby, a jewel. I confess I adore you. Maybe that's why you infuriate me so, infuriate us all. Even your poor husband."

"Lucy . . ."

"Let me finish. Your only fault that I can see is a huge one. You're disgustingly self-centered. You decide some-thing and that's it, no one else has any say, least of all poor

Maynard. He had tears in his eyes last night telling us about this sorry business, how he feels about you, how desperately worried he is he'll lose you. It would kill him."

"That's enough."

"I'm not through. You don't care about him, about any of us. You care about you, your 'obligations,' your 'duty.' You're a fool, Abigail Havers, he deserves better than an ox for a wife. What he doesn't deserve is a martyr to the cause of getting to Oregon. Have you once asked yourself what he'd ever do up there without you? On his own this late in life? Your being sick and the way you behave makes me sick. I'm going back."

Abby's mouth remained open as Lucy turned and walked away, stepping on an unseen stone, reacting angrily at the pain, hopping for a few steps and hurrying on.

Five days later, in the afternoon, the emigrants passed Independence Rock and crossed the Sweetwater River over a bridge. Each wagon paid a three-dollar toll and the oxen and others animals swam across. The river was high and much swifter than the Platte at any point, but no oxen were lost. The water lived up to its name, the emigrants replenished their supply.

Abigail Havers condition grew worse over the rest of the day and the day following her dressing-down by Lucy. Then, miraculously, she began to improve. She coughed less and less, the color slowly returned to her cheeks; by the time Independence Rock appeared in the distance, she had completely recovered.

To Lucy and Marcia she attributed the return of her health . . .

"To exercise."

Which was hard to argue, inasmuch as she had yet to ride in the couple's wagon.

"The funny thing is," commented Noah, "Maynard doesn't seem at all surprised."

"Maybe because he's seen it before," said Marcia.

"But he was coming apart he was so worried."

Marcia laughed. "He's a deep one. So is she."

Lucy said nothing; she was too busy wondering if Abigail would forgive her for her harsh words. Then decided she would, she wasn't the type to hold a grudge. At this point Abby probably thought it was all very funny.

TWENTY-TWO

The crest of the continent made the Laramie Range look like rubble. A billion years earlier, from deep within an inland sea, the chain of mountains began pushing upward, to intercept the clouds and send their rain to the two largest oceans of the world. And the Rockies were born.

We keep on, the land once again rising and all of us shivering in midsummer. We came today to a place called the Ice Slough, seventy-seven miles west of Independence Rock. Here a bed of ice lays about a foot under the sod even at high noon. Schwimmer says that some travelers chop out big chunks for their water casks. (We topped off all our containers at the Sweetwater River.) The ice resists melting because we're so high up—more than seven thousand feet.

Ahead is the vaunted South Pass. A few miles

beyond there is a place called Pacific Springs. Just beyond there is where the three of us will actually be leaving the train, the others heading northwest, continuing on the Oregon Trail while we turn off to the southwest and Fort Bridger through the Wasatch Mountains.

I'll miss everyone so terribly, especially Abby and Marcia. I just know all three of us'll be crying our eyes out. Marcia and I will, Abby will play the stoic. But dear Lord I'll miss her, she's such a marvelous human being. She forgave me for ordering her into the wagon. She never did get in; I knew she wouldn't. Noah says she got well purely to spite us all, that Mother Nature jumps at her command. Which is not hard to believe, considering how things turned out.

Marcia is already down in the dumps over our separating. I pray I'll hear from her; there's got to be some way to make contact between the Willamette Valley and the Sacramento. Only, neither of us has a specific landing place and both valleys are so enormous. It's hard on a person to make such a good friend only to lose her. All the time you're close you know that it has to come to that eventually. We'll just never see each other again. And that's so sad.

Look at that, if that doesn't beat all, a tear on the word "sad."

I can't help worrying about the three of us after we leave the others, there's still so far to go. We've come so far and we're just over halfway there. To Fort Bridger, to Salt Lake City, across that hideous Basin and desert, then over the Donner Mountains. That's what I've begun calling them, only not in front of Noah.

Schwimmer keeps saying that Noah and I are the lucky ones. The others, keeping to the Oregon Trail, will

have to take Sublette's Cutoff, which is a fifty-mile
stretch across a grassless tableland. The only available
water is on its far side in the Green River. While they're
crossing the cutoff we'll be heading southwest for Fort
Bridger, with good water and forage all the way.

Whatever the landscape, however high the mountains or
flat the lowlands the wagon train continued to pass graves
on both sides of the trail, one grave every eighty yards on
average between the Missouri River and the Willamette
Valley, according to Schwimmer. Lucy got to talking with
the wagon master one evening, while Noah was busy greasing the wheels.

"I'm curious," she said, "why are you heading up to
Oregon all by yourself?"

A smile ignited Schwimmer's round face. "On account I
got no wife."

"But where are you going?"

"Fort Vancouver on the Columbia River. I'm going to
work for the Hudson's Bay Company. My roaming days are
over, I'm settling down. I'll make steady money, I'll build
me a cabin, find me a Cowlitz bride."

"Cow? . . ."

"That's a tribe. Fort Vancouver is Cowlitz redskin country, prettiest women west o' the Big Muddy. Present company excepted, o' course."

"You don't like cities do you, Herman?"

"Can't stand 'em. Give me the woods any time. And I'm
sick of rolling. I've had my fill o' alkali dust, dry rations
and . . ."

"Emigrants."

He grinned. "Not you folks, you're the easiest I ever
worked with. You should see some of them, I could tell you

stories. . . . I've seen easterners start out from jumping-off places with their wagons pulled by horses—and refuse to believe they can't make it halfway to Fort Kearny. Women so spoiled they never set foot out of the wagon even when the trail's at its steepest; they just lounge about all day prettying and pampering themselves, letting their servants do the cooking and cleaning and everything. I've seen a whole train, nineteen wagons, hit their first real rain, turn around and start back. I've seen more folks die on the trail than I care to remember. And most for stupid reasons: wandering off where the redskins are thickest, drinking poisoned water, getting themselves run over by their own rig, bit by snakes, trampled by buffalo. People are amazing, out to get themselves for sure. Not you folks, o' course, except I was a mite worried about Missus Havers. How was I to know she got a railroad rail for a spine. Woman's got more ox in her than human, I swear."

Lucy laughed. Noah was done greasing, the stopover was ended, the trek resumed.

"What were you and Herman talking about?" asked Noah.

"Him, mostly, his aspirations. He's a good soul, I'll miss him. I can't think of attempting something like this without his help and guidance, his experience."

"Lucy . . ."

"Mmmmm?"

"That's exactly what we'll be doing after Pacific Springs."

"Oh. That's true. For a minute there I forgot."

He laughed.

TWENTY-THREE

Wild roses, geraniums and amaranth littered the wayside, bringing color to the glorious scenery until the trail began to rise again. Soon, patches of snow appeared and the never-resting wind took on a sharp edge. It seeped through the two blankets Lucy pulled tightly around her and invaded marrow and bone. Getting up in the morning her teeth chattered until she and Marcia got the fire going.

Ahead loomed South Pass, the "Great Crossing"; not rocky, as Lucy had envisioned it, but a sandy, saddlelike valley with here and there drifting snow that looked as permanent as the cliffs and crags reaching for the clouds far ahead.

"I pictured a great gorge," murmured Noah, his eyes fixed on the mountain crest from which the morning mist had almost completely dissolved.

The pass stretched twenty miles, arching over a broad grassy meadow, its opposite side dipping down toward the Pacific. From there all the rivers flowed west.

And four miles from the distant end of South Pass lay Pacific Springs. To Lucy it seemed to take only a few fleet minutes to reach there. There were springs where supplies of water could be replenished, a few trees and wildflowers, but Pacific Springs was no Ash Hollow. Seeing it materialize saddened Lucy; she could feel tears come into her eyes. Noah's hand found hers and Marcia, sitting on her other side, put her arm around her.

Good-byes were as sad as Lucy anticipated. As she spoke with Ruth Willoughby she thought of Anson, Ruth's Boaz, and though he continued to dominate her and she let him, it struck Lucy that despite the inequities in their marriage

Ruth was content; there was a bond between them. Who was she to judge their relationship?

"Be careful, you two," said Ruth.

Lucy managed a smile. "You and Anson, too. I wish we could stick together. I'd as soon end up in Oregon as California. I don't see any difference, except for the gold." Ruth tittered. It was the first time Lucy had seen her express amusement over anything, and Ruth's face said that she wanted to explain her reaction. Anson stood close by talking to Schwimmer; Ruth lowered her voice.

"Between the two of us, I wish Anson and I were going to California. Not to prospect for gold, only because it's so much warmer than Oregon. I left Canada to get away from the cold; now here I am heading right back into it. They say Oregon winters can be brutal."

"Does he know how you feel?"

"Oh no. And I wouldn't tell him. He decides for us, far be it for me to confuse things."

"Mmmmm, you're only his wife."

"That's right."

Abigail Havers came over. Ruth impulsively kissed Lucy on the cheek, squeezing both her hands, and then almost ran to Anson to grab his arm. Abigail watched her, shook her head, but made no comment. She smiled fondly at Lucy, she was by now completely recovered, her vigorous, tireless self again. Lucy felt almost foolish appraising her: her ruddy cheeks, clear eyes, imposing appearance exuding health.

"So we part company, Mrs. Mitchum."

"So we do, *Mrs.* Havers." They hugged. "I'll miss you dreadfully, Abby; who do I run to with my troubles now?"

"Stop it, you make me sound like a big sister. You never complained, never had any real problems." She winked and laughed. "Not yet."

"What?"

"I do wish you were already there; us, too. All of us have carried the burden so long. . . . I've read about the Great Basin, even though Mr. Havers and I get to avoid it. The heat, the dryness, the distance, how hard it is on oxen. You and Noah have got to fix these things in mind, accept them and put them to one side. Bow your heads and press on and on and on. Once you reach the Carson River you can celebrate; crossing the Devil's Kingdom is the hardest thing you'll have to do. But you can do it and your Noah can, too. He's pulled himself up by the bootstraps since Council Bluffs—what a change! And he can pull even higher when he needs to. Don't tell him I said that, it'll go right to his head. Not because he's Noah, because he's a man."

"I really worry about the oxen."

"You'll be trading for fresh ones at Fort Bridger."

"Definitely. Abby, are there lots of Indians around Fort Bridger?"

"Around the whole route, till you get to the Basin. Mostly Utes."

Lucy knew the name to be only one syllable, but Abby got all her information from her reading.

"Are they as bad as the Sioux?"

"All Indians are dangerous, that's the safest assumption. Stay clear of them if you possibly can."

"Would that they stay clear of us. They're bound to pick on us, aren't they?"

"Why do you say that?"

"A single wagon, only one man. Easy pickings." The look on Abby's face agreed emphatically. "Are there no Indians in the Basin? I mean that's where we'll be our most vulnerable, the weakest. . . ."

"Utes, they come to harvest the crickets."

"Crickets?"

"To eat."

"Oh my Lord."

"Everyone to his own taste, right? My dear, I don't mean to frighten you, I just want you on your guard. Hundreds of emigrants, thousands, have crossed the Great Basin and climbed the Sierra Nevadas and live in the Sacramento Valley. They made it—so will you; with flying colors."

The men came over to say good-bye to Lucy. When Marcia walked up they withdrew.

"So . . ." said Marcia.

"So."

"Listen closely, this is important. There's a place called Oregon City in the Willamette Valley. It's near the Willamette Falls, for whatever that's worth. But I've been thinking: if you were to send a letter care of the Hudson's Bay Company in Fort Vancouver, where Schwimmer's heading, I'm sure they'd send it down to Oregon City. They forward mail all over the West."

"It makes sense," said Lucy. "I haven't the remotest idea where we'll be settling; it could be two hundred miles from the nearest post office. But as soon as I have an address I'll write. By then my letter will probably weigh four pounds."

"Mine, too."

"We'll be terribly far apart."

"A million miles."

Lucy responded with a weak smile. "Last night I thought about ten years from now; we'll both be long settled. You'll be teaching and married."

Marcia laughed thinly. "I wouldn't be too sure about that."

"Oh, you will be. Abby says there's thirty men for every white woman in Oregon."

"I hear red is the color of preference up there."

"Seriously, you'll have children: I predict a boy and a girl."

"By then you'll have a houseful. Have you thought at all about what we discussed? About teaching?"

"I'd love to, I just don't have the qualifications. I never made it to college."

"Lucy, you're as educated as I am; you sure know as much. You're very bright and believe me, 'qualifications' in the Sacramento Valley aren't going to be demanding. Anybody who can write a simple declarative sentence without misspelling more than four words can teach."

"Thank you."

Both grinned, both sobered.

"I hate this," murmured Lucy. Out of the corner of her eye she saw Herman Schwimmer heading their way; she blessed him for interrupting. Marcia, too, looked relieved. She moved to go, Lucy caught her arm. "Stay." Schwimmer came up tipping his disreputable hat. Noah joined them.

"One last thing before we split up," said the wagon master. "After Fort Bridger you'll come to Salt Lake City. I should warn you: the Mormons can be a mite . . . confusing. Watch yourselves."

"They're not to be trusted?" asked Noah.

"They're very shrewd dealing with 'em. They don't much like gentiles; that's us, that's anybody who ain't Mormon. They're God-fearing, hardworking, good-hearted, generous. They're also intolerant, unforgiving and strict as the worst schoolmarm of your childhood nightmares. Leastwise Brigham Young is, and he's in charge. They took a terrible beating from outsiders just getting here. Most folks are deeply prejudiced 'gainst 'em, mostly on account of the men take more'n one wife at a time. But they been through hell and the highest water getting here and they claim it as all their own. Anybody—even just passing through there—ain't all that welcome, if you follow my meaning."

"Are you saying we'll be in danger?" asked Lucy.

Schwimmer grinned. "Not o' your skins, just pay strict attention in any business deals you have with 'em. In lotsa ways they're an amazing people. They come from the banks o' the Mississippi fourteen hundred mile to Salt Lake City. How they done it is the amazing part. They moved in small groups. The first groups planted fields, sowed crops. Groups that come after them harvested the food and left behind new plantings for them that followed.

"This was three years back. By midfall more'n a few thousand had traveled four hundred mile to winter quarters in redskin country on the Missouri River, just west o' where we left from. There come a winter o' sheer misery. Starvation and cholera killed more'n six hundred. But by spring they was ready to push on. When you get to Salt Lake City and see what they 'complished in so few months your eyes'll pop outta your heads. Just be careful in your business dealings with 'em. They'll slicker you outta your boots while you're standing in 'em, Noah. Good luck and Godspeed to you both, all o' us are losing two good friends. We'll miss you mightily, but that's the way o' the trail."

Lucy and Marcia hugged again; both fought to hold back tears. Lucy could feel Noah watching, Lynette standing beside him holding his hand. Marcia had already said good-bye to both.

"I'll write as soon as we're settled," murmured Lucy.

"Please. Don't let time pass and put it off and never get around to it."

"That won't happen, I promise."

Marcia nodded. "Yes." Spoken tonelessly as if other thoughts had suddenly whisked her away.

"What is it, Marcia?"

"I don't know; as welcome as it is, a letter's just thoughts on paper. If only we could get together once in awhile. Once a year, even."

"Maybe someday."

"Maybe. I'll think of you every day, Lucy, and pray you're well, and Noah and Lynette. It's not a million miles. They say more and more boats are traveling up and down the coast. Maybe I could come down. There's a new town, Sacramento . . ."

"Is it near the coast?" Lucy asked.

"I don't know."

"That's our whole trouble, neither of us knows anything about where we're heading; I guess because there's so little there, so few settlements." Schwimmer called; the other emigrants were up on their wagons; Marcia would be back riding with Olin Coombs and his children. "This is it," said Lucy.

They hugged and held each other one last time. Marcia broke away, spinning about, striding swiftly to her wagon. Olin helped her up. Lucy, Noah and Lynette got up on their driver's seat. Noah pulled out first, heading southwest. Lucy peered back around the bonnet, but there was no point in waving, the Coombs' wagon had already moved behind the trees and started heading back toward the Oregon Trail.

Noah closed his hand over Lucy's hands in her lap.

TWENTY-FOUR

From Pacific Springs to Fort Bridger was over a hundred miles; more than five days' travel with the oxen so weary. On they rolled between dawn and darkness . . . until they reached a point Noah estimated was ten miles from the fort. No sooner had he spoken than the skies began blackening and thunder rumbled through the peaks; the wind from the east blew harder and the rains came.

Lucy was still glum, and the weather helped her mood not at all. Barely able to make himself heard above the thunder and the rain drumming the canvas, Noah said, "At least in weather like this the Indians stay home."

"Probably."

He sighed. "I know you miss her like hell, Lucy."

"Don't swear in front of your daughter, Noah Mitchum."

"Sorry. 'pologize, Lynette. But honey you do. Still, you'll see her again."

"Oh sure. . . ."

"You will. I'll come back with our gold, we'll take a vacation. Don't we deserve it after all this? We'll take a packet up the coast to Oregon. By then you'll know where she's landed; we'll track her down and you two can have yourselves a great old visit. Two weeks, three, whatever you say."

"And if you don't find any gold?"

"Everybody's finding gold. Nobody leaves the goldfields empty-handed."

"Who told you that?"

"I just know. It's lying all over California."

"If that's so, why do you have to go running off? Why not pick it up in your own backyard?"

"Please, I know you're down, but . . ."

"I shouldn't take it out on you. You're right, I'm sorry."

Within the hour everything was soaked through. Noah announced that he would buy a new canvas at Fort Bridger, which didn't help at the moment. The mud slowed the oxen so, he finally gave up, pulling the wagon to one side so that the beasts could rest. The canvas showed dozens of leaks; droplets plunked down on bedding, clothing, and an all-pervading dampness filled the wagon. Lucy poked in the cornmeal barrel, its contents reduced by two-thirds. She brought up an egg.

"The last one; shall we divide it three ways raw?"

"We'll buy eggs at Fort Bridger."

"You don't understand."

"Understand what?"

"This." She indicated the egg. "The last one; we're out of practically everything. Of course this is no egg, it's a symbol. It's the sand running out of the hourglass, it's our lives running out."

"Lucy . . ."

"I've taken it, taken it and taken it; I don't know how much more I can stand."

"Darling, when the rain lets up we'll be at Fort Bridger in two hours, maybe less."

"In this mud? The poor oxen can barely pull themselves, let alone the wagon. I don't know, I'm just suddenly full up to my throat with discouragement. So we get there, stock up, change oxen, start out again. And it's the same old thing—hundreds and hundreds of miles; the Great Basin, the Sierra Nevadas."

"And the Sacramento Valley." He came to her and put his arm around her lovingly. Lynette wedged into her mother's arms. "Home, ladies. A new world, a fresh start. This, the last egg, the weather, the discouragement, all of it'll pass. We're coming into a new day. We're together, we're happy, healthy, there's nothing but the future. No past, no present."

"Onward and upward."

"Exactly!"

She kissed him. "You're right, what's the matter with me?"

As if in agreement with Noah's assessment of the situation, the rain stopped abruptly; within seconds the sun came out dazzlingly bright. Noah cheered, Lynette squealed, Lucy laughed. And restored the egg to the cornmeal.

TWENTY-FIVE

From a distance of about two hundred yards Fort Bridger looked desperately neglected. It consisted of two large, squat, chinked log houses with ramshackle roofs joined by a pen. The pen was divided at its center by a fence, with mustangs on one side and oxen milling about on the other. Surrounding the entire installation was a stockade fence about twenty feet high. The tops of the houses and the pen could be clearly seen from the crest of the hill where Noah stopped the wagon.

"There it is!" he whooped.

"Impressive," murmured Lucy, and poked her cheek with her tongue to keep from laughing out loud. Fort Jim Bridger looked as if it had been thrown up in a day. Noah saw her reaction.

"What did you expect, marble and Corinthian columns? What matters is what he has to sell. Those oxen certainly look healthy."

"You can tell from here?"

"We can count on spending at least a hundred dollars...."

"Oh no."

"Lucy, we've got to replenish food supplies, swap oxen, get us a new canvas top and four new tires. Look at the crack in the second yoke, it runs clear through, it has to be replaced. The new oxen have to be shod, we could use four new wheels, but I'll settle for the tires. Maybe just replace the left front wheel. It's ground down almost to kindling from the constant wobbling; blame that rock we hit coming down out of the Laramies."

Lucy pointed high beyond the fort. "What are those mountains?"

"The Wasatches. There's been plenty of traffic over the trail through them, it shouldn't be hard."

"They look awfully steep; I wonder how far they run north and south?"

"Why?"

"It might be easier to go around them."

"Forget that, if we tried we'd probably get to the Sierra Nevadas Christmas morning. Besides, if trains went around them Herman Schwimmer would have told us. We'll go over like everybody else—with fresh oxen, remember. And if we take it easy in the Wasatches they'll still be fresh for the Great Basin. Have you got your grocery list?"

"I've had it ever since we left Fort Laramie. What was left of it to leave."

"I'm being serious, don't be miserly with the famous Mr. Bridger——"

"Dear, I think we should tighten our belts. Now's as good as time as any to start. It's not just the money, it's the weight. As it is we'll probably have to jettison more things getting over the Wasatch Mountains."

"Take heart, once they're behind us and we start across the Great Basin the only real mountains left won't show up until California."

"We still shouldn't go spending hog-wild. We still have to buy land, build and furnish a cabin——"

"House. My wife and daughter aren't living in any 'cabin.' "

"Beggars can't be choosers starting out. I'll bet prices in the Valley are outrageous."

"Who cares? We'll be paying in gold!"

He had gotten down and was preparing to crack the whip over the oxen to start them down the grade when the fort's gate swung wide and Indians came rushing out. Heavily armed, yelling shrilly.

"Good God!" burst Lucy.

Noah groaned. "No."

TWENTY-SIX

"Snakes . . ."

Jim Bridger was rangy with a well-worn saddle-leather face strapped with a short scruffy beard going to salt-and-pepper. He was forty-five; from wrinkled throat to deeply creased forehead he looked seventy. His hands, Lucy noticed, were huge; each knuckle looked as if it had been broken and in healing swollen to twice normal size. He stood well over six feet despite his slouch. His shoulders were impressively wide—it looked to her as if he could comfortably seat a fully grown man on each one.

"Friendlies," he added, Noah's hand vanishing inside his. "They work for my partner, Louis Vasquez, and me. I'd interduce you to Señor Vasquez but he's over to Salt Lake City doing business with Saints. I'm sorry our Snakes scared you. I'm told you seemed froze to the trail, rig and all, when they climbed up to escort you down."

"We had a bad experience with the Cheyenne at Fort Laramie," said Lucy.

"That'd be Black Fox and his Dog Soldiers; we heard. Oh, we got unfriendlies 'round here, too: Sioux, Cheyenne, Utes—not the Snakes. Some folks call 'em Shoshones but they prefer Snakes. They really scared you?"

Noah and Lucy exchanged glances. The Indians had escorted them inside the fort, animals, wagon and all. The Mitchums were brought to the larger of the two log houses, to Bridger, who resumed his seat behind a rickety maple table. He was going over bills, pounding them with a rubber stamp. Lucy could see that reading was not one of the man's talents. He appeared to be concentrating on credits and debits indicated by plus and minus signs.

"Scared us out of two years growth," said Lucy.

"I'm sorry, you got my 'pology. Where be the rest o' your wagon train?"

"We're it," said Noah.

The interior smelled of a combination of stale whiskey and tobacco. The furnishings were uniformly crude with no evidence of a woman's touch; the windows were bare of curtains, the dirt floor uncovered, a large, ceiling-high wall cupboard displayed no bric-a-brac. Three rifles and a musket with its powder horn were displayed on the walls.

"You're alone?" Bridger asked, an anxious expression

displacing his brown-toothed grin. He began chewing on his lower lip as he considered this revelation.

"Bound for California," said Noah.

Lucy explained. "We split up with the others at Pacific Springs." She tendered her grocery list. He squinted at it, a look of defeat taking over for his worry.

"My eyes ain't what they used to be, would you mind reading it?"

She ran down the list, each item prompting a nod from him except for when she got to fresh eggs.

"No hens, no eggs."

Everything else on the list was available.

"You need cattle," said Bridger, coming around the table. "You want six or eight? I personally advise eight to get across the Basin."

"Don't some people make it with three yoke?" Noah asked.

"It has been done, it's up to you."

"How much?"

"Fifty dollars per head. Plus your oxen."

"I paid fifty each in Council Bluffs. You won't swap?"

"Our prices ain't Council Bluffs' prices. Everything you see for sale here has to be brought in from Kansas City, St. Louis—transport costs money. All our prices is as fair as we can fix 'em. The fifty includes new shoes, no makeovers; put on free o' charge."

"We'll need other things for the wagon."

"We likely got 'em; if not, you can deal for 'em with the Saints further on." He noticed the studying his wall cupboard. "That there's mahogany from Germany."

"Very nice."

"What I really and truly want is a armor."

"A what?"

"Armor. You know, a closet on legs."

She thought ruefully of her armoire sold in Council
Bluffs for a fraction of its worth to diminish the weight of
the wagon load. And the grandfather clock she'd seen standing on a flat rock in the mountains, the double bed complete with mattress and countless other pieces of furniture
abandoned by the wayside.

There appeared no way they could keep expenses under
the hundred dollars. Noah excused them and took Lucy to
the far end of the room, leaving Lynette with Bridger. He
talked animatedly to her, bringing her out of her shyness.

"He's dealing fairly," whispered Noah, "I feel it in my
bones."

"I agree."

"We're not buying anything we don't really need—I
mean for the wagon. I did think the oxen would be cheaper,
around twenty-five dollars, but . . ." He shrugged.

"Do you think we'd be shortsighted not to buy a fourth
pair?" she asked.

"You heard him, people do get across the Basin with
only three. A fourth pair would be a hundred and fifty for
the oxen alone."

"They're only fifty apiece."

"That's when you can swap. Then there's the yoke."

She nodded grimly. "We'll make it with three pairs."

A squat squaw came in wearing trousers and a serape,
her jet black hair bound in twin braids that descended below
her waist. She shuffled toward Bridger and he put his arm
around her.

"Folks, this is my wife, Little Bird. Little Bird . . ." He
went on in Indian, indicating the Mitchums, then Lynette.
Mrs. Bridger smiled down at the child and greeted Lucy
and Noah cordially. Then she addressed her husband.

"Little Bird's been looking over the cattle; she says she got eight good-looking animals for you."

"Six," said Lucy.

"Whatever."

A thudding sound struck high on the wall near the door; a second and a third thud followed.

"Oh boy, here we go. . . ."

"What?" asked Noah and Lucy together as Lynette rejoined her mother.

"Injuns. Drunken Utes, likely, wanting whiskey and horses. Don't worry, your wagon and cattle are safe inside. My boys have already closed the gate. Miz Mitchum, I'll ask you to stay here with your daughter and Little Bird; you'll be safe. Mr. Mitchum, would you come with me? We could use another rifle; what are you carrying?"

"A Hawken forty-four."

Bridger grunted. "A fifty-three is twice't as powerful, but no mind. Fetch it and meet me out by the gate. I got to rally the troops. Mind your step on the way to your rig—arrers coming over. They're drunk and they can't see, but you never can tell."

Noah disguised a swallow and cast a worried look at Lucy, which she returned in kind. Bridger, she noticed, seemed not at all worried; on the contrary, he looked eager. She looked over at Little Bird, who grinned and yawned as two more arrows thumped into the side of the house. *Did attacks come every other day?*

Driving the wagon into the fort with the Snake Indians swarming about, Noah had failed to notice the shoulder-level loopholes in the stockade. By the time he and Bridger got outside, Snakes were already manning the loopholes and returning fire. Noah picked his way carefully to where he'd parked the wagon, got out his rifle, crammed his pockets with shells and rejoined the frontiersman at the second loophole to the right of the entrance gate, which was barred by a roughly squared timber six inches thick.

Bridger had removed his hat and was pressing his cheek against the stockade, squinting through his loophole. He turned, a grin spreading across his leathery face.

"Hear 'em circling us on their cayuses? Beggarly scum. Listen to that whooping, you can always tell a drunken whoop from a war cry."

"How many are there?"

Bridger returned his eye to the loophole. Noah waited, holding his breath; the frontiersman turned back. "No more'n fifty or sixty."

"How many men do you have?"

"About twenty."

"Oh."

Bridger cackled. "Don't look so, emigrant; they only got about six rusty rifles; they don't dare dismount—too easy to pick 'em off—and they can't hit the sky riding, one-handing and aiming, rifle or bow. Comanches can, not Utes." He paused as two arrows came flying over, lodging in the bonnet of Noah's wagon. "They can rain in arrers all day, all they're doing is supplying our Snakes."

An arrow struck the stockade; in one motion Bridger pulled back, ducked.

"That was close," murmured Noah.

"Inch lower and you'da seen the point coming out the back o' my head." Noah glanced nervously at his wagon. "Don't worry, you was going to replace your cover anyways; just hope they don't start sending over fire arrers. Okay, emigrant, find yourself a loophole, start picking off your share. You can sneak a peek between shots, but make it

lightning fast; look and pull clear. After you fire they expect
you to check, so they'll be aiming at your aperchoor."

"Ap . . ."

"Loophole. Get busy, son, make your wife and daughter
proud."

Noah sighed as he ran toward an unoccupied loophole.
His aim had improved markedly since he first tried the rifle
shortly after Nancy Coombs broke her arm, before the
wagon train reached Fort Kearny. But since then, even
though he practiced daily, he had yet to kill so much as a
jackrabbit, let alone a human being. He could handle the
weight of the Hawken, could aim, ease back the trigger
instead of snapping it—the question was, could he shoot to
kill? Suddenly he was expected to; Bridger would have one
eye on him and likely be appalled if he failed to dispatch at
least one of the attackers. The Utes were circling the fort
close enough to permit Lucy, who'd never even picked up
any kind of weapon, to hit one.

He had to help defend the place, defend his family; he had
to challenge his nature and do his best to kill. If the Utes got
the upper hand and broke in, his failure to do his part would
haunt him the rest of his days. His cowardice would infuriate
Bridger. And if he did survive, how would he face Lucy?

"Dear Lord," he murmured, "just don't let me kill a
horse."

He peered out and to the right, at a sharp angle; a brave
waved his rifle and, howling at the top of his lungs, came
galloping into view. Noah shoved his thirty-four-inch
octagonal barrel through the hole, gauged the time it would
take to bring the Ute directly opposite him, closed his eyes,
pulled the trigger. The rifle jumped so he was afraid the
barrel would snap in two. It did not. When he pulled it

clear, smoke pouring from the muzzle, the stink of cordite stinging his nose, he waved away the smoke and looked out.

The brave lay with part of his face blown off, his horse having galloped on. Noah wondered, had he killed him? As he speculated, an arrow came whirring from a sharp angle, striking dangerously close to his eye, the shaft vibrating as he jerked clear.

"I got one!" he called to Bridger.

"I got six so far and two wounded. They're thinning out, they'll give it up soon!"

Just then a barrage of fire arrows came arcing over the top of the stockade, most of them coming to rest in the ground behind the defenders, one narrowly missing the wagon. Noah gulped. Even shooting blindly the Utes could easily hit it—and destroy everything they owned in seconds. Two fire arrows found the roof of the house in which Lucy, Lynette and Little Bird waited, one of the arrows rolling down the roof, tumbling harmlessly to the ground and extinguishing. The second arrow lodged in a shake, the breeze blowing the fire back from its head. Noah stared as Little Bird came waddling out carrying two sloshing buckets of water. She pulled a ladder from under a pile of scrap lumber at the end of the house, and, ascending it carrying one of the buckets, doused the fire. Two more arrows barely missed her as she dropped the bucket and scurried back down.

Bridger called to her in Shoshone, obviously thanking her. She dismissed him with both pudgy hands, as if annoyed and blaming him for the attack. Noah returned to firing; he missed his next three shots, but then managed to kill a second brave. Moments later, the survivors gave up the attack and rode away.

Bridger took stock as the Snakes wandered about retrieving enemy arrows. Not one of the Indian defenders had been even slightly wounded. It wasn't an attack, decided Noah, it was a shooting gallery.

"How many did you get?" Noah asked him.

"Only nine. They didn't stay very long, did they? Some days it just isn' worth gettin' outta bed."

Bridger laughed at his own joke. The entrance gate was swung wide and a round dozen of the dead Utes' horses were roped and led inside, into the corral.

Lucy, meanwhile, came out of the house with Lynette and Little Bird. Noah was leaning against the stockade catching his breath, resting his rifle butt on the ground. The sigh of relief Lucy heaved was audible to everyone. Bridger saw her staring at Noah and smirked, winking at Little Bird.

"Sweetheart!" Lucy waved and started toward Noah. He waved back, turned his face from her view and threw up.

Bridger slapped his knee and broke into raucous laughter, the Snakes joining him.

TWENTY-SEVEN

Jim Bridger appreciated the tenderfoot's contribution to the defense of the fort. He gave the Mitchums a brand new canvas for their wagon as an outright gift; he also cut in half the price of the six fresh oxen. Noah demurred, but a frown from Lucy quieted his objections. The Mitchums finished stocking up, all necessary repairs were made to the wagon, the new oxen were yoked and they started out, Bridger and Little Bird waving them away.

"Cutting the price of the oxen in half was too generous," commented Noah.

Lucy shook her head. "I disagree. Look at it this way, you risked your life to help him acquire a dozen horses. I'd say Mr. Bridger is well ahead of the game."

"You forget, I got a quick lesson in how to use the rifle. Experience that could come in handy up the line."

"I sincerely hope not. He's quite a character, isn't he?"

"Very colorful."

"Abby told me all about him. He started out as an apprentice blacksmith, at eighteen got itchy feet and came west from Virginia to trap beaver. He built the fort six years ago. He doesn't get along too well with the Mormons, they're constantly bickering. They claim he sells whiskey to the Indians."

"He wasn't selling any whiskey yesterday." Noah shook his head. "I'm beginning to wonder about the Mormons; from all I hear they don't get along with anybody."

"Possibly, but in their defense, everybody treats them shabbily, all because of their religious beliefs."

"Because they're different. Well, my love, it won't be long now before we see for ourselves how 'different.' We won't be lingering in Salt Lake City, no need, about the only thing we couldn't get at Bridger's was your eggs."

The mountains of the Wasatch Range loomed ahead, rising to a height of nearly two-and-a-half miles. Lucy eyed them apprehensively. Like the mountains they had already crossed, between the towering peaks were yawning, seemingly bottomless chasms littered with emigrant wagons and oxen and human bones. The human sacrifice demanded by westering was all but incalculable.

Three days after leaving Fort Bridger the Mitchums started up into the Wasatches. In spite of the slightly parched-looking vegetation, the foothills were uniformly beautiful, the detritus giving way to woodland stretches.

Trees rose to block out the burning sun; nightfall brought impenetrable darkness, the blackness of a mineshaft. Nights became colder the higher they climbed, lasting past sunrise and well into morning. Fierce and constant was the wind, threatening to rip the new bonnet from its bows and rattling the wagon on its axles. Lucy decided that the wagons at the bottoms of gorges and ravines had not wandered off the trail in darkness and fallen, but rather the bullying wind had blown them to their destruction.

The Mitchums walked and pushed while the oxen strained and stumbled up a steep grade, rested briefly and started up a steeper one. The year was now well into August, the fourteenth day, a Tuesday, and getting over the Wasatches would take upwards of two more weeks. Moreover, the western face was reputedly treacherously steep, forcing a careful and very slow descent to the Salt Lake Valley.

On Monday, August 27, they completed their descent. Before the arrival of the Mormons, the Salt Lake Valley was so dry, desolate and sun-scorched, the soil so hard, that an iron plow bent before breaking the surface. Emigrants and prospectors, for the most part, even Indians, shunned it. Since then, the Saints had diverted water from the mountains to irrigate it; now grasses and crops flourished.

This was the edge of the dreaded Great Basin; when the Mormons arrived, to be confronted by a sea of knee-high sagebrush, with legions of crickets the size of a man's thumb the only living creatures, Brigham Young had struck the ground at his feet with his cane and declared "Here will be our temple of God."

And around the temple the city was raised, a massive fort enclosing twenty-nine houses, a smithy, corral and communal storehouse. Now, two years later, Salt Lake City was burgeoning, thriving. And with the Rocky Mountains to protect him from gentile America's disapproval, Brigham Young took twenty-seven wives, setting a precedent for his followers that was to help sustain the prejudice against them from their fellow countrymen living on all four sides.

Noah stopped the wagon, they surveyed the neatly plotted city. Lucy marveled at the sight, but Noah had other things on his mind.

"Stagecoaches have brakes," he muttered as they moved forward. "Why not wagons? Just run the handle down through the floorboards, attach a shoe and make contact with the right front wheel."

"We got down safely, dear," said Lucy, "our next-to-last mountains. That's all I care about." She shaded her eyes from the sun. "Why stop here, why not drive on through?"

"Let's not rush things. The information we've gotten about the Great Basin up to now has been fairly sketchy. If it wasn't so enormous I wouldn't worry, but we really should find out all we can before starting across. Most important of all, we have to make sure we follow the best route. And we'll need to stock up on all the forage we can carry."

"And all the water. The oxen soak it up like sponges."

He snapped the whip, the oxen plodded on.

TWENTY-EIGHT

Josiah Wilfred Riley was one of a mere handful of non-Mormons in Salt Lake City. The Saints treated him cordially, knowing that he did not find himself in their midst through choice. Somewhere between Fort Bridger and the

Wasatches he had been set upon by Utes, his oxen slaugh-
tered, his possessions looted, his wagon burned; miraculously, he escaped in the dead of night. He made his way
over the mountains to the city, where he'd been stuck for
more than two months.

Lucy judged Josiah to be well into his sixties. He was
spry, clear-eyed and had a surprisingly quick mind. But the
long trek from Independence, Missouri, had taken its toll
on his lungs.

"I must have inhaled close to sixty pounds of alkali dust
since Alcove Springs. I started out with a twenty-two wagon
train but broke an axle three days past Fort Kearny. Had to
walk all the way back leading my oxen to get a replacement.
The train couldn't wait, they went on." His weathered face
took on an expression of appeal as he looked from Lucy to
Noah back to Lucy. "I still want to get to California, I just
hesitate to attempt it on my own."

Noah engaged Josiah in conversation, with Lucy firing
an occasional question while Lynette hung over the tailgate
watching them. Noah had parked in front of the Deseret
Store to purchase eggs, met Josiah inside and they got to
talking. When the conversation moved outside, Lucy, waiting on the driver's seat, got down and joined them. Between
Josiah's battered sombrero and snow white beard, shaped
like a quilt frame clamp, an honest face presented itself. It
touched Lucy's heart when Noah recounted Josiah's misfor-
tunes. But the old man's happy-go-lucky attitude made him
endearing almost immediately. And the fact that he had
already been to California nearly ten years before could be
helpful. Her questioning launched him into a dramatic
description of the Great Basin and the perils awaiting ill-
prepared and fainthearted emigrants.

Josiah was an impressive speaker; he may have resembled a typical prairie rat but he proved highly intelligent and his English was exemplary.

"The Great Basin is extremely arid; you got a sampling of it before entering the city, but that was nothing. Crossing it is both a test and a unique experience. Sagebrush and saltbush, saltbush and sagebrush; and heat like you've never imagined."

"Can anything live out there other than crickets?" Lucy asked.

"Oh yes: coyotes, mule deer, pronghorn antelope, jackrabbit, rattlesnakes, the kangaroo rat."

"Without water . . ."

"With very little. Animals know where to find it, few people do. Still, most of the animals survive on dew. The kangaroo rat drinks no water, it lives on seeds that give it all the water it requires internally. There's plant life, too—other than sagebrush and saltbush, which predominate—greasewood, prickly pear cactus, shad scale. There's even flowers: mariposa, sego lily. Nevertheless, it's no place to be marooned, without water, without forage for your oxen."

"Can I ask a personal question?" asked Noah. "You're unusually well-spoken, are you or were you a teacher?"

Josiah laughed. "I left school in the third grade. No, what I am is a voracious reader. I devour books. My tastes are vicarious but selective. I prefer natural history. I suffered the loss of my life when the Indians looted my wagon; they burned Thackeray, Fielding, Smollett, Laurence Sterne, many of the giants of literature."

Lucy got him back onto the subject of the Great Basin. Isolated, prehistoric in appearance, covering an area of approximately two hundred thousand square miles, it presented "a simmering cauldron of white-hot salt sands, baked clay wastes and circling mountains reflecting the sun's heat like a parabolic mirror."

For all its variations in topography, it was classified as a desert. The barrenness extended into the surrounding mountains themselves, where there were bare rock cliffs, stony slopes and little vegetation.

"You've crossed it, do you remember your exact route?"

"It's etched here." Josiah poked his temple. "Leaving here, you head straight for the Sink."

"I've heard that word before," murmured Noah. He turned to Lucy. "Herman Schwimmer."

"It's the popular term for the lower end of the Humboldt River." Down on his knees Josiah drew a large oval in the sand with his finger. "You start out crossing in a straight line, you come to the Sink about here."

Noting the western rim of the Basin, Noah frowned. "That still leaves a long way to go."

"It does, only, from the Sink on there's no established direct route to the Carson River. You have to, so to speak, pick your way. Carefully, as there's no shortage of bad places to camp and water is scarce. What you must keep in mind is that by the time you reach the Sink you'll be low on water and forage." He stood up, his eyes narrowing. "Now, if you were to take me with you—and I'd bring my own food and water—I could guide you from the Sink to the river. There is no map, if there were it would be useless, it's impossible to map."

Husband and wife eyed him slightly suspiciously.

"Really. The reason is you've got to zigzag in your search for water. And where there was water three months ago there may not be next week or next month."

"So," said Lucy, "the availability of water dictates your route."

"Exactly. But remember, you can't waste too much time wandering about looking for it; people have died of thirst looking." He eyed Noah. "Are you a good hunter?"

"He killed two Indians back at Fort Bridger."

"That's self-defense, not hunting."

Noah grinned sheepishly. "I'm a neophyte."

"*I* can shoot the eyes out of a bird at a hundred yards. If I had a rifle I could. The Indians got mine. What kind of rifle do you have?"

"A Hawken forty-four."

"A fifty-three is much more powerful, but a forty-four will do," said Josiah. "I bet you bought it from a city store."

"Mmmmm."

"It'll do for jackrabbit, pronghorns, mule deer. If you're lucky enough to bring down an animal, cook and eat as much as you can on the spot. In that heat meat rots in an hour." Josiah craned his neck to look over the Mitchums' oxen. "Only three yoke?"

"It's all we could afford coming out of Fort Bridger," said Noah.

"With a little luck they should get you to the Carson River; watch them drink it dry when they get there. May I ask how heavy is your load?"

"Fairly heavy," said Lucy.

"You might think about lightening it. You could sell some of your food."

"Food and water are the last things we'd get rid of," said Lucy.

Josiah's response was a smile. "It's only that most people carry just enough to last them across the Great Basin and over the Sierra Nevadas. There's no shortage of food in the Sacramento Valley. People allocate what they pack so as to arrive with barely enough rations for a day or so."

He paused, looking up the street. A stern-looking individual in his late forties, his blocky jaw clean-shaven, his long black hair whipped by the breeze, was approaching in a top buggy. Men doffed their hats as he passed and he waved with his eyes fixed straight ahead.

"The emperor himself," muttered Josiah.

"So that's the great Brigham Young," said Noah.

Young drove past them without so much as a glance in their direction. Josiah chuckled.

"His Majesty and I have never had the pleasure. As contrary and contradictory as they come, he is. Rules with the proverbial iron fist. And brilliantly. Zachary Taylor should be admired and respected half as much. His followers claim their Brigham and the Almighty are on the friendliest terms."

"He certainly looks formidable," said Lucy.

"He has more courage and more gall than any six politicians. A few weeks back he applied to Washington for statehood. He's still waiting to hear. The sovereign State of Deseret. He doesn't stand a chance."

"Deseret?" asked Lucy.

"The Mormon word for the honeybee. They admire it above all other creatures. They admire its industry. They compare themselves with the honeybee: they're highly social, tightly knit, they get along, they're tireless workers, they want above all else to be left alone. . . ." His eyes shifted from wife to husband. "And any outsider poking into their hive can suffer a most painful experience."

"I hear they don't get along with any outsiders," said Noah.

"They get along among themselves, that's all that matters to them."

Josiah gave them directions to a campground on

Brigham Street, an area allocated to transients where they could park the wagon overnight without charge. Lucy invited him to come around at sunup and share breakfast. He beamed gratefully and walked off.

"He's dying to travel with us," she said, "should we invite him? He does know the route."

"He claims he can find it, there's a difference."

"I believe him, Noah."

"He does sound sincere. I feel sorry for him. The only problem I can see is his age, and his health isn't good. What if he were to die on us out there?"

"The odds against that are pretty long, and it's a pretty selfish reason not to take him. What did he say inside the store?"

"Nothing much, pleasant conversation. He spotted me as a gentile immediately."

"He's obviously desperate to get to California. To look for gold, I'm sure."

"I don't think so; he has a son near Sacramento, he wants to join him. I doubt he's interested in prospecting. He just wants to settle down, live out his life in the sun. So, do we ask him to join us?"

"I say yes. Here it's been less than half an hour and he's already made himself an old friend."

"He's clever that way, isn't he?" Noah made a clucking sound and shook his head.

"What are you thinking?"

"I don't know, I just wish we knew more about him than what he told us."

"Which, other than telling you he has a son, was next to nothing."

═══ TWENTY-NINE ═══

The Mormons are cordial: not cold but not warm. Quite subtly they remind us that we're outsiders just passing through. In all things they're pretty much as Josiah Riley characterizes them.

Their city is a miracle, built and thriving in by far the harshest climate we've encountered since starting out. But they've gradually succeeded in reducing the harshness by irrigating the land, planting to hold the water. The city is surrounded by farms and newly planted orchards which in a year or so will begin bearing fruit. What a marvelous place to live. No smokestacks belching foulness and soot; no cramped row houses or tenements, no suffering poor, none of the disadvantages in living back East. I should qualify "what a marvelous place," however; it is if you're a Mormon. I do envy the women their city, but not their polygamy, and Mormonism is too demanding and too rigorous for my taste. I wish Daddy could see this place and talk to Brigham Young and some of the elders. I don't know whether he'd be amazed or appalled.

We're staying at a campground for emigrants in the heart of the city; ours is the only wagon here, so we have our choice of fire sites. No one comes near us and I feel safer than I have at any time since we left Council Bluffs. Josiah will be coming back for breakfast first thing tomorrow. He sounds very knowledgeable about the Great Basin; since he left us this afternoon Noah managed to get hold of a pamphlet on the Great Basin. It's filled with interesting facts. I just hope he doesn't use *it tomorrow to test Josiah. He's very bright, he'll know we got hold of the pamphlet and it could turn out embarrassing.*

As to the Great Basin itself, it's dimensions are prodigious. According to the pamphlet, it encompasses an area about the size of Texas. Neither of us has any idea how big that is, only that it's enormous. The Basin is situated between the Rocky Mountains on the east, the Colorado River on the south, the Sierra Nevada Mountains beyond the Carson River on the west and the watershed of the Columbia River on the north.

Josiah was barely out of sight yesterday when Noah and I agreed we should heed his advice and get rid of much of the food we bought at Fort Bridger. You'd have thought Bridger himself would have warned us, but of course that's no way to stay in business. The clerk in the Deseret Store was most obliging; I'm sure he's dealt with a lot of emigrants before us the same way. He gave us cash for a lot of canned goods, flour, sugar and other staples. Noah estimates we've lightened our load by a good seventy-five to eighty pounds. I think it's more like thirty-five. Forage for the oxen is very important, but even more precious is water, of course. They consume so much! And the hotter it gets out there . . . oh well . . .

Sitting writing while Noah sleeps beside me and Lynette in the wagon, my thoughts keep going back to Marcia. I miss her dreadfully; I keep thinking about how she kept harping on my taking up teaching once we're settled out there. I'm not even going to think about it until Noah gets back from the goldfields and is cured of

his "fever." I know one thing, once he's back he'll never
get out of my sight again!

As to teaching, I'd probably have to build my own
schoolhouse; true, there'd be no shortage of pupils; on
the other hand, how can I be sure the place isn't over-
run with teachers? Competent ones with college educa-
tions, like Marcia? It's all daydreaming at this stage, I'll
just put it aside.

But it is interesting.

We leave day after tomorrow. We'll be skirting the
Oquirrh Mountains around their southern end and then
heading out into the dreaded Great Basin. Noah wants
tomorrow for a number of things: to get to know Josiah
Riley better, check the wagon, make sure the oxen are
fit, top off our water casks and more.

According to the pamphlet, unless your party
includes a second wagon carrying nothing but water,
you should depend on running out long before the
Carson River. Which means, as Josiah said, water has
to be found en route. Would we find it without him?
Still, I trust he's not claiming water-witch powers
just to hitch a ride, though if he is he'll end up suffer-
ing as much as we three. I must say, the fact that so
many emigrants have already gotten across does allay
my fears. I keep reminding Noah of that, but the
worry stays in his eyes despite the optimism in his
words.

Lucy closed her diary and prepared to go to sleep. Thinking
back once more, Marcia's devotion to the cause of equal
rights for women came to mind. They had talked about
women's rights a number of times out of the others' hear-

ing. Marcia was not militant in her convictions; she didn't down men, didn't treat them coolly, despite the failure of her marriage. Her idea was to win them over to women's rights, not bully them into conceding them. Lucy agreed wholeheartedly.

She lay back and was soon asleep. . . .

And dreaming . . . she was in an audience: hundreds of women of all ages and no more than ten or twelve men. The hall was huge. Up on the stage at a podium was a small woman with black hair pulled sharply back and pinned. Just as dark were her eyes—arresting, probing eyes, the type that drill opponents into agreeing. Her lips were all but nonexistent and her skin unusually fair . . . Lucretia Mott lecturing on women's rights. . . . At the moment reading from her "Declaration of Sentiments," a statement of grievances and demands patterned after the Declaration of Independence.

It had turned out an evening that was to coalesce Lucy's own personal feelings about women's rights. And Lucretia Mott had fired her zeal. The few men in attendance— among them Mrs. Mott's husband, who supported her in every way—were as avid in their interest in equal rights for women as were the women themselves. Many women shouted, not a few stood up and scathingly criticized the male sex for perpetuating their domination socially, politically and in every other way.

Lucy awoke, sitting up; Noah slept on. She thought back to the lecture and the Seneca Falls Convention the month before, which she had read about in the Baltimore newspapers. The "Declaration of Sentiments" called upon women to organize and actively petition for their rights. Daddy agreed wholeheartedly that they were entitled to equality, as did Noah. But most wives found strong opposition to equal rights under their roofs. The Seneca Falls Convention had passed twelve resolutions, eleven unanimously. The ninth resolution was key; it demanded the right to vote; it passed narrowly upon the insistence of Elizabeth Cady Stanton, Lucretia Mott's partner, who had helped her to conceive and direct the convention. But insistence on the right to vote was to subject the convention to wide ridicule and caused many backers of women's rights to withdraw their support. Even Noah confessed to being leery of giving women the vote. Lucy recalled their conversation almost word for word.

"I don't understand, what do you need with the vote? Husbands vote . . . "

"What about unmarried women? Besides, what makes you think every wife agrees with her husband's political views?"

"Isn't that one of the cornerstones of the family, complete agreement on everything?"

"I don't know if it's a 'cornerstone,' I know it's nonsense. Be honest, Noah, you don't think women can think for themselves. They're not bright enough?"

"I didn't say that."

"You only think it. There's only one thing that stands in the way of the vote: entrenched tradition."

"Most men put great stock in tradition; live by it."

"Not Daddy. Not in this; he's all for giving women the vote. And when a woman has the right to vote she has true equality. Only then, and tradition be damned!"

"Lucy . . ."

"I mean it." To her amazement he was suddenly grinning. "What's funny?"

"Nothing."

"Something is."

"You have to admit it *is* amusing; have you seen the cartoons in the newspapers? Especially the drawings of Mrs. Stanton."

"You think she's a joke? A woman who single-handedly helped pass a law in New York State giving property rights to married women, who pushed through the resolution demanding the right to vote, which even Lucretia Mott was opposed to in the beginning? Elizabeth is not to be taken seriously?"

"I . . . I'm sorry. . . ."

"Also blissfully uninformed."

"Wait just a minute, I keep an open mind."

"Dear, open it a little bit wider, would you?"

"I will, I will."

Daddy, not she, won Noah over. How many fathers or fathers-in-law sold other men on women's rights? Sadly, very few. But she did manage to convince Noah that there was nothing funny in the movement, despite the newspaper cartoons. The only "funny" thing proved to be Daddy's unswerving support of equal rights for women and Mother's wishy-washy attitude. Tradition, it seemed, had a cautionary hand on her shoulder.

Lucy lay back and looked over at Noah, studying his profile in the dim light of the moon filtering through the canvas. He now subscribed to women's rights without reservation. And the newspaper cartoons that were once amusing he now thought unfair. She could say in all honesty that she hadn't forced her views onto him, he'd embraced them of his own volition.

Of course he would find it awkward living with her if he

didn't change his attitude. Was that the case in many house-
holds?

It definitely wasn't in Salt Lake City. Imagine the differences of political opinion between a husband and twenty
wives? Now that was funny.*

═══════════ THIRTY ═══════════

Josiah accepted a third fried egg from Lucy. The old man
looked tired, as if he hadn't slept more than an hour or two
the previous night. Lucy wondered where he slept, how he
survived, how he earned money to get through his enforced
layover in the city. He didn't say, she didn't ask.

Noah was staring at her, then turned his eyes on Josiah.
"Josiah, you're welcome to come with us to California."

The old man gasped and swallowed and smiled—in too-
obvious relief decided Lucy. Her heart warmed for him.

"I appreciate that more than you can imagine, Noah.
Others have come through since I landed here and not

---

*A misassumption on Lucy's part. Ten years later, in 1869, political action in
Congress was initiated to eradicate polygamy. The stratagem of Congressman
George Washington Julian of Indiana was novel, if not ingenious . . . if ultimately
unsuccessful. Congressman Julian introduced a bill in Congress that would give
Mormon women the right to vote, believing that since they outnumbered their
men by a rate of three to two, they would take advantage of the ballot and join to
outlaw plural marriage.

Brigham Young knew more about Mormon women than did Congressman Julian.
The Mormons advocated polygamy as essential to eternal happiness. In 1870,
before Congress could act on Julian's bill, the Utah territorial legislature granted
the vote to women. Refuting the nationwide opinion that Mormon women had no
voice in their religion, the women went to the polls and voted with their men,
ensuring more ballots to maintain territorial control, where an increasing number
of gentiles were beginning to settle.

one family has been willing to . . . you know."

"Say no more."

"We're glad to have you," added Lucy.

"Oh, I'll earn my keep, I won't eat your food, drink your water. And I promise I'll help get you to the Carson River, not to mention over the mountains. You won't be sorry, you won't be. When do you plan to leave?"

"Tomorrow at sunup," said Noah, "there'll be lots to do today."

"I'll help. Sunrise is the best time, before the heat gets fierce." He finished his coffee and declined more with a wave of his cup and a thank you.

"Except for the six hours before and after high noon you can move fast. As fast as oxen move. We can take turns cracking the whip over them. One thing I didn't mention, we should keep our hats on; around noon we'll be sweating furiously, but keep your hats on and shade your eyes from the sun throughout the afternoon. People without eyeshade have gone blind. The sun reflects off the salt flats like it does off water. And the heat rises from the ground shimmering in waves that can hypnotize you if you let them. You'll adapt. Let me ask you, did you stop for a noonday meal coming out?"

"No," said Lucy, "just breakfast and supper."

"We did make short rest stops for the oxen between," said Noah.

"Mmmmm. Now you should start feeding them at breakfast and at night, too."

"Both?"

"Definitely. They'll be working harder than ever, even in the mountains, they'll need all the energy they can store. And the only stops between meals should be to water them. Be prepared, about the third day you'll be shocked to see how much water they can drink."

AGAINST ALL ODDS   159

"I can imagine," said Lucy.

Josiah shook his head. "I don't want to sound rude, but you can't imagine. And there's nothing I'm telling you that's exaggeration. Cross your fingers you don't lose any oxen due to suffocation. They raise a lot of alkali dust with their hooves alone, but what's dangerous is the wind. It can come up and blow for hours. Some people stop to cover their oxens' faces. Waste of time and effort; unless it's blowing so you can't see ten feet in front of you don't stop. Keep going, keep going. They'll be willing, they want to get across as badly as we do."

Josiah stayed after breakfast to help prepare the wagon; together he and Noah greased the wheels, checked every spoke, every inch of the wagon. Josiah found a tire that was working loose.

"We can fix it," said Noah, "we'll take it off and shrink it in the embers of the breakfast fire."

"That'll work, but it's a last resort. Trouble is it weakens the iron. I suggest we remove the wheel, take it over to Harmony Street to the blacksmith and get him to shrink the tire."

Noah nodded. "I saw them use a tire shrinker at Bridger's fort. But how do we get the wheel off without upsetting the wagon; I don't have a jack."

"You don't need one. We'll get out a couple of your full water casks and use them to prop up the axle."

"We'll have to empty the load."

"No we won't."

"Won't the weight smash the casks?"

"They're oak, metal hooped, they'll bear the weight."

"I must not be fully awake or stupid, but I don't understand; how do we place them under the axle and at the same time lift the wheel clear so we can pull it off."

"That's the easy part, watch . . ."

Together they wrestled two twenty-gallon casks down out of the load. Crawling under the wagon, Josiah scooped out a depression under the rear axle; the casks were set into place, their tops coming to within an inch of the axle.

"Now what?" asked Noah.

"Help me here. . . ."

Together they dug dirt out from under the wheel, slowly lowering the axle until it rested on the two casks. Digging deeper, they freed the wheel from contact so that it turned easily. It was then removed.

"While we're at it," said Josiah, "we should walk your oxen over and have the smith check their shoes."

"Good idea."

They left Lucy and Lynette leading the ox team and carrying the wheel. At the smith's, while one man was checking the oxshoes, a device was utilized to shrink the tire. Noah watched the process like a man watching a dowser raise water from parched ground. Josiah laughed.

"Life is easier when you know what you're doing."

They returned to the campgrounds. Lucy approached as they came up leading the oxen.

"One dollar and the tire's tight as a tick," said Noah.

The remainder of the morning was taken up with unloading the wagon and carefully reloading to utilize all possible space for the water casks. The addition of four new twenty-gallon casks brought the total water weight up to twelve hundred pounds, plus the combined weight of their containers.

"It can't be helped," said Josiah. "Water and forage are the two things you can't stint on crossing."

When they completed reloading he left to return an hour later with his own food and water. His food consisted of Arbuckle's Coffee, two slabs of bacon, a quantity of buffalo jerky and three types of biscuits. That night

Lynette slept in the tent with her parents. Josiah slept on three bales of hay.

Above the rim of the Wasatch Range the unseen sun was sending up the pink of crepe myrtle blossoms when the Mitchums and Josiah Riley, their stomachs warmed with breakfast against the lingering chill of night, drove their wagon back onto Main Street and headed southwest toward the Great Basin.

THIRTY-ONE

Thursday, September 6. Having circled the southern end of the Oquirrh Mountains, the Mitchums now found themselves well out into the Great Basin. The miles slipped from under the wheels; Josiah pointed out that it was to be expected starting out, with the oxen in good shape after their two-and-a-half day rest. Lucy sat between the two men while Lynette stood on a box of canned peaches peering over her mother's shoulder at the white landscape stretching into invisibility.

Josiah was talking; Josiah never stopped talking; he had to be the most tireless talker in the thirty states, decided Lucy. He did seem enormously relieved to get out of Salt Lake City. Not relieved at finally resuming the trek to California, but just leaving. Since first introducing himself in the Deseret Store he had been very helpful to Noah; he was agreeable, polite, all in all a gentleman. But he talked too much and was less than conscientious about personal cleanliness. And the Mitchums still knew next to nothing about him other than that his grown son lived near Sacramento.

"Brigham Young is like a coin, two distinctly different

sides. He can be a slave driver, harsh, vindictive, unforgiving, a temper like you wouldn't believe, like the worst tyrant in history. But his other side . . . When they were leaving their Elkhorn encampment on the way here a woman tried to climb out of her wagon while it was moving. She'd just given birth a few days earlier and was still weak. She slipped and fell in front of the front wheel. It ran over her and broke three ribs. Her husband pulled her out from under to avoid the rear wheel rolling over her. But she'd broken a leg as well. They say Brigham set her leg as good as any doctor could have.

"Because her bed took up all the space in the wagon, from then on her three children had to walk. On the ninth day on the trail, when it seemed her leg was knitting properly, her daughter accidentally stumbled over her leg, breaking it a second time. She was in agony with every step the oxen took. She begged her husband to pull out of line and stop. When Brigham saw the wagon pulling to the side he stopped the whole train. When she explained to him he ordered the train to make camp for the night; then he rolled up his sleeves and sawed off the tops and bottoms of the legs of her poster bed, leaving only the frame and the mattress and springs. He hung this from the cover bows, so it swung like a hammock. He rode along beside the wagon for the next few days to make sure she had no further trouble."

Lucy could tell from Noah's face that he wasn't interested in Brigham Young, or anymore stories about the Mormons.

"Here's another story," began Josiah, barely pausing for breath.

"Excuse me," said Noah, "I think we should talk about water. You weren't exaggerating when you said the oxen drink it by the bucket out here. We started out with about a hundred and fifty gallons, it's going very fast."

"It's the heat. . . ."

"I know; we water them four times a day, each of the six drinks about two gallons a day. That's twelve gallons daily, not counting what we use."

"Nothing like twelve gallons," said Lucy.

"My point is, at the rate we're going we'll be lucky to get thirteen days out of our supply."

"Oh we'll find water before it gives out," Josiah assured him. He looked overhead, shielding his eyes from the glare. High and directly above them a large bird rested on a thermal. "Golden eagle," he said pointing.

"All I can see is black," said Lucy.

"You can tell by the size of the wings and how they soar. Horizontal, not like buzzards. They raise their wings slightly."

"How do you propose to find water?" Noah asked. "And if we do and it turns out salty . . ."

"It won't, it won't be surface water, it'll come from underground." Josiah laughed. "When it bubbles up you can catch it in your hat."

"Are there many springs?" Lucy asked.

"Nobody knows how many. The trick is to find them. Which is where I come in."

"We're down under a hundred gallons," said Noah, "shouldn't we start looking?"

"Relax," said Josiah, "we'll find water before we get to Nelson's Creek."

"How far is that?" Lucy asked.

"Not far. Less than eighty—eighty-five miles?"

"Are you asking me?"

"Eighty-five or ninety miles. We should see to it we're back up to full capacity before we leave Nelson's Creek. From there on it's a long haul to the Humboldt Sink."

"How far?" asked Noah.

"Over two hundred miles. And if you think it's hot now, you'll think we've traveled through hellfire by the time we reach the Sink."

Again Lucy looked skyward; the eagle had vanished. In this, the hottest and driest flatland on the continent, she felt like she was confined in a furnace. She had long since learned not to gulp breaths, the result was a sharp burning sensation in the throat; all four of them inhaled small amounts of air between lips pressed nearly together and never breathed through their noses.

They cooked as they moved along—or so it felt—while at night the temperature plummeted close to eighty degrees or more, necessitating bundling up in blankets and comforters. And the wind cut like an icy sword.

But by 8:00 A.M. the sun was clear of the mountains behind them and pouring down its merciless heat. The land, so white it resembled pure salt, began sloping upward. There were valleys below the tilted mountain blocks that were smooth, often troughlike, and were the source of shallow salt lakes.

That afternoon, after a brief stop to water the oxen, Josiah came up with a clever suggestion calculated to allay their fear of running out of water.

"You could start out each day one or two hours before sunrise. And stop for the night when the first shadows show instead of waiting until dark."

"Why do that?" Lucy asked.

"You haven't been watching the animals. Different species are active at different times. During the day, eagles, hawks, buzzards, insects, lizards, they're about the only living things you'll see on a sagebrush flat. But when evening comes jackrabbits, kangaroo rats and other creatures come out of their burrows. The thing is, a lot of night activity takes place around waterholes, lakes or streams; like Nelson Creek ahead. The best source you can find is a spring; the animals find them. Even the burrowers among them lose water during the day and congregate around water at night to replenish it."

"What do you think, dear?" Lucy asked Noah.

"It's up to you."

"What it's up to is common sense," said Josiah, almost snapping.

Was it the heat, the unrelieved aridity or her imagination; but was he beginning to lose some of his admirable patience with his tenderfoot hosts? Before, he took pains to apologize for anything that could be taken two ways. No longer.

"We're not arguing the point," said Lucy.

"You can see activity around a waterhole, a bubbling spring, at a fair distance. Of course if the oxen smell it they'll head for it, but if they're full at the time they won't bother. When the animals hear a wagon they usually drink up and disperse. My idea is to pull up, find the water—you can see it by moonlight—and take as long as is necessary to top off the casks. Does that make sense to you two?"

The Mitchums agreed. The oxen's thirst assuaged, together consuming half a cask and half a gallon out of a full cask, they set forth. Lucy now had Lynette sit up front in the mornings, out of the direct rays of the sun, and back by the tailgate in the afternoons when the sun was in front of them. Up to this point Lucy had kept a firm rein on her curiosity about Josiah; now she saw no reason to continue doing so.

"Where do you come from originally?" she asked.

"Ohio, why?"

"Where in Ohio?"

"Ah, Mansfield, Richmond City."

"Do you really? My ears must be deceiving me, I thought I detected a slight southern drawl."

"I spent a lot of time down South."

He was hurrying his responses; his expression said he'd prefer she stopped questioning him. Why? Lucy wondered.

"And you went out to California ten years ago. Was your son living there then?"

"No."

"You came by yourself?"

"With a small wagon train."

"It must have been hard," said Noah, "whatever trails there were being so little used. I'll bet it was especially hard getting through the Wasatch Mountains. They were the hardest for us."

"Yes."

"You said your son lives near Sacramento," said Lucy. "What does he do for a living?"

"Farmer."

"What did you do back in Ohio?"

"The curiosity beetle has bitten you badly, hasn't he?" Josiah laughed, but there was no amusement in it, no smile on his face.

"I'm being very nosy, forgive me."

"It's all right. The heat is fierce out here, and the dryness. Thirdly, comes boredom."

The Mitchums retired early that night, planning to get up two hours earlier than usual. Noah wanted to sleep, but Lucy was wide awake. Lynette fell asleep almost the instant she lay down.

"He really resents my questioning him, Noah."

"So would I. Some people are very private. Some people are born invaders of privacy."

"We invited him along out of the kindness of our hearts."

"We invited him along because he knows the way and how to deal with this steaming bowl of soup they call the Great Basin."

"It's strange, the more I question him the tighter he closes up; like a clam."

"Isn't that natural? Wouldn't you if somebody kept hammering at you?"

"I'm not hammering."

"Lucy, he doesn't want to talk about himself. He's a man of many secrets." He chuckled.

"Something's fishy; we've told him everything. People with nothing to hide are wide open. And it's not as if we're strangers. By now? Really, what is he hiding?"

"Ask him. Say to him, Josiah, what . . ."

"Stop it. He said he *had* to get to California; I think he *had* to get out of Salt Lake City."

"Why? I didn't see anybody harassing him; not inside the store, outside, at the blacksmith's. You have a vivid imagination."

"It's called woman's intuition. Do you think he could be on the run from the law?"

"He's too old to be a criminal."

"There's an age limit on crime?"

"He must be sixty-eight if he's a day. What do you think he does for a living, travel about strangling women for their wedding rings?"

"Why doesn't he want us to know what he does to keep from starving?"

"Simple, it's none of our business."

"He's hiding something."

"I want to go to sleep."

"You're a big help."

Noah raised onto his elbow frowning. "Look, I just don't want to alienate him. We asked him along because we need him."

"Are you saying he doesn't need us?"

"All right, it's mutually beneficial. I say leave him alone, stop poking into his privacy."

She sighed. "You're right."

"What?" he looked surprised.

"I said . . ."

"I heard you, for a second there I just didn't believe my ears."

"I'm tired, go to sleep."

They kissed good night.

THIRTY-TWO

It was still dark and the night wind quite cold when the Mitchums and Josiah finished breakfast and started forth the next day. Since raising the Oquirrh Mountains behind them blocking out the last view of Salt Lake City they had seen not a sign of potable water. Slimy salt shallows appeared every so often, but the brackish water could not even be used for cooking, and was poisonous to the oxen.

Lucy was getting more and more accustomed to the sterile landscape and progressively indifferent to it. She took refuge from the monotony in memories of Baltimore; it was nearing the middle of September; back home on damp, chill evenings Noah would bring in wood, they would kindle a fire and sit in front of it for hours. September 30 would be Lynette's fifth birthday; it seemed sad only the two of them would be celebrating with her. And Riley, who, for some reason, Lynette had not warmed up to as she had Herman Schwimmer and Abby Havers.

Yes, only the three of them at this birthday party; but they were together, their family, east, west and in between.

Lucy sighed. With the onset of fall she'd be missing many of its wonders: the leaves dressing in their motley, the crispness in the air, the distinctive pungent aroma of that precious few weeks; the sky's limitless blue, in the evenings the fading afterglow assuming the orange of a polished pumpkin that sent shadows spilling down the buildings and flooding the streets.

But it was the leaves that costumed the season and gave it its distinction; she would miss that more than anything else. She summoned up visions of the gold-and-copper hillsides outside the city and a trillion leaves, whipped loose by the mischievous wind, falling in flights. Often, in a normal breath, a thousand leaves would fall at a time like a ball of swallows swiveling suddenly in flight, as one. Mostly, though, they fell slowly, lazying down, pirouetting in ones and pairs.

And when the soft rain fell it fastened the leaves to the sidewalks and streets, to windowpanes and steps and fenceposts, wrapping the city in color. And naked branches guided by the wind scratched invisible messages on the fat clouds scudding by overhead.

Already she missed Noah's fires, and Daddy's in the parsonage: the delicate smell of white oak, the faintly sweet fragrance of beech, the even sweeter scent of paper birch and the intoxicating heavy smell of olives that comes from freshly split red oak.

The oxen were slowing. Noticing snapped her out of her reverie.

"They're hanging their heads lower," said Josiah, "starting to plod. That dust that whipped up yesterday didn't do them any good. If the alkali doesn't suffocate them when they inhale it it goes right to their lungs." A gnarled hand shot out. "What's that over there?"

He squinted through the darkness. A mule deer turned tail and bounded lightly away, its silhouette distinct against the fading night sky. A second deer raised its head, moving off in another direction.

"Water!" Noah got down quickly.

"No," cautioned Josiah, "let them go on another ten or fifteen yards. Stop right across from it."

They moved through luxuriant saltbush down a slope to a mass of rubble, Josiah in the lead. The rocks looked as if a giant cairn had been tumbled to form a mound a good forty feet across in the depression. The sound of burbling water broke the silence; then a soft rattling sound. Josiah stopped short, reaching back, setting his fingers against Noah's chest. The rattling repeated, triggering a chorus around them.

Slowly lowering his eyes, Josiah saw a snake coiled, rearing, preparing to strike. Fangs gleamed in the moonlight, it hissed ominously; as if to encourage it to strike the rattling chorus grew louder. Noah and Josiah turned and ran like men possessed back up the slope toward the wagon. In his haste, Noah streaked nearly past it while Josiah came staggering up, his hand to his heart, blowing loudly.

"Diamondbacks," he gasped to Lucy. "There must be a hundred. . . ."

Noah frowned. "I don't understand, they didn't bother those two deer."

"They don't bother what doesn't bother them. Don't you know anything about snakes, either?" His rudeness was wholly unexpected; before either husband or wife could react, he went on, without anger. "It was a miracle," he said to Lucy. "I mean that neither of us stepped on one. Unbelievable!"

Noah confronted him. "Snakes or no, Riley, we need that water."

"Not that badly, *Mitchum*."

"We could wait for a little more light, then I'll fire a few shots into those rocks."

"You do that, you just might kill one. What, you think that'll scatter them? Not a chance, they'll just burrow and come back up when you move in among them. You, not me. Wait, you don't have any birdshot do you? What am I saying, you don't even have a shotgun. You know you should have bought a rifle *and* a shotgun. I made sure I had both."

"We know, as presents for your friends the Utes."

Lucy had gotten down. "Will you two stop sniping? Josiah, is there any way of clearing them out of there?"

"Ten pounds of black powder might help, only who would we get to plant it? It's a little like belling the cat. Those rocks are their home. They live under them, bask in the sun on them; when it gets too hot they go down into their holes. I say we give it up as a bad job and move on."

"You say . . ."

"Noah!" Lucy snapped.

"I'm sorry. I apologize, Josiah. Our first water, it's . . . upsetting."

"It's a disappointment, that's all. It won't be the last. Don't look so, we'll find another spring."

"I wonder how far to the next one?"

"Are you asking? Again?" He was suddenly bristling; as frustrated as Noah at their failure, thought Lucy. "It could be three hundred yards," Josiah went on, "it could be a hundred miles. Except for one thing." His annoyance gave way to a grin. He waved a finger. "We're no more than twenty-five miles from Nelson's Creek. At the rate we've been moving that's sometime around noon tomorrow. How much water left?"

"I'd guess under forty gallons, about a quarter of what we started out with."

"We'll be fine, Noah, stop worrying."

═══ THIRTY-THREE ═══

Farther, and farther into the white saucer of the Great Basin they inched. So brilliant was the glare, Lucy could no longer look directly at the sky. The harsh conditions began taking their toll on Lynette.

"I'm burning up, Mommy."

"We all are, little tyke," said Josiah, "don't complain."

"She's a child," said Lucy, "keep that in mind. Sweetheart, dip your cloth in what's left of the water in the enameled pitcher."

"Water's too hot."

"It'll cool on your face, go ahead . . ."

Lynette scrambled back to where the half-filled pitcher sat on the cornmeal barrel.

"How far now to this Nelson's Creek?" Noah asked Josiah.

"No more than a mile or so."

"Where is its source located?" Lucy asked.

Josiah pointed downward. "It just decides to surface and lo and behold, a creek."

"Do you mind my asking how old you are?" asked Lucy.

"How old are you?"

"Twenty-four."

"I've got you by thirty years." She suppressed a gasp but could do nothing about the surprise that took over her face. He laughed. "I look seventy, is that what you're thinking? Rough life."

"Time to stop for the oxen," said Noah, checking his Waterbury watch.

Josiah narrowed his eyes. "You haven't much faith in your pilot, do you?"

They kept on. Josiah shielded his eyes from the blistering sun with both hands, looking off to his right. He said nothing, which set Lucy to wondering how long he could go without talking, at the same time appreciating the respite. After nearly thirty minutes of silence he spoke.

"There . . ."

He pointed at a trough. They stopped and got down. Noah knelt, sifting the sand through his fingers.

"Dry as a bone."

Josiah clucked. "Dry summer." Noah got up, turning on him. "Is that all you have to say?"

"It's dried up, what would you like me to do? It happens out here. It was a fair-sized creek last time I came through."

"Ten years ago; the whole topography of the land has to have changed in ten years."

"Probably; something else I had no control over."

"You're funny," muttered Noah.

Lucy laid a hand on each one's arm. "Stop before you start, you two."

They started out; no one spoke, each of them sitting mired in his own thoughts: the same thought, the rapidly dwindling water supply. Noah broke the silence.

"We'll have to cut the oxen down to two waterings a day instead of four," he murmured.

To Lucy's surprise Josiah agreed.

"Keep your eyes peeled," he said at length. "Look for a distinct dark spot in the sand. We may not find surface water, but it's down underneath somewhere. Keep looking."

It was late afternoon. The three adults were each submerged in speculation regarding the immediate future when Lynette's shrill voice startled them.

"It's dark there, Daddy!"

They watched Josiah walk about the discolored spot and then call for a shovel. Both men dug. Water bubbled to the surface. Lucy cheered; the echo rang off a nearby outcropping. In ten minutes water was rising two feet. In that time the washtub was positioned to catch the fall before the sand could steal it back and the empty casks were brought up. They were quickly filled and one, barely half-full, topped off. When all the water they could carry had been collected and the casks restored to the wagon Lucy spoke.

"We should take advantage of this and wash ourselves before going on. We may not get another chance until the Carson River."

The suggestion elicited agreement from Noah, nothing from Josiah. Lucy got out a half-used bar of Mottled Castile Soap and a new bar of Pears. She gave the Castile to Noah and took a bucket of water, the Pears and Lynette behind the outcropping. Despite it being late afternoon the sun was still blistering hot, causing the cold water to feel even colder.

"It's freezing," complained Lynette.

"Hold still, you've a quarter inch of salt on you. Grit your teeth, you'll feel glorious when I'm done."

*   *   *

Lucy and Noah lay on their mattress in the tent while Lynette slept at their feet as usual, since Josiah joined them.

"It's amazing," murmured Lucy, "how bathing can change one's whole outlook."

"Please, do I have to hear that whole tribute to the splendors of the bathtub again?"

"Did he wash himself? When Lynette and I came back from behind the rock he didn't look as if he did."

"His face and hands; under his arms. Some people are just not that conscientious about personal hygiene."

"He's intelligent, he has a sort of—I don't know what you'd call it—primitive breeding. You'd think he'd keep himself cleaner. Did you ask how far it is from here to the Sink?"

"You already know that: over two hundred miles."

"Dear Lord . . ." She paused as the wind came up buffeting the little tent, testing the solidity of the upright poles. "Nearly two weeks to the end of nowhere. Where water may or may not collect. And if it does it's probably brine."

"I'm afraid he used that very word. But we found this water, we'll find more. Lucy?"

"Mmmmm."

"What did you think when he told you he was only fifty-four? That he was lying?"

"I was shocked."

"He does look seventy, but he could be telling the truth."

"If he is it's a first."

"You don't much like him anymore, do you?"

"Just disappointed; not because he's a bore, it's the flashes of arrogance, the sarcasm. He was such a gentleman back in Salt Lake City."

"It's his age, and living alone for so long; somewhere along the way he's lost tactfulness."

He was about to go on when they heard muffled stumbling sounds outside. In the next instant a pole snapped in two under the weight of a man falling; and the tent collapsed, burying them in its folds. Lynette woke up screaming.

THIRTY-FOUR

Noah cradled Josiah in his arms.

"My chest, it's like a boulder crushing——"

"Don't talk. . . ."

He was fighting for breath, his normally ruddy cheeks white and assuming a faint bluish cast; he sweat furiously.

"I'm dying. . . ."

"No you're not. Don't try to talk; breathe easier, slower."

"Can't . . ."

"Hold him all the way up in a sitting position," said Lucy.

"Won't do any good; it's my heart, as if you didn't know. Not much time." He gestured them closer. "Listen, I lied; I have no son in California, no relatives anywhere. Lucky for the world, eh?"

"Get water," murmured Noah to Lucy.

"Don't trouble yourself, too late. I lied about almost everything. I've never been near Ohio. I . . ."

He shivered, became rigid, his mouth fell wide, his eyes bulged, he was still. Noah let him down slowly.

"Dear Lord," murmured Lucy.

The wind had come up stronger, tearing flames from the dying embers of the supper fire. Sand whisked about. Lynette was on her knees, capping them with her slender hands, rocking back and forth, staring at the dead man.

"Sweetheart," said Lucy, "go, get in the wagon."

"I want to stay with you." She could not take her eyes off Josiah.

"Do as your mother says," said Noah.

"My bed's in the tent."

Lucy smoothed back the child's hair. "Just wrap up in blankets. I'll be there in a little bit to tuck you in. Go on now."

Lynette left pouting.

"We should bury him right away," said Noah. "Before sunrise. I can get it done a lot faster in this cold air."

"Yes, only you mustn't mark the grave. That way the Indians won't find it."

"What Indians?"

"The Utes; they do come out here looking for crickets. Don't you remember he told us that?"

"He told us a lot of things."

Noah got out the shovel; it took him about an hour to get down five feet. Lucy wrapped the body in a blanket; together they lowered it into the grave. They stood at Josiah's feet looking down.

"I hate to just start throwing the sand back in. Shouldn't we say something before . . . before . . . ?"

Lucy nodded. "I'll tuck Lynette in and get the Bible."

She found the passage she wanted: 1 Corinthians 15.

" 'O death, where *is* thy sting? O grave, where *is* thy victory? The sting of death *is* sin; and the strength of sin *is* the law. But thanks *be* to God, which giveth us the victory through our Lord Jesus Christ. Therefore, my beloved brethren, be ye steadfast, unmoveable, always abounding in the work of the Lord, forasmuch as ye know that your labour is not in vain in the Lord.' Amen."

"Amen."

He began to fill in the hole. Two shovelfuls and he paused, looking inquiringly at her. "Was that passage appropriate do you think?"

"I've no idea what's 'appropriate,' Noah, I didn't really know the poor man."

═══════ THIRTY-FIVE ═══════

The sun was already clear of the horizon when they finished breakfast, which included some of Josiah's bacon and coffee. Before starting out, Lucy went through the dead man's few belongings—mainly extra clothing. The least worn and ragged was a sheepskin jacket, which for some reason they had never seen him wear, even on the coldest night. There was a gold-filled stickpin and, curiously, a buckle without a belt: silver-plated with an eagle grasping a globe stamped on it. Everything was collected in a small wooden box with brass hinges and latch. Josiah Riley's entire estate, to be inherited by no one. There was also a well-smudged manila envelope with a tie string.

"Open it," said Noah as they took their seats.

"I'll feel like I'm prying."

"He's dead."

"All right, all right."

In the envelope were three worn photographs even more smudged than the envelope. Two of them were of the same woman. Young, posing with her face at a slight angle, eyes dark and morose-looking, her hair in neatly aligned pipe curls. She wore a white blouse with a ruffle collar and a long string of black beads. Her features were well formed; looking at her for a few minutes Lucy decided she was pretty-approaching-beautiful; but almost desperately unhappy-looking, the sort of look people who endure great tragedy display. On her other picture she was face forward but again unsmiling, suffering. The third picture was of a doughty, aggressive-looking older woman. She could have been the younger one's mother, although her features were not nearly as attractive; still, there was a resemblance. The older woman's photo was yellowed, and a diagonal crack where it had been folded ran through her right eye, across the bridge of her nose and down her left cheek.

In the envelope as well was a clipping from a newspaper, brown with age. Lucy took it out carefully, fearful it might disintegrate in her hand, so dried out was it. There was no way to tell what paper it had been clipped out of.

New Braunfels Farmers and Merchants Bank Robbed. A robber, disdaining the customary folded neckerchief disguise, yesterday held up the Farmers and Merchants Bank of New Braunfels, getting away with more than three thousand dollars. Comal County Marshal A. D. Squiers organized a posse within the hour and gave chase, but the culprit escaped capture. Eli Higgenbotham, president of the bank, was quoted as saying the man took everyone by surprise, giving no hint of his intention upon entering the bank. He walked in calmly sans gun-belt and wearing no disguise. His pistol was in a satchel he forced the tellers to fill with money. He is described as clean-shaven, with dark eyes, wavy black hair, high cheekbones and a ruddy complexion. Witnesses various-

ly describe his height as between five foot six and six feet
with a lanky frame and narrow shoulders.

Mr. Higgenbotham has offered a two-hundred-dollar
reward for information leading to the arrest and conviction
of the robber. Marshal Squiers has stated his belief that the
robber was heading toward the New Mexico border.

"It's him," said Noah, "it has to be. Why else would he hang
onto that?"

"Three thousand dollars. He's described as clean-
shaven. It's definitely Josiah, just not the beard. Strange . . ."

"What is?"

"He wasn't the ideal passenger but he didn't seem the
criminal type."

"What is 'the criminal type,' Lucy. What distinguishes
them?"

Lucy frowned. "You know what I mean. . . ."

"Not really."

"Most bank robbers don't just steal, they kill: innocent
bystanders, lawmen, anyone in their way. I didn't like certain things about him, but he was no killer."

"Who says he was? The clipping didn't. Who do you
suppose the women are? The older one could be his mother . . ."

"I don't see even a remote resemblance between him
and either one. Maybe the older one raised him. She looks
eighty, old to be his wife; the other is too young."

"His daughter do you think?" Noah asked.

"He said he had no relatives; in his dying words."

"He could have been lying to spare them embarrassment."

"What 'embarrassment'? They're probably a thousand

miles away and haven't seen him in eons. This clipping is very old. Besides, dying people don't lie—so everybody says."

He shrugged. She restored the photographs and clipping to the envelope.

"What'll we do with it?" Noah asked. "And his belongings?"

"I do wish we held off burying him; we should have looked through all this first, and buried everything with him."

"Mmmmm. It's over for him, Lucy, and now we're on our own."

"We'll be all right: just follow this road to the Humboldt Sink. And from there on to the river."

"Sounds a snap," he muttered.

"Are you afraid we might lose our way from the Sink on?"

"Not really. Still, he never did get around to describing that last leg to the river in any great detail. He said it's hot as blazes and that's it."

"How far did he say from the Humboldt Sink to the Carson River?" Lucy asked.

"He didn't. I'd guess less than a hundred miles."

"You'd *guess?*"

"Darling, don't start worrying."

"You're the one who sounds worried."

"Nonsense. We're well over halfway there, we're experienced, seasoned, we've plenty of water——"

"Not enough to get us to the river. And we've used up more than half the forage."

"There, see? You *are* starting to worry. Out here the oxen don't need food half as much as water."

"They have to eat, dear, you don't get energy from water."

"I know, I know, I know!"

"Don't be upset . . ."

Four days later Lucy was the first to spot dust rising about a mile off to their right. They watched it approach; out of it two men rode up, one on a horse, the other astride a mule. Men and animals alike were whitened with alkali dust. They hailed Lucy and Noah; she groaned.

"What's the matter?" Noah asked.

"I hope they don't want to ride with us."

Noah stopped the wagon. The taller man dismounted, touched the brim of his vaquero-style hat to Lucy and nodded to Noah.

"Deputy Marshal Hale Bagby," he said, showing his badge. "Comal County, Texas. This here is Fred Petra, deputy. Hope you can help us, sir."

"If we can," said Noah, looking askance at Lucy.

Bagby, a broad-chested man with twinkling eyes and sharply sculptured features, dug into his saddlebag and produced a folded wanted dodger. He held it up for appraisal. "Have you folks seen this man?" Lucy swallowed to hide a gasp; unquestionably, it was Josiah, only without hat or beard, his face showing fewer lines, but it was a drawing, not a photograph. "We don't know his name," Bagby went on. "But we think this is a fair likeness. He may have grown a beard, a lot do. He's wanted for bank robbery and murder, as it says."

"Murder?" Lucy felt her right eyebrow arc upward.

The deputy spoke for the first time. He looked no more

than fifteen to Lucy, a face as round as a pan, front teeth going from yellow to brown, one absent. Under his skin of alkali dust, which, as she eyed him, he self-consciously tried to wipe off, were pimples and cheeks and a jaw that had yet to feel a razor.

"Robbed the bank in New Braunfels and before that killed two ranch hands over to Caldwell. Terrorized the citizenry in New Braunfels something fierce in the less than fifteen minutes he was there. He doesn't look it, but he's cold as a snake and mean as they come."

"We . . . know him," said Lucy.

Both men started.

"You do?" asked Bagby.

"He's dead," said Noah, and explained.

The two lawmen exchanged glances.

"How far behind you did you bury the corpse?" Bagby asked.

"Does it matter? It was him all right, and he was quite dead. A heart attack."

"It's just that we got to be certain sure."

Lucy got out Josiah's box. The deputies examined the contents. Bagby took particular interest in the younger woman's photographs. He studied each one at some length, turning them over repeatedly as if hoping that information of some sort might magically leap out of the blankness. There was nothing, not even a date.

"You've come all the way up from Texas after him?" Lucy asked, thinking as the words came out that it was a silly question.

Incredible! The three of them had traveled all the way from Salt Lake City with a murderer. Talking to him by the hour, working with him, sharing food and necessities, old comrades on the trail. And affording him the easiest victims he'd ever find if he turned on them. She would never have believed that he was a killer. Why should she? He didn't even carry a weapon.

"We lost his trail at the border," said Bagby, breaking into her musing. "Then this past spring a tip come in to the office from La Junta, on the Arkansas, in Colorado. Some local up there matched this dodger with a stranger in the area. Fred here and me rode up there faster'n deer in a forest fire——"

"But he was gone by the time we showed," added Petra.

"We wandered 'round all summer hoping to pick up his tracks, but it wasn't till last month we got lucky. Got another tip. Only by the time we got to Salt Lake City he was long gone." He smiled grimly. "With you, it turns out."

"You been with him all the way since there," said Petra, "did he give you any kinda hint he was a fugitive? Act suspicious in any way?"

They shook their heads.

"He *was* very secretive about himself," said Lucy. "I must say I thought he was hiding *something.*"

"More'n you can imagine, ma'am," said Bagby. "Them two ranch hands wasn't his first victims; he killed over to Oklahoma, and who knows how many poor souls before that. Killer first, bank robber second, that's him."

Lucy reserved comment, thinking, what could she say?

"What name did he give you?" Petra asked.

"Josiah Wilbur Riley," said Noah. "An alias, no doubt."

"No doubt," said Bagby, smiling again.

THIRTY-SIX

The Texans accepted Lucy's invitation to share supper before heading back up the trail to Josiah's grave. Noah didn't know the exact distance back, but told them that they couldn't miss the freshly turned mound in the middle of the trail. Listening to him, it struck Lucy that the mound was as good as a marker, if any Utes happened by.

Before the deputies rode away Noah asked if either knew the route from the Humboldt Sink to the Carson River. Neither did; as Lucy suspected, both were as far west as they'd ever ridden.

September 25, four days into a leafless fall, found the Mitchums nearing the approximate three-quarter point from dried up Nelson's Creek to the Sink. Ever the optimist, Noah figured the Sink to be roughly fifty miles ahead. Telling herself that one of them should assume the role of realist, Lucy added twenty-five miles to his figure. Which meant that they could expect to see the Sink sometime on Lynette's birthday—the oxen slowed a good five miles a day since the death and burial of Josiah Riley.

Lucy was already planning Lynette's party; she had brought along four presents, keeping them well hidden. She planned to bake a cake, frosting and all, but neglected to bring candles. That night after supper she took Lynette aside.

"Do you know whose birthday is coming in five days?"

"Mine!"

"And you'll be four years old."

"Five!"

"Oh my, you're right."

"Stop teasing; will I have a party?"

"Of course, a birthday's not a birthday without a party."

"With a cake and presents and friends? Oh, no friends——"

"Why not?"

"Out here?"

"Oh, are you ever in for a surprise."

"Who's coming, who's coming?"

"Don't ask me, you're the birthday girl; you get to invite whomever you please."

A frown shadowed Lynette's face. "That's not fair, you know I can't."

"There's a way. But you have to help; in fact, it's all up to you. Think about all your dearest friends, sweetheart, your best friends in your books."

Her eyes lit up. "Yes, yes, it'll be make-believe!"

Noah had finished feeding the oxen; he came over.

"What are you two getting so all worked up about?"

"My birthday party, Daddy, and who's coming. . . ."

Noah glanced quickly at Lucy.

"Storybook friends," she said.

"Buster Bear, Princess Mathilda, the Frog family. How many can I ask, how many?"

"Ask everybody," said her father. He swept his arm. "We won't be cramped for space."

"Oh yes, yes; oh this'll be the best birthday party in the world! It will!" She hugged her fists, first dancing on one foot and then the other, then whirling about. "Part real and part make-believe!"

Lucy finished tucking her in. Noah stuck his head in the tent and kissed Lynette good night, then husband and wife sat by the flap to talk and relax before retiring themselves.

"We're getting low on water again," murmured Noah.

"Even lower on forage."

He exhaled exasperation. "All the grass is filled with salt. At least, I can't find any that isn't. But don't worry, there'll be plenty at the foot of the mountains."

"Three weeks from here. Darling, what'll we do?"

"We've got enough for them for five, maybe six more days. Well past the Sink. If we still don't find any, if worse comes to worst, we'll have to break up the mattresses."

"Oh dear . . ."

"You knew it might come to that. Last resort."

"We might be ruining them for nothing, the stuffing's so dry it has to be absolutely tasteless. What if they refuse to eat it?"

"They'll take 'tasteless' over starving, dear; though I can't imagine it'll come to that," he added hastily.

"They can't work if they don't eat; they'll die."

Noah slapped his knee. "We'll *find* grass. Damn, I wish I had a horse; I could scout out grass, water, everything."

"You mean ride off and leave the two of us? Me with the rifle on my lap, is that it?"

"I wouldn't ride so far as to put you in danger."

"That's a relief." She laughed lightly to dispel the weariness in his face.

"Lucy . . ."

"Mmmmmm?"

He edged closer, slipping his arm around her, hugging. "We'll make it with bells on. We will, we're getting closer and closer."

"Oh, we'll make it all right, I've never doubted it."

"Really?"

She wished he didn't look so amazed. It strongly hinted that he'd been worrying all along. Hiding it. At that, wasn't it always in his eyes? Especially now that they were without Josiah?

Or was she being too hard on Noah? She was. And they *would* make it; one day a month from now, more or less, the three of them would stand atop the west face of the Sierra Nevadas, shade their eyes from the sun sinking into the Pacific Ocean and look down on the Sacramento Valley.

THIRTY-SEVEN

Buster Bear spilled his milk, the Frog family children acted up, as undisciplined children will; other than that, Lynette's birthday party was a rousing success. She loved the two dolls, the peg-board game and the tea set she got for presents. Lucy tried to put her heart into the celebration; she did her best—as did Noah—but both were getting increasingly anxious. Here it was, the last day of September, and no sign of the Humboldt Sink. Even more worrisome, they would be out of forage by the end of the day. They were down to their last two casks of water, one barely half-full: thirty gallons for beast and man.

Their nerves were becoming taut and their fatigue increased daily. They had resumed their journey the day after Lynette's birthday and had been moving less than ten minutes when they spotted horses and pack mules dusting toward them. Four Mormons were heading back across the Great Basin to the city. All were young men, all wore full beards, so little of their faces showing they could have been brothers. They had come from digging gold all summer. With Lynette's permission Lucy offered them what was left of the birthday cake.

"Can you help us?" Noah asked. "We're looking for the Humboldt Sink and then from there the shortest route to the Carson River.

The man he addressed, who appeared to be older than his three companions, knelt and drew in the sand with a stick. The others with Lucy and Lynette gathered around.

"This is the way you've come, following the Humboldt River."

Noah frowned. "We didn't see any river. . . ."

"It's there, all the same. Oozing along until up ahead it disappears in the Sink. We're about here now."

"Excuse me," said Lucy, "but is there any grass ahead? Any at all?"

"There is."

"Not in the desert," said another man.

"No grass there, not a drop of water," added the man wielding the stick. "You'll need to detour to find both. Follow me now." He paused. "You may want to copy this on a piece of paper, ma'am."

He waited while she got pencil and paper.

"Any luck in the diggings?" Noah asked.

Two of the other Mormons dug in their pockets and brought out small black cloth bags; they bulged.

"Lots. All good," said one. "Makes up for all the alkali dust."

Lucy returned with the pencil and paper.

"It's a little tricky," said the man drawing the map. "The Sink is just ahead."

"You may not see a blessed thing," said another man, "this time of year it's so dried up it takes a sharp eye to spot it. We didn't see it."

"We didn't look," said the other man. "Can I please finish this? Pilgrim, ma'am, beyond the Sink look for a plain wagon track off to your left. Follow the track. About three miles from the main road you'll come to a grassy meadow. You'll find plenty of feed there and wells with clean, fresh water."

"Plan on staying at least one day," said another man. "To feed and rest your cattle. While you cut as much grass as you can carry and top off your casks."

"When you leave there you'll be fine with both all the way to the Carson River and beyond. I should warn you, crossing the desert the heat will be fierce; much worse than the Great Basin. No grass, no water, nothing. Get across fast as you can—it's only about fifty miles.

"When you get to the mountains, your oxen'll have to work harder than at any time since you started—even harder than when you came over the Wasatches. And they'll already be dog-tired."

"You know," said another man, "it's seventy miles up to the top of the Sierra Nevadas."

"Seventy?" Noah slapped his forehead and gawked in astonishment.

The man with the stick nodded. "Do you have rope, chains, at least a couple winches, pulleys?"

"Everything."

"You'll need them to get you to the top."

"Can one man handle it?" Lucy asked.

"I can handle it," said Noah.

The Mormons smiled. "I'm sure you can," said one.

The man with the stick went on. "I hate to say it, but when you get to the top it's another hundred miles, zigzagging all around Robin Hood's barn until you get to where you can look down and see the Sacramento Valley."

Noah was suddenly looking slightly pale, reflected Lucy. She sighed silently.

"I knew about having to hoist the wagon over certain spots," he murmured. "I had no idea how far it was climbing up and crossing."

"A hundred and seventy miles," said the map man, standing. "Not counting getting down the other side. Best of luck, pilgrim, and don't be discouraged, you've made it this far, you'll make it to the Valley. Only next time I wouldn't attempt it by yourself."

"Just be careful crossing the desert," said another.

"It's only fifty miles," said Lucy.

"A brutal fifty miles. It's true you'll want to get across fast as you can, but don't go killing your cattle to do it. You'll need all three yoke to get you up and over the mountains."

Lucy and Noah watched the dust roll out from under their hooves into a pillar that rose and hung in the pale sky before gradually dissipating.

"Shall we?" asked Noah.

The miserable stream that identified itself to mapmakers as the Humboldt River was too salty to drink. It oozed along without a course, without an outlet, without any discernible reason for existence, before disappearing into a viscous mass of alkali dust.

As the Mormons had mentioned, it was late in the dry season, the river had vanished without a trace, the keenest eyesight could not see where it disappeared.

"We'll see the Sink in a few more miles," said Noah, trying to inject assurance in his tone.

"They didn't."

"They weren't looking for it, you heard."

The Mitchums did, most diligently, but failed to see it.

Because they had already passed it.

THIRTY-EIGHT

"We'll keep going," said Noah.

"I don't know, it's getting dark fast."

"Not that fast; if we do miss the Sink in passing we'll still see the wagon track off to the left."

"I'd forgotten all about that, looking so hard for the Sink. Noah, it's really getting dark."

"We can't stop now."

"Why not?"

"We don't have a sprig of grass to feed the oxen. They've got to have forage, look at the way they're dragging."

"Driving them into the ground won't help any."

"Just a little farther."

They went on in silence, until she could no longer contain herself.

"Noah, this is crazy, stop the wagon."

"Are you really looking?"

"Stop!"

They got down, Lynette joined them.

"What's the matter, Mommy?"

"Nothing, sweetheart. Did you put your dollies to bed? You should. Go and tuck them in." Lynette left them. "You know what we have to do," she said to Noah.

"I guess . . ."

"Let's get to it."

They pulled down the big mattress; Lucy slit it at one end while Noah unyoked the oxen. They watered them, but when they tried to feed them the dried-out straw the oxen refused it, turning their heads this way and that and lowing.

"Maybe if we soak it in water," said Lucy.

The oxen consumed the moistened stuffing down to the last wisp, protesting volubly when they couldn't have more.

"We'll have to sleep on the ground tonight," said Noah, "and until we find that wagon track."

"You make it sound like it'll take us days."

He looked about. "I guess we can camp here."

"Start a fire, I'll make supper. Tomorrow we turn around."

"I wonder how far past it we've come——"

She was frowning, biting her lip gently, suddenly deep in thought. "Darling, do you suppose . . . I know it sounds crazy."

"What are you thinking?"

"Do you think it's possible those Mormons would deliberately mislead us?"

"No."

"You know how they feel about outsiders; some of them despise us with a passion."

"Did they act like they 'despised' us?"

"They saw us coming from a mile away, plenty of time to devise a plan."

"That's ridiculous. Lucy, this isn't you talking; next you'll be believing in ghosts. It's just too far-fetched. Think about it, there's one chance in a thousand they'd deceive me, but not one in a million you and Lynette. Josiah would, but not Mormons. What's for supper?"

"Oh, the whole menu from Purdy's in Baltimore; nine courses, a fabulous selection of wines. You're right, I'm sorry, I shouldn't be so mistrusting, it's childish. Blame all this, I'm out at the end of every nerve."

"Of course; me, too."

"What'll we do if the oxen die on us?"

"It won't come to that. The grass is here, we'll find it."

"They—the Mormons—claim it is."

"Please, let's not get back on that."

"No." She tried a smile of apology.

"I'm not blaming you, it's Josiah. He'd shake the Good Samaritan's faith in his fellow man."

"I sure haven't had mine 'shaken' like that in a long time." She kissed him.

"What's that for?"

"The man of my heart. And there's more where that came from when we get to bed, mattress or no. And tomorrow we'll find that meadow."

"Load up on forage, water."

She tittered. "And restuff the mattress."

THIRTY-NINE

Noah watered the oxen while Lucy finished cleaning up after breakfast. But when he failed to offer them forage, instead yoking them and readying to leave, they began lowing loudly and refused to budge.

"What now?" Lucy asked.

"How should I know? It's never happened before, I'm no authority on ungulates."

"It's never happened before because they've always been fed before; and don't get mad at me."

He began cracking the whip repeatedly above their rumps; they still refused to move.

"Maybe if I gave them more water——"

"They're full, Noah, they want their breakfast."

"Maybe I could take the mattress tick, walk back up the road, find that wagon track . . ."

Lucy shook her head. "You're not making sense, it could be ten miles back. Double that; add six miles back and forth on the wagon track . . ."

He cursed and, in a sudden burst of anger, began whipping the lead team's rumps. They stirred, lowing loudly.

"Noah!"

He waved her away, continuing to beat them; it was as if all his frustration, his helplessness, were surging and surfacing at once. He was shouting now, but to her surprise, and his, both oxen moved forward. The other two pair quit balking; he turned them about, they started back.

Noah figured it to be about ten miles back to where we would find the elusive wagon track. I think it was farther. The exact distance doesn't matter now. We lost a full day here; and we won't be back to where we turned around till early tomorrow afternoon. At this rate we won't see the crest of the mountains until well past the middle of October. God help us if we run into heavy snows! Shades of the Donner Pass!

The bright side is that we finally located the meadow. We fed the oxen to bursting, first laying the cut grass out in the sun to dry a little—Noah was afraid they'd get cramps wolfing down moist, fresh grass. We stuffed all the grass we could in the wagon while Lynette filled the tick. Plenty of fresh water here, but it wasn't until late afternoon that we were done filling our empty casks. Noah got the bright idea of leaving them in the wagon bed and bringing the mountain to Mohammed—they're so heavy to boost up over the tailgate when full. The three of us bathed; by that time it was so late in the day it seemed pointless to leave, so we're spending the night here. It reminds me of Ash

*Hollow, only without the trees, without any shade—
just acres upon acres of sweet grass bending in the
wind. If the oxen had their way we'd never leave.*

*Noah wanted to start out at midnight tonight,
which would get us about a quarter the way across the
desert before the sun cleared the mountains behind us.
It did make sense until we both started thinking about
conditions after that: it's doubtful the oxen could keep
going for such a long stretch; from midnight to sundown would be around eighteen hours, for we could
hardly camp in the desert while the sun is high. Even
rest and water stops would have to be brief. All in all, it
seems a sure way of killing the poor creatures, working
them so long, so it was finally agreed that we leave after
breakfast.*

*Fifty miles doesn't seem terribly far when you con-
sider how far we've come already, but it'll be by far the
hottest and hardest stretch we've had to cross. And
Noah worries about losing one or more oxen. There
won't be any alkali dust, but who's to say the sand
won't be just as hard on them when the wind comes
up?*

*Lynette, bless her heart, has been a Trojan all the
way from Baltimore. Her only bad time was when we
pulled her tooth, and who could blame her for acting up
at that? When I think of how some children her age do
little more than whine and complain over next to nothing, and of the way she's put up with this drudgery—
the dust, the sand, the heat, the myriad discomforts
and inconveniences—we both feel blessed that she's
our flesh and blood.*

*There's one problem—one more—that looms and is
beginning to assume phantom shape the farther we*

*proceed: the farther, the less we know about what lies
ahead. It can happen when one family attempts this
alone. Josiah mentioned that there are half a dozen
trails over the Sierra Nevadas, but never did specify
which one was the best or if any of them is preferable to
the others. All of them have been used by emigrants
before; all, I'm sure, present similar dangers and difficulties.*

*But seventy miles to reach the top, then a hundred
more to cross before we get to see the western slope, is
as daunting as the Great Basin. I can still see Noah's
cheeks paling when the Mormons told us.*

*So, should I end this entry by asking that God be
with us? Or is it more fitting to say, fools rush in where
angels fear to tread?*

FORTY

Lucy imagined she could hear the heat crackling. In every
direction the landscape looked veiled in shimmering, rising,
watery waves. The oxen moved so slowly with their heads so
low, that Noah had to slow his pace to a lazy amble so they
could keep up with him.

"They want water," called Lucy from the driver's seat.

He cracked his whip over the lead pair. "It's not even an
hour and a half since the last time."

"Look at them, Noah."

He stopped the wagon. This time he didn't bother to
unyoke them; each one consumed a full bucket.

"They could die of cramps as easily as from thirst," he
said.

Lucy looked back into the curtain of heat, then forward. "How far have we come?"

"We're moving so slowly I don't think we're even halfway across yet."

"Maybe if we give them less water more often: say half a bucket every half hour . . ."

"If we do that it'll take us three days to get across. One thing we *can* do: keep going after nightfall."

To his surprise, she agreed. "I guess. Only I can't believe they'll pick up speed when the sun goes down and it begins getting cooler. The big question is will they have the stamina to keep on?"

"If they'd move even a little faster there's a chance we could reach the Carson before sunup; at least before it gets too hot."

"A chance. God forbid they collapse from exhaustion and die on us."

His hat restored to his head, he moved closer to her; he could not conceal the anxiety in his eyes, he did not try. "This has been nothing but a long drawn-out gamble since Council Bluffs: crossing rivers, plodding on looking for the next water, going over trails no wider than your hand and nearly falling into ravines half a dozen times."

"Inviting a stranger along who turns out to be a wanted killer . . ."

"Do you blame me for him?"

"Of course not, we discussed it, we agreed. The irony is he actually turned out a big help in a dozen ways."

"Only to end up beating the hangman when his heart gave out, poor man."

" 'Poor man'?"

"It's small charity to feel sorry for somebody, even his sort; we did get to know him."

They finished watering the oxen and went on. In silence for a time, each inside his own thoughts of survival and their chances. Then Lucy got to thinking about the others in the original train.

"I wonder how far they've gotten. . . ."

"They do have farther to go, so Schwimmer claimed. And mountains almost all the way to the Willamette Valley."

"I envy them, it does sound easier than what we've been through. Mostly because they can help each other. I wonder what Marcia's doing at this very moment? I hope she doesn't have to ride with your bosom friend Olin."

"Why shouldn't she? Is he a leper? Did he ever do anything to her?"

"You don't understand, do you, Noah? What he did to Sarah he did to every woman. Any man who brutalizes a woman does it to the sex as a whole. I'm sure that given the chance he'd take his frustration out on anyone. Never a man of course, he's too much of a coward. Nancy's the one I feel sorry for."

"You honestly think she's in danger from her own father?"

"Of the worst kind, if you know what I mean. Thank God she has Abby and Marcia to protect her on the road."

"He really upsets you, doesn't he?"

"He has no right to live; you kill someone, you forfeit that right."

"Maybe what happened to Sarah changed him. I mean what he did to her. He sure sounded like it did; he was still drowning in guilt when we parted company."

"Don't be naive. His kind never changes, their attitudes are much too deeply ingrained."

"My, we're in a judgmental mood today."

"I'm not being 'judgmental.' Oh, maybe I am, only, he's

the king of the snakes. I wish he were here right now, I'd bash him with the shovel!"

Noah laughed.

"You think that's funny? What really infuriates me is he calls himself a man of God. Conducting Sunday services, spouting the Bible, that bogus humility of his. Disgusting fraud! Why did you have to bring him up, of all people?"

"You brought him up talking about Marcia."

"I wonder how Abby's health is . . ."

"Better than yours or mine, the woman's a draft horse; if something happens to them and only one survives—she'll be it. She fascinated you, didn't she? What was the big attraction?"

"I guess it was the combination of everything about her. She was cheerful, she oozed motherliness, she was colorful, bubbling over with personality. And underneath it all, a real soldier—all the women going through this should be like her. The jewel of her good points was that she liked and loved Maynard; they were as happy as newlyweds, and neither felt the need to dominate the other. The difference between Abby and Olin Coombs——"

"Please, we're done talking about him."

"I can't help but think that when we left them, Ruth Willoughby was beginning to change for the better because of Abby. Ruth sees her every day, sees what equality in a marriage is, how fair, how right it is, sees how much Maynard does for Abby, how little Anson does. I know Ruth idolizes him almost to a point of nausea, but she's not stupid."

"So Abby's pulling the scales off her eyes."

"I'm being serious."

"Me, too, darling."

"We're talking about a woman's life. I pray that by the

time they get to the valley Abby will influence Ruth just by example. Take on a whole new set of attitudes toward herself as much as Anson."

"What about Marcia?"

"What about her? She doesn't need new attitudes; her head is on as straight as Abby's. I'll tell you one thing, she learned a hard lesson, she'll never marry the wrong man again."

"Too bad she won't have you there to make sure she doesn't." He elbowed her playfully; she slapped his knee.

They went on, but only a short distance; time to water the oxen again. It was an hour past noon, their second day in the desert. The oxen were moving much more deliberately than when they crossed the Great Basin, as if instinctively preserving their remaining strength. Noah had figured that at the very most it would take five days to cross. At their present pace it would take at least that.

Somewhere too far ahead, beyond the tantalizing mirages, on the other side of the shimmering veil that joined burning sky to burning sands, the Carson River meandered in and out of the shadow of the Sierra Nevadas. And waited. On trundled the wagon.

FORTY-ONE

Approaching their fourth nightfall in the desert, Noah decided that it was time, once again, to gamble. They would stop to eat, feed and water the oxen, then continue on.

"Averaging ten miles a day, even eight, that leaves only eighteen miles to the river."

"*Only.*"

"I think that in the cool of the night we can get that far easily. Be there before sunrise."

"You're ignoring the fact that the oxen are more tired than ever. Whether it's hot or cool won't make any difference if they collapse and die on us. Losing just one pair, the others will have to work twice as hard."

"Not *twice.*"

"Don't split hairs. You know what I'm saying."

"So what do we do?"

"I say we stop when it gets dark, as usual; go on in the morning, and when the sun goes down tomorrow *then* we keep going. I mean, if your figuring is right, that'll make it only ten miles to the river, not eighteen."

"And the oxen one more day more weary. I don't agree."

"Noah!"

"Why are you yelling, Mommy?"

Lynette pushed her head between them.

"I'm not. Back inside."

"It's boiling inside."

"Get your rag, daub some water on your face and neck."

"But . . ."

"Just do it!" Lynette started and withdrew. "Listen to me. One more day traveling normally—that's all I'm asking."

"It doesn't make sense."

"It makes perfect sense!"

"Your daughter's right, you are having a loud day."

"Blame yourself, why are you so obstinate?"

"Self-defense, it sounds like. Why are we fighting?"

"Discussing——"

"Fighting! All right! Have it your way."

He got down and stopped the team, grumbling to himself. She couldn't make out a word. She watched him. One of them was right—which obviously made the other dead wrong. If they lost even one oxen doing it her way, she'd never hear the end of it. It was all so absurd; like performing a play without rehearsal; neither of them knew what they were doing; both were learning on the move, making mistakes at every turn . . . gambling, guessing, hoping.

The sun hadn't really come out since they left Council Bluffs; since that rainy day, they'd been in the darkness of ignorance every mile of the way—definitely since Pacific Springs.

They'd never have gotten this far had it not been for Bridger, Josiah Riley and the four Mormons. Still, wasn't it the same for everyone preceding them, everyone coming after? What were any emigrants doing but pushing on with their eyes on the horizon, their dreams in their hearts, their hearts in their mouths? What, after all, was this pilgrims' progress but nature at its most hostile, weather at its varied worst and risk, risk, risk?

And all these graves; they'd doubled in number here in the desert. So many people gambling and losing. Meanwhile the Lord of Hosts looked down and decided who would make it, who fail.

"Not us," she muttered.

"Not us?"

"We'll make it. . . ."

FORTY-TWO

Sleep, abundant forage and all the water they could drink the next morning did not restore the oxens' energy nearly as much as the Mitchums fervently hoped they would.

"Maybe we should just stay put," suggested Lucy. "Just for one day."

"Out here? Are you crazy?"

"We've plenty of food and water for them, what they need more than anything is prolonged rest."

"Lucy, if they stand in the sun all day it'll only sap what little energy they have left; which is all we've got to get us to the river. Are you serious? You'd like us to sit out here in the blazing sun all day? The heat must be getting to you."

"Don't be sarcastic."

"Are you fighting?" Lynette asked.

"No, sweetheart," said Lucy keeping her eyes on Noah. "Daddy just thinks Mommy's being stupid."

"Lucy . . ."

"Forgive me, that's no way to begin another glorious day of traveling."

She scraped what was left of the fried eggs into his plate. He cut them in half and scraped the half into Lynette's plate. He cleared his throat.

"Maybe it's time we put all the cards faceup, shall we?" Lucy frowned, not understanding. "Deep down, you really and truly resent me for this: dragging the three of us to the Promised Land. Correction—trying to, and not doing a very good job of it. Doing a disastrous job."

"You're wrong."

"I don't think so."

"If that's how you really think, don't blame me; better you blame your lack of confidence in yourself."

"Lucy, I don't lack confidence, I never would have left Baltimore if I did."

"Don't you mean *we* never would have left?"

"I twisted your arm, dragged you to Iowa kicking and screaming."

"I don't recall doing either; that's disgusting, you are."

"Don't fight," said Lynette.

"I apologize," said Noah. "What are we doing? My God, we're almost there!"

"Almost to the wall, you mean. Have you stopped to think about how in heaven's name the two of us will ever lift the wagon over the rocks on this side?"

"We did it in the Wasatches——"

"And lucky we didn't lose everything down that ravine."

He came to her and slipped his arm around her. "We can do it, we can. . . ."

"If we can't—what then? Turn around and go back? It's just so discouragingly frustrating; to come all this way and end up against a thousand-foot wall."

He grinned, hugging her. "Some of the highest points are eleven to fourteen thousand feet—that was intended to be funny. But aren't you overlooking something? Aren't you forgetting how many others before us have made it? How many Noahs, Lucys and Lynettes?"

"They weren't alone."

"How do you know? I'll bet some families were; and some have even crossed in the dead of winter."

"The Donner Party for one. My God, will you listen to me? One of my more supportive days. Getting back to what we were talking about, I'll admit I was . . . less than enthusiastic about coming . . . but hardly 'kicking and screaming.' I agreed to come, I've been willing to go on every step of the way. My confidence is in *both* of us. It's been hell at times, it's also been fascinating beyond anything I imagined.

We've both found patience, optimism and courage neither of us dreamed we had in us.

"You know something, Noah Mitchum, we should be patting ourselves on the back. What *I* shouldn't be doing is moaning and groaning."

"I do just as much."

"We didn't before—even after Pacific Springs when the going got rougher."

"We do now because we're tired; who wouldn't be? What the three of us really need is a vacation. A long trip." He laughed. "No, a month in the country without moving more than a few steps across a room; out of sight of oxen and wagon, mountains and deserts, sun and storm. Nothing but shade and pink lemonade. We owe ourselves a vacation; once we've settled into our new home we'll take it. In the parlor."

"Sounds delicious. The sun's coming up; forget what I said about resting today, let's get moving."

Noah estimated that they made all of five miles that day. When darkness fell they stopped, took care of the oxen, ate a hurried supper and continued westward. Sundown had brought a welcome coolness as usual. Around nine, Noah stopped to water the oxen. The stars cluttered the heavens, the moon was full, the omnipresent shimmering veil of heat had long since vanished and the Sierra Nevadas could be clearly seen darker than the sky ahead—a great granite blade rising, threatening to slice the sky.

On dragged the oxen. It was well past midnight when abruptly they picked up their heads, began bellowing softly, and, to Lucy's amazement, increased their pace. Faster and faster they moved.

"They smell water!" exclaimed Noah. "The river! Darling, we've made it, we've made it!"

Lucy's sigh of relief was prolonged and came forth on a gradually descending note. It expressed her feelings without any need for words.

═══ FORTY-THREE ═══

Willows and alders dominated the trees on both sides of the river. It descended the eastern slope to level ground and headed northward. Somewhere over eight thousand feet above was Carson Pass, so the Mormon prospectors had informed Noah. A trail had to lead up to and through the pass and through the peaks to the western slope.

"That does make sense," said Lucy when they discussed the situation the next morning.

Noah turned to dismantling the tent while she prepared a breakfast of bacon and soda bread. The coffee made from river water tasted very good; Noah broke his habit and took a third cup. He helped Lucy clean up after breakfast, then all three stood where there was a break in the trees gazing up at the final obstacle, its peaks still mantled in haze. Lucy could not help noting Noah's guilty expression.

"Is something bothering you?"

"Me?"

"What is it?"

"Sell the house, pack up and leave. I should have taken the time to plan this last phase down to the last detail. I don't know what I must have been thinking back there. I guess I thought that we'd hook up with another wagon train."

"We haven't even seen 'another train' since we broke up with the others. And ours was the only wagon at the campgrounds in Salt Lake City."

"Obviously because it's so late in the year." He shook his head. "I wanted us to make it to the top before October fifteenth. We'll be lucky to get there by November. I wonder if it's started snowing up there yet?"

He was beginning to depress her. He of all people—the tireless voice of optimism. Once again a gamble confronted them, pure chance would dictate their fate. The winter high up could begin early; it could have arrived already. It could come at its normal time, sometime in November. It was even possible that it would be late.

"It's a game of three-card monte," he said. "You get one pick only."

Lucy managed a laugh. "Except that three-card monte is rigged; this, at least, will be fair."

"On second thought, we're actually faced with *two* chances out of three. A normal winter or a late one, either one would work in our favor. But the one other choice could turn out . . ."

"Disastrous. Don't be afraid to say it—the Donner Party."

"No, the Donner Party was an extreme case. Their luck, their planning, their timing, the advice they got, the weather—all were bad; nothing favorable or helpful."

"If you remember, Josiah said that some years it does snow in October up top, but that it's unusual. So what are we waiting for? Let's look for where the trail starts."

He pondered this. "Let's wait, steal at least two days."

"You mean give it even a better chance to start snowing up there?"

"Lucy, look at the oxen, they need rest desperately. They'll need all their strength to get us past the obstacles up there. If we force them to start out still tired . . ."

She nodded. "You're right, we'll rest them."

"But only two days. Today's the sixth; Monday, the eighth, we move out."

They needed a break themselves. The oxen grazed in the shade, Lynette played with her birthday gifts, Noah inspected the wagon. The desert heat had taken a heavy toll on the wheels. None of the iron tires had worked loose, but all four were badly worn.

"Will the wheels give out going over the mountains?" Lucy asked.

Noah pointed skyward. "Ask him, not me. If we do lose a tire we'll have to just keep going on bare wheels. The only thing that'll stop us is if a wheel shatters. Too bad we used up the spare replacing that wobbly front wheel."

He set about greasing the wheels while Lucy sat under a tree and wrote in her diary.

> It's so restful here, so peaceful, even more beautiful than Ash Hollow: the oxen grazing, birds singing spiritedly, the river flowing by in soft, friendly tones. Lynette playing, Noah working. My Noah, who started out as green as new grass and got us to this point, and himself hardened, experienced, as capable as any wagon master. Herman Schwimmer would be proud, Abby, too. . . .

A sound broke through the melody of the river: hooves drifting down the slope behind her. Two riders came splash-

ing across the river, their horses leading two fully loaded
pack mules. The water washed the dust from the men's
trouser legs and the lower halves of all four animals.

"No . . ."

She stiffened. No more company, please. No strangers
pushing into this, the most hazardous and critical phase of
the trek. She watched them rein up, dismount in separate
dust clouds and approach Noah.

She got up to join them. Lynette, meanwhile, was acting
as if she hadn't even seen them, continuing to sip her make-
believe tea and talk with her make-believe party guests.
Both men looked about the same age. One was huge, standing more than a head taller than Noah and outweighing him
by sixty or seventy pounds. His wrists looked the size and
squareness of bricks, and his shoulders, separated by his
thick neck, approached the width of the tailgate. His red
face showed a week's beard.

His companion was as tall as he but narrow-shouldered
and as skinny as a rifle, his chest caved in, face gaunt, cheeks
hollow. He stood leaning slightly forward, his hands spilling
from his cuffs showing long, slender fingers. On the left side
of his jaw the flesh was bunched to the size of a thumbnail,
as if a knifepoint had dug at it and it had healed imperfectly.

The bigger man introduced them.

"Gordon Wirth's my name, this is my partner Slade
Bellows." He held up a small leather folder; it dropped
open; Lucy held her breath.

"Relief Committee?" Noah read aloud.

"Yes sir, sent out by the U.S. government to help late
emigrants over the mountains. We assume that is your
intention, Mr. . . ."

Noah introduced them. "It is," he said, "we intend to

start out day after tomorrow. We wanted to rest our oxen for a couple days."

Bellows spoke for the first time, around a sprig of grass he had started chewing. "Everybody's cattle are worn down to the knees by the time they get to here. But you won't need no two days to rest 'em, one'll do nicely."

"Two days is sure to spoil them," added Wirth grinning.

"Wait just a minute," said Lucy, "you're not with any Relief Committee." They gaped, she laughed and, turning, pointed up the slope. "You're angels come down from heaven."

"Hallelujah!" burst Noah.

Lucy brewed fresh coffee and offered the visitors what remained of the batch of soda bread.

"Has it started snowing yet up top?" Noah asked.

"Just a dusting a few days ago," said Wirth, "nothing to slow anybody down. Although we haven't seen a single wagon in the past two weeks."

"I know we're late. . . ."

"You're on the edge of being late." The big man was staring at Noah. "You planned to climb all by yourself? Oh, it's been done—though not that often. And you do have to know your way around up there."

The conversation turned to the choice of trails.

"The trail up to Carson Pass starts not far from here," said Wirth, "but it's not the easiest to follow. At the summit it's the toughest of all. The descent on the other side is gradual for several miles, but getting up on this side it becomes very steep nearing the top."

Bellows nodded. "It gets so just when your oxen are plumb tuckered out."

"Not to mention you," added Wirth. "At one time or

another Slade and I have tried all eight trails, and there are better ones than up the Carson." He pointed. "There's a second branch of the river about twelve miles south of here. We think the best trail starts just beyond the branch."

"Whatever you say," said Noah.

Bellows got out a map and spread it on the tailgate. Lucy and Noah followed his finger to the second branch of the Carson River and the beginning of the trail both men recommended. It zigzagged up the eastern slope in what appeared to be fairly easy stages, reached the top and undulated across to the west face.

"From here," said Wirth, "the worst and the hardest will be behind us and right about here—if there's no haze—you can look down into the Valley."

"You got a particular destination in mind?" Bellows asked.

"The Sacramento Valley," said Noah.

Bellows laughed, Wirth smiled. "Mister," said Bellows, "the Central Valley o' California, which the Sacramento is the north half of, is two-hundred-fifty-odd miles long, forget how wide."

"Good," said Noah, matching smirk for smirk, "that means we can't miss it."

The representatives of the Rescue Committee turned to inspecting the wagon. Lucy noted that neither appeared impressed with the condition of the tires.

"You get these at Bridger's fort?" Bellows asked. Noah nodded. "They're bad wore. You say you come from Council Bluffs, did you happen to notice how your original tires looked when they took 'em off?"

"Not really. You think they replaced them with used tires?"

"It's hard to say, only that your originals coulda been in better shape than his 'new.' "

"Will these hold out long enough to get us over the mountains?" Lucy asked.

"Hard to say," said Bellows. "They ain't loose but they're mighty thin."

Wirth ran a thumb down the tire and nodded. "Lose a tire and you can split a wheel in no time."

"We'll just have to cross our fingers," muttered Noah.

Wirth smiled. "And pray . . ."

Bellows grunted. "And keep a sharp eye out for a rig down the bottom of a ravine; maybe climb down and salvage a unbusted wheel or two."

Lucy groaned silently, turning her head to hide her expression. Did it *ever* get any easier? *Was* there such a thing as a natural balance between good and bad? You couldn't prove it by this journey!

"Another thing," said Bellows, "best brace yourselves. High up the chill gets colder than the desert gets hot. It's like they blocked the way to the sunshine with a piece o' the North Pole. It gets so cold it can fracture your bones."

Wirth laughed. "Slade here has a gift for exaggeration. But he's right, it can get very very cold."

FORTY-FOUR

By Gordon Wirth's estimation they had reached a height of close to two thousand feet when they were stopped by a sheer wall of granite about twenty feet high. To the right of the narrow trail was a sheer drop that plunged into darkness; to the left, a thick stand of trees, with the largest of them perched on the top of the obstructing rock. The oxen were unhitched and the four adults set about unloading the wagon.

"Everything?" Lucy asked.

"Every stick," said Bellows. "Mr. Mitchum, get out your rope, pulleys, block and tackle, whatever you got."

Piece by piece Noah lay the equipment out between Lucy's churn and two chests of drawers. When the wagon bed had been emptied it was unbolted from the axles and three ropes were passed under it and joined over the top.

"I've about thirty feet of chain," said Noah to Wirth.

"No chains, not this time; they chafe the sides where rope won't. Chains can even break a board or two if they're mishandled, or if the wagon should drop even a few feet in pulling it up and over."

The ropes and block and tackle were made fast to the tree at the summit and the wagon bed eased slowly up the side of the rock to the top. The carriage assembly was raised in the same manner. Hauling up the Mitchum's heavier belongings, carrying up the lighter ones with even Lynette helping, and lifting the oxen up one by one, took all day. The wagon was reassembled, reloaded, the supper fire lit, the oxen fed and watered and camp was made for the night.

They huddled around it against the cold.

"Someday," said Wirth, removing his gloves to warm his hands, "assuming emigrants continue to use this way, the government'll send a crew up here to build a dirt and log ramp up to the top of the rock. It'll still be steep, there's just not enough room for a gradual approach, but it'll do away with the need to unload wagons and dismantle them."

"You could even drive your oxen up without having to unyoke and separate them," said Lucy.

Wirth agreed. "Speaking of oxen, before we continue on tomorrow, we should collect some grass to add to your supply of forage. All you can comfortably carry. Water's no problem, there are sources all over these mountains, but the grass gets sparser and sparser the higher you climb."

Wirth and Bellows insisted on eating their own rations, drinking their own water, but both readily accepted Lucy's offer of coffee. Slade Bellows played Lynette's board game with her until it was her bedtime. By then she was calling him Uncle Slade.

The next day, the wagon rolled up an extended series of gradual slopes following the rock- and boulder-walled trail. It was so narrow that if another wagon were to appear coming their way it would have been impossible to pass. It was late afternoon when Bellows, riding well ahead of his partner and the wagon, momentarily disappeared around a bend and seconds later sent up a shout. He came riding back.

"A rig, Gordon, down a crevass. Locked in place like a vise, canvas and all!"

"How far down?" asked Noah.

"No more'n a hundred feet. Both right side wheels sticking up in the clear; both look to be in prime shape."

"You can't see the tires," said Lucy.

"I can if I climb down."

They continued on around the bend. The wagon below looked identical to theirs, decided Lucy, which meant the wheels were the same size. A rope was tied around Bellows' waist and Wirth and Noah let him slowly down carrying the monkey wrench from the wagon's jockey box. Alighting on the slightly slanting side of the stricken wagon he inspected each of the wheels, then signaled upward.

"Good shape; send down the light rope."

Half-inch Manila rope was let down as he set about loosening the square nut on the front wheel, then removed the wheel, tied the rope to it and watched it hauled up.

Noah and Wirth inspected the wheel and tire. The tire looked newer than Noah's four tires.

"How do we take it off?" he asked.

"Why bother? If and when you need it, why not just replace it wheel and all."

A week later they camped one night between two enormous boulders out of the relentless and bitter cold wind. Noah climbed to the top of one rock to see what he could of the trail ahead. It brought him to a wide notch through which he could see the setting sun igniting the sky in various shades of gold beneath a blanket of royal purple clouds. He offered to help Lucy up to see, but she demurred.

"Time enough to see the sunset when we get to the top."

Noah was helped down. "We're almost to the top. By tomorrow?" He looked for affirmation from Wirth and got a nod.

"Then," said the big man, "only a hundred-odd miles to go before we start down."

"Easier miles than climbing, you can bet," said Bellows, beating himself briefly with his arms and edging nearer the fire.

Lucy couldn't blame him, she felt frozen to the marrow, and the wind howling about them made it even colder. A hundred more miles of this . . . As the discouraging thought moved through her mind, she felt a dart of cold strike her cheek.

A snowflake.

FORTY-FIVE

So well were the oxen bearing up that even the two guides commented on it. Wirth disclosed that at their present rate they would reach the top sometime tomorrow.

"This snow's just a dusting——"

"I don't know how he can be so sure of that now that winter's sneaked up on us," said Lucy to Noah minutes later in the privacy of their tent.

"Who says it has? It's just a flurry. Look . . ." He sat up in bed, slipped out from under the covers and scrambled forward untying and easing open the flap. It was snowing, not flurrying.

"Close that! It's cold enough without letting the wind in here. Are you satisfied? We could get three feet by morning, then what'll we do?"

"What we don't do tonight is conjure up all sorts of problems before we go to sleep."

"Snow . . . And we're not even to the top. And the wind's so fierce and uncertain it'll blow eight-foot drifts in our way, you just watch."

"Lucy, stop it; look at the bright side: the oxen are healthy, we've made it almost to the top—in record time, according to our guides. Getting across to the west face has to be a snap compared with climbing up here."

All true. And it wasn't like her to let the first snow push her into pessimism. It really could turn out no more than a dusting. Still, mention of the oxen got her to worrying about them. With the horses and mules the men had herded all six oxen into a break in the rocks where they were cramped for space, but out of the wind and the worst of the cold. And biting it was, becoming more and more brutal the higher they climbed.

Three nights before, somebody had carelessly left a half-filled water cask outside in the wind. Upon arising in the morning, it was found sprung and its contents solid ice. The casks in the wagon might also freeze, Bellows warned, but Wirth hastened to add that as long as they were kept out of the wind the temperature would have to plunge for that to happen.

Wirth and Bellows—ideal partners they were. Every pearl of pessimism that fell from Bellows' lips Wirth countered with something as rosy-sounding as he could make it without straying into exaggeration. They got along well; up to now, at least, not once had either sniped at the other in a difference of opinion. And their job was not easy. Getting over the mountains only once was more than enough for Lucy; riding back and forth over them for a living had to be grueling. Bellows mentioned that he personally wore out four horses a year on average; Wirth was listening at the time and didn't disagree, so it must have been true. She would have guessed at least six horses.

Between the worrisome snowfall and consciously striving to fall asleep Lucy was wide awake. Lynette and Noah had no such difficulty. Half an hour after Noah dropped off, Lucy drew her fur robe around her shoulders and moved on her knees to the entrance, undoing the flap and peering out. It was still snowing, but not nearly as heavily. As she watched it a gust snatched a handful of snow and flung it toward her. She ducked just in time, turtling back her head.

Lulled by the now moaning wind she finally dropped off. . . . And into a dream. She saw herself standing in front of a blackboard. She was wearing glasses and in her hand was a pointer. When she turned her head her hair was done up in a bun at the back—a hairdo she'd never liked, never tried. Back and forth she strode, talking without letup, although no sound came out. Now and then she would stop, turn to the blank blackboard and tap the pointer.

The point of view switched; now she could see her bun, her back and her hand gripping the pointer. Before her was the classroom, chairs in neat rows and in the rear a waist-high bookcase stretching from the door to the corner. On the opposite side of the door was a flagstand; Old Glory drooped on its staff.

But what surprised her was that she had only one pupil: sitting in the center of the classroom, hands dutifully folded in her lap, her shiny black shoes unable to reach the floor. She listened attentively, her eyes concentrating on her teacher above well-scrubbed cheeks. A pretty child, she looked familiar.

Lynette.

Lynette woke her. "Mommy, Mommy, come see the snow!"

Lucy yawned, she felt groggy and stiff all over. The other side of the mattress was empty. Lynette was bundled up for outside, her scarf—the plaid one Grandmother Scott had knit for her last Christmas—up to her eyes.

"Come! Come!"

"How much?" Lucy asked.

"Heaps and heaps and heaps!"

Lucy groaned. Noah stuck his head in, sending in a cloud of vapor. "A few inches."

"Ten? Fifteen?"

"Four or five. And it's warming up. Gordon says that's

good, the surface'll melt. Later it's sure to get colder, it'll form a crust so it can't drift on us."

"And is more snow threatening?"

"The sky's bluer than your eyes; the sun's out."

It was dazzling, striking Lucy's unprotected eyes like darts. She winced.

Snow mantled everything in sight. Wirth and Bellows came up; Noah, the first one out of bed, had made breakfast for everyone.

"Why didn't you wake me?" Lucy asked, feeling embarrassed.

"I didn't have the heart, you were sleeping so soundly. Come and eat before it gets cold. We have to get moving. The animals are all fine, raring to go. Come, today's the day we go over the top!"

Lynette squealed joyfully. Lucy yawned and managed a smile. Dear Lord it was cold!

═══════ FORTY-SIX ═══════

It took the Mitchums and their guides nearly twelve full days to cross to the summit of the west face of the Sierra Nevadas. Despite the welcome absence of steep climbs and drops that characterized the ascent, it turned out an arduous trek; the trail twisted and turned so often it seemed to Lucy that the estimated distance of a hundred miles was doubled. The snow stayed away; not the wind. The heights were its playground; it blasted tirelessly, bringing numbing cold even with the sun burning brightly at high noon. The wind burned the travelers' cheeks, sent them into narrow slits in the rocks to build their fires, rocked the wagon unceasingly, threatening to spring it free of its axles, and crept boldly into the tents at night. It made Lucy very nearly long for the heat of the desert.

They had ascended through the thick forest belt, up to where there was more rock than soil, where the growing season lasted no more than two months a year. But the sun had melted the snow of two weeks earlier, plants clung to life and animals were active. Here the night wind began to blow soon after dark, starting in tolerable gusts, but increasing in velocity toward midnight to a powerful gale.

Up high in the Alpine Belt meadows, trees and rock intermingled, and unlike the slopes, there was no real forest. Lodgepole pines grew alone, stunted by the cold. Silver pines and western white pines survived at the heights, and on the most exposed places the white-bark pine reached a height of forty feet.

The high meadows, some bare, some with scattered trees growing around them, provided welcome relief from the rocky landscape. No lush green pastures, their grasses were sparse and stunted, useless for forage.

It was the trees that drew Lucy's attention. They were uniformly ugly, partially stripped of their bark, bleached of their color, gnarled and twisted by the wind; trunks and branches alike often grew horizontally. But seeds had found clutch in the impoverished soil pocketed on uninviting granite, saplings sprouted and matured in defiance of the harsh environment. Wind and weather, however, avenged the intrusion, robbing the trees of their stateliness, reducing them to cripples.

On the tenth day, two days from the end of the horizontal trek, Lucy spied a particularly tortuous specimen and realized she'd seen others with its groups of elongated needles on the slopes. Wirth identified it as a Jeffrey pine.

"The ones you saw below stand tall and straight, shielded from this wind and in much healthier soil," he explained.

This was a dwarf, root bound and prostrate on a ledge. Like other Alpine trees, much of its bark was missing. No birds ventured near, rodents shunned the fallen needles collected around the base. It was a thing of no beauty, of no usefulness; but it survived. Lucy marveled at its tenacity, at the grasp of every growing thing clinging to precarious existence, and in many cases thriving. There were grasses, like those in the meadows, too stunted to be used to feed the oxen, and there were sedges and rushes; all adapted to the elevation, the lack of rain and the short growing season.

The trees that succeeded in standing close to straight hosted a variety of birds, while different breeds of mice and other vermin competed for the meager food supply with mule deer and bighorns. Overhead hawks, eagles, condors rode high winds and looked down on the scurrying life below, selecting their food.

Midafternoon of the twelfth day, Bellows broke away from the group, riding forward, reining up suddenly, lifting his hat high and calling back.

"Come see, Noah, Miz Mitchum, little princess . . ."

He indicated a wide, almost perfectly level ledge. Lucy scrambled up onto it on all fours, gripping Lynette by the wrist.

"Your new home," said Bellows, pointing. "All yours, all the way up to Mount Shasta."

Lucy gasped. The Sacramento Valley! The land undulated to the south, portions of it hidden by majestic groves; spreading northward it gradually changed into flat, treeless prairies, much like those in the Midwest. Buttes rose on the eastern side of a dominant river whose banks were lined with trees, their dark green foliage splashing color against the dull browns of distant, low volcanic hills.

"That there's the Sacramento River with all her tributaries. You like to fish, Noah? Them waters teem with salmon and steelhead trout. You want to farm? Best soil on the whole continent. Plenty o' water and sun; warm and comfortable year-round. The Promised Land for sure."

"Is that gold down there?" Noah asked.

"Wheat—a few folks are starting to farm."

"Are there Indians?" asked Lucy.

Wirth nodded, "Yokuts, Miwok, Maidu, Washo, Yana— a dozen tribes. Down there around Sacramento are the Miwoks——"

"Are they warlike?" Lucy pressed him. "Like the Sioux and the Pawnees?"

He shook his head. "They're friendly, as gentle as well-behaved children. They hunt, they fish, they harvest acorns and they leave emigrants alone, except to trade. If there's any trouble it generally springs up in the gold diggings. And some drunken prospector's usually at fault."

Lucy turned to look at Noah; he averted his eyes.

"So all the danger's out where they're hunting for gold."

Wirth looked between husband and wife, realizing he'd touched a sore point. "It's dangerous wherever men compete for something of value," he murmured.

They rested before starting down the west face. The plan was for Wirth and Bellows to accompany them only about a third of the way down.

"We'll come to a fork," said Bellows. "You'll keep on, we'll cut right and head north."

"To where?" Lucy asked.

"Home base," said Wirth. "Down near Marysville. You're our last assignment of the season. We start again in the spring."

"I'm curious," said Lucy. "How did you know we were coming?"

"We didn't," said Bellows. "We stay near the base of the west slope till we spot wagons." He patted the lump in one saddlebag; Lucy knew it was a telescope.

"Then we ride up and introduce ourselves," said Wirth. "Your government here to serve you."

"You saved our lives," said Noah.

Wirth grinned. "I wouldn't go that far."

"Is Marysville a town?" Lucy asked.

"A trading post. It will be a town some day soon, all the posts will be. Have you thought any further about where you'll settle?"

"We're open to suggestions," said Noah.

"South o' Sacramento is nice country," said Bellows. "A widow lady I know lives there. Small house painted white; stands out like a sore thumb, nothing but land, land, land around it. Her name is Brady . . . Elvira. She's——"

"His aunt," said Wirth.

Bellows went on. "She just lost her husband and she's looking to sell. Wants to move to San Francisco to live with her sister, Aunt Mina. It's a pretty house, Miz Mitchum, and well-built. I wouldn't want to pressure you folks none, but it is worth looking into. That is, if you like what you see in the area."

"How much is she asking?" Noah asked.

"I couldn't begin to guess. Prices ain't cheap anywhere in the Valley."

"Too much gold around," said Lucy.

He nodded. "And there's the chance it could already be sold."

"We'll check into it," said Noah, looking Lucy's way.

Wirth scanned the sky. "It's getting late. We should camp and get an early start down tomorrow."

═══════ FORTY-SEVEN ═══════

Descending toward the Sacramento Valley Lucy sensed the gradual warming in the air. Ever since the rain stopped near Omaha, shortly after the wagon train departed Council Bluffs, they had been assaulted by extremes: of heat and cold, dampness and aridity, drenching storms and blistering sun.

The air was so sweet she fancied she could taste it. When she felt the light breeze coming in from the distant Pacific that picked up the warmth of the Valley, she thought back to Baltimore: to the soot, the noxious stenches from mills, factories, neglected sewage and uncollected refuse. Living in the city one developed an insensitivity to offensive smells, sights and sounds. . . . Also to the unrelieved congestion in the streets. The absence of orderliness and cleanliness made all the Baltimore of the East unpleasant places in which to live.

They had parted with Gordon Wirth and Slade Bellows two days earlier. Wirth had given Noah a crude map showing the best camping places descending the west face. Once they reached level ground it was only about twelve hours travel to Sacramento. The idea of locating near there appealed to Lucy; Marcia had mentioned Fort Vancouver as a place from which mail was sent out all over the Pacific area. Wirth had described Sacramento as mushrooming; it must have a post office.

"Ten years back John Augustus Sutter built a fort there," he had told her. "It's still standing. He shrewdly located it on the direct line of emigration from the East. They didn't start selling town lots until January of this year, but when you get there you'll be amazed at how big it is. Its population is already more than two thousand and it'll double by next summer.

"A city government was organized this past August. Almost any place in the Valley has great possibilities for growth, but Sacramento is the cream. They've already offered a million dollars for the honor of being the state capital."

"What are you thinking about?" Noah asked.

"I'll be amazed if the Brady house is still available, the way the town is growing," she said.

"How come you're so smitten with Sacramento?"

"There are people there; you heard Gordon, most of the other places are just trading posts. And all men."

"You realize, if we do buy the Brady house we'll be out of town."

"The way it's growing it'll reach us in no time."

He laughed. "Shades of Baltimore."

"Not really. Oh, in fifty, a hundred years, there'll be big cities like in the East, but in this climate they'll be lots healthier to live in. And there's so much land, they won't be cramped like Baltimore, Washington or New York."

"I wonder how much land the widow Brady has?"

"We don't need miles and miles, you're not planning to raise cattle or wheat."

"Do I look like a farmer?"

"I would like a vegetable garden out back; and flowers, of course. We could plant trees."

"Whoa, whoa. Let's first see if the property's still available."

"If it's not, we'll find something. But near Sacramento, Noah. I'd really prefer it."

"You don't have to tell me, I saw your face when Bellows mentioned the house. I wonder, do you think he tried to lead us down the garden path?"

"In what way?"

"That if we do buy his Aunt Elvira's house he'll get a finder's fee?"

"Who cares if he does? *If* the house turns out decent and the price is fair."

They circled a large lake fed by mountain streams; Wirth had told them that it provided the headwaters to a river that led to Sacramento. Noah indicated.

"That's the American River."

"How far to Sacramento?"

"Roughly twenty-five miles. We'll camp here tonight. If we start at first light, we should make it to Sacramento before sundown tomorrow. I'll walk beside the lead oxen and keep whispering that we're getting closer and closer to the end of the trail; that should speed them up like they did coming out of the desert when they smelled the Carson River."

"You're in buoyant spirits, aren't you?"

"Glorious spirits, top of the world! Lucy, we made it!"

They had! And a profound change came over him the instant the front wheels touched level ground. The anxiety in his eyes since they crossed the Missouri vanished; his whole face relaxed; the weight fell from his shoulders; his posture changed visibly, he stuck out his chest. His nerves unknotted, his upper body, his limbs, his whole demeanor, even his tone of voice, magically shed the pressures of the trek.

She recalled her father that day in the parsonage office comparing westering to circumnavigate the globe. Now they'd accomplished it; Noah had. With help along the way to be sure, and at the times when it was most needed; but in no way did that minimize what he'd done. He'd kept his head high, his eyes on the horizon, his comments laced with optimism—even if occasionally he had to bolster it with exaggeration for her sake.

Now—bless him—the end of the ordeal was at hand. He could take his well-deserved credit; he could also tell the world's skeptics that his decision to Go West had been right.

"Forgive me, but I have to say it, Lucy."

"What?"

"I was right all along, wasn't I? Not that you disagreed, nor your father; but everybody at work did, all our friends . . ."

"You were right. And I knew you would; why else would I agree to come?"

"You're kidding. . . ."

"Am I?"

She pushed him playfully; they laughed so loudly Lynette shoved between them.

"Daddy and I are just celebrating, sweetheart," said Lucy.

"Have you noticed something?" Noah asked. "We've been pushing, pushing, pushing to reach the Sacramento Valley. Now part of it's behind us!"

FORTY-EIGHT

Sacramento was considerably larger than Wirth had described, but then, he hadn't seen it since early that summer. Stores and shops, livery stables and rooming houses flanked a main street twice the width of any street Lucy knew of in Baltimore. Behind the buildings facing the street were jumbles of additional structures facing in all different directions, as if they had been hurriedly set down to be properly lined up at some later date. They included businesses of one sort or another, homes, barns, sheds, tents, even lean-tos.

Commercial buildings facing the river formed a row broken only by the beginning of the main street and were set well back from the water's edge, to protect them against spring flooding. There were hotels, a theater, a bank, the gold exchange, provision houses, a drugstore and various other stores.

Freighters and a paddle wheeler crowded the riverbank. Freight wagons jostled to get close to gangplanks, men loaded and unloaded the vessels; a loaded two-master's whistle pierced the warm air as it moved slowly out into midstream.

Noah asked no fewer than four people for directions to the Brady house before someone recognized the name. They had stopped by a tent pitched near the river, its canvas advertising coffee and hotcakes for sale. He was told that the house was situated about two miles south of town.

"You can't miss it," said a boy about sixteen with dusty, rumpled clothing. His buttonless jacket was fastened by a strange-looking device, his face and hands badly in need of soap and water. "It's white and pretty and neat. You'll spot it almost as soon as you leave town, they's no houses around it."

Noah thanked him. The boy's dull eyes were fixed on the oxen.

"You looking to sell them? I know somebody who'll give you a fair price."

"Be back after we get settled, I'll want to sell the wagon, too."

"May I ask you something?" began Lucy. "What is that metal thing holding your jacket closed?"

"New invention, ma'am; it's called a safety pin. I got the onliest one in town, maybe in the whole valley. Swapped for it."

Lucy had pictured Elvira Brady as about Abigail Havers' age, but shorter, plumper and with spectacles that rested on the tip of her nose. They found her collecting wash from the clothesline in the backyard. She looked not at all like Abigail; she was a little more than half as tall, and weighed well under a hundred pounds, a skinny knot of pure nervous energy—plucking clothespins from the line with machinelike speed and dexterity, bunching bedsheets and other pieces and flinging them into her basket without even looking.

"Be-through-in-two-shakes-Sit-on-the-doorsill-out-of-the-sun-why-don'tcha-Rest-yourselves-You-must-be-worn-to-a-frazzle-coming-over-the-big-hills."

The house with not a neighbor to be seen for a mile in any direction was still for sale. Elvira showed them through it, first cautioning Lynette not to touch "anything-china-or-glass."

The dying sun sent orange light to every corner of every

room save the kitchen. Elvira was obviously a fanatic house-keeper; the pine plank floor had been scrubbed so often the nail heads gleamed like mica. The kitchen featured a zinc basin sink with a close-top pitcher spout pump and side-board under a double window which overlooked a backyard enclosed by a split-rail fence. Beyond the fence was a fresh-ly painted red barn.

"Pump's-got-a-brass-lined-cylinder-Try-it-if-you-like."

Both politely declined. The stove, an Orr-Painter Othello Range exactly like her mother's, was not a particu-lar favorite of Lucy's. Far too much filigree for her taste, but reliable.

"Note-it's-got-an-extra-large-oven-It-stays."

Furnishings in the other rooms were of little interest to Lucy. The floral wallpaper in the front room was attractive, however; according to Elvira, any type of wallpaper was a rarity in the Valley. The tapestry curtains in both the front room and bedroom drew a compliment from Noah. Lucy liked them, but was more reserved in her comments. Like the stove, they would come with the house, and she didn't want the price increased because of enthusiasm from the two of them.

"Curtains-stay-too," announced Elvira.

The house, she explained, was a Compton Ready-Made. Noah and Lucy stared. On she rattled. Most of the homes in the area were prefabricated. Compton offered a variety of models.

"This-one-is-dwelling-number-sixteen-Cost-a-pretty-penny-new-but-included-all-materials-all-hardware-ready-to-assemble-Came-from-New-York-City-by-ship-to-San-Francisco-and-on-a-freight-wagon-from-there-Cost-another-two-hundred-to-put-it-up-plus-two-fifty-for-my-special-beautiful-custom-made-flooring-I'm-prepared-to-

sell-for-two-thousand-dollars-twelve-hundred-down-and-
a-note-for-the-rest-Includes-stove-floor-and-curtains-plus-
one-hundred-fifty-dollars-for-my-twenty-acres-which-is-
dirt-cheap-you-can-ask-anybody-Property-all-staked-
registered-with-the-town-clerk-in-Sacramento-Copy-
obtainable-on-request-Any-questions-No-questions-Fine-
When-can-you-move-in?"

"I have a question," said Noah. "How far is it from here
to the goldfields?"

FORTY-NINE

Elvira Brady accepted $1,200 cash for the house, plus a note
on the Sacramento Farmers and Miners Bank for the remainder. After waving her on her way, it took Noah and Lucy a little more than an hour to move in. She set out for San
Francisco in her box-brake wagon with her $425 parlor
organ surrounded by everything else she owned in the world.

Noah drove the wagon to town, sold it and the team and
bought everything he would need for the Great Gold Hunt:
pick and shovel, a gold pan, provisions for three weeks, a
horse and gear; and a mule to carry his equipment, along
with extra clothing, blankets and his rifle.

Lucy greeted him glumly. She was in the backyard hanging her first wash. He came through the gate leading horse
and mule.

"Aren't you jumping into this? You don't know the first
thing about mining gold: where to look, what it looks like,
the legalities of staking a claim . . ."

"Calm down, I may be in a hurry, darling, but I'm no

fool. I bought everything you see except the horse and mule
at Tabor's Provision House down by the river. Arthur—
Arthur Tabor—was very helpful. He told me nine out of ten
fellows start out not knowing one end of a pick from the
other, but you learn fast. Everybody does. Finding gold
doesn't exactly call for an engineering degree. And most
men out there find some . . . "

"I'm sure."

"Lucy, why so skeptical?"

She finished pinning a sheet to the line and moved the
half-filled basket down. "Believe me, I'm not nearly as skeptical as I am afraid. Look at you, you might as well have a
sprig of straw sticking out each ear. You *look* green as grass."

"Nine out of ten . . ."

"I heard you."

"May I finish? Arthur knows a couple of fellows who are
going back out tomorrow morning. He offered to speak to
them, ask if they'd mind if I go along with them, introduce
me . . ."

"Total strangers."

"Not to him."

"*He* is. To you."

"He's an honest storekeeper, one of the first citizens of
Sacramento; like a town father. Lucy, look at me." He took
hold of her hand, bringing it down from the clothesline, and
turned her toward him. "Green as grass maybe, but do I
look like an idiot? You think I can't talk to someone for ten
minutes and not be able to judge if they're honest or not?
Why don't you come into town right now? I'll introduce
you to Arthur."

"Noah . . ."

"Ask him anything you please, judge for yourself. Other

wives must be just as worried when they land here and their husbands want to go off to the goldfields. . . ."

"Sweetheart, please. I don't want to dash cold water on your dream, but I can't help worrying. You won't know a soul out there. The nicest, friendliest, most intelligent man you meet could be a murderer or thief on the run. Does the name Josiah Riley strike a chord? Dear God, they're probably some out there who never lift a finger prospecting; all they do is look around for people like you who do all the work, find the gold . . ."

"Lucy, stop it!"

They stared at each other for a time, not speaking; the breeze came up and whipped the wash on the line. She averted her eyes, pretending interest in the summer-browned meadow beyond the back fence.

"I hate this."

"Do you want to come with me?"

"And bring Lynette? Oh, of course, I'd like nothing better."

"You're welcome to."

"And you're being ridiculous."

"I'm leaving in the morning."

"It's insane. For how long?"

"I'm meeting Easterly and Delvecchio at the store at seven. Arthur says most fellows go out for two or three weeks."

"And which do you intend?"

"I can't say until I talk to them, it's sort of up to them."

"Sort of . . ."

"Lucy, it's done all the time: perfect strangers hooking up to go out. Safety in numbers, you know. And whatever they find they divide equally."

"I hate it."

"I know, you keep saying . . ."

"*It*. Not you. It's almost as if you'll be walking into . . . I don't know, up the gangplank onto a ship full of pirates. Cutthroats standing around just waiting for you to step on board. And, God forbid, if anything does happen, how will I ever find out? I wouldn't know who to ask, where to begin to look . . ."

"Nothing will happen. It's not exactly crowded out there; Arthur says you can search for days on end and never run into another soul. The goldfields stretch all the way from Elk Creek up north down to Tranquility. Remember the four Mormons? Remember the bags and bags of gold dust they showed us? They picked up a fortune in just a few weeks."

"*Four* Mormons, safety in numbers."

"And there'll be three of us."

"The Mormons at least knew one another."

"So will we; by the time we get back we'll be the Three Musketeers. Rich musketeers!"

"Tell me one thing: if there's so much gold out there, if it's lying around on the ground just waiting to be picked up, why is there a single, solitary soul in town? Why isn't everybody, including your friend Arthur, out looking?"

"Be reasonable, you do have to find it."

He was like a racehorse that had to run or die. Tied up to a stake it pranced about, tossed its head and ached furiously to break free and run till it dropped. She'd never seen his eyes so wide, so sparkling; so excited he couldn't breathe normally. It was far past the point of trying to talk him out of it. Hug him, kiss him, wish him luck, let him go. And he'd be back the sooner.

Only sitting home waiting the proposed three weeks would be like months in the desert.

That night her worry shared the bed with them. If he noticed when they made love he said nothing. She made him breakfast before dawn. When the sun freed itself from the horizon, spreading its brilliance all over the Valley, he set out for town, for Tabor's Provision House, for the meeting with Delvecchio and Easterly and his destiny.

Her last words brought a wry smile to his guilty expression.

"And keep an eye out for snakes, especially the two-legged kind."

FIFTY

Jack Easterly reminded Noah of Josiah Riley, though he was a few years younger. Like Riley, Easterly wore a beard, and his eyes were the same color, but he was not nearly as disheveled in appearance nor as neglectful of his personal hygiene. Easterly's eyes betrayed him as a two-fisted drinker, but he had a ready smile and his handshake was firm. Was a firm handshake an honest one? What a man said had to be a more reliable indicator. Easterly was not stingy with words; Noah listened, and studied him, and tried to decide.

Unlike Lucy, he had no knack for judging character. Would Easterly turn out to be another Josiah? The thought brought a slight and brief grimace. It wasn't like him to deny his fellow man the benefit of doubt, but the situation did involve gold, which made it special. How many men who prided themselves on their honesty and integrity had been found wanting when the elusive shiny key to untold riches was tempting them?

Abel Delvecchio was about Noah's own age. After they'd been introduced, Delvecchio had little to say, little for Noah to judge him by, preferring to leave the indoctrination to his partner. The three stood outside Tabor's place. Arthur had introduced Noah and then gone back inside to wait on a customer.

"I been out four times," said Easterly. "First three I come up empty as a bucket with no bottom, but last time I come across a small hidden creek near Hangtown; I mean small, no bigger'n a puddle stretched out long. I poked in the bottom and sure 'nough. I panned that puddle down to the last flake. Come to near seven hundred dollars."

"We're not going out panning this trip," said Delvecchio to Noah. His tone suggested that he'd brook no disagreement from his partner. He lit a cheroot, tilting his head back and blowing smoke at the sky. "Myself, I ain't found jack shit in creeks or rivers."

"There's them that has," said Easterly.

"Besides, it's too much work and too hard on the god-damned knees."

Noah noticed a curving scar hammocking Delvecchio's neck; a rope burn? He had taken pains to look deep into Delvecchio's eyes when Arthur introduced them. Delvecchio had gazed in similar fashion into his eyes; so he must have suspicions of his own. This made Noah feel better.

Unfortunately, studying a man—even listening to him—told you little about him. One had to eat, drink, work and relax with a stranger for an extended time before getting to know his character. One thing Noah did notice: Delvecchio wore a loaded pistol, so he had to be practical. Easterly wore none; did that mean he was trusting? Or was it in his saddlebag?

Noah had arrived at the store minutes before Easterly and Delvecchio, just as Arthur Tabor was opening for the day. Admitting he was curious about the two, he apologized for his "suspicious nature." But Arthur assured him that he understood. He praised both men as honest, reliable and hard-working. Not, he was quick to add, the commonest combination of personal assets in the goldfields. Not that the majority of gold seekers were untrustworthy, only that too many were lazy.

"Either that or they really believe the gold's lying around out there just waiting to be picked up." He laughed. "And all anybody needs is a burlap sack and a strong back."

Easterly was speaking. "Me and Abe here talked it over last night after old Arthur mentioned about you wanting to throw in with us. We could use another hand if you know how to use a pick and shovel. Anything we find we divvy three ways."

"Only we'll be looking strictly for a lode," interposed Delvecchio. "No panning, no rocking, no winnowing."*

"When we find our lode," Easterly went on, "we stake out the area, hightail it back here and file our claim with the district recorder." He indicated the end of the street. "Savvy? All three of us come back on account all three have to sign the claim. That makes it legal-like. Once we do, Mister, we are in business! Mind you, we got to mark it and file faster'n greased lightning even if it's as small as ten square foot."

"That way no jumper can touch it," said Delvecchio.

---

*A rocker was used to shake down creek or stream sand leaving the gold flakes. Winnowing involved tossing gold-bearing sand in a blanket. The wind blew away the sand leaving the gold.

Easterly nodded. "We file the date of discovery, the location and our names with Moses Ascher, the district recorder." Again he pointed up the street. "Next door to Basset's Funeral Parlor. Then back we ride and get to work."

"What happens if we make more than one strike, separate? Say a hundred yards from each other?" Noah asked.

"You stake 'em both; only you dasn't stake and just leave it and move on. To keep title to your claim you got to work it at least one day in three. Don't show up for a couple weeks and anybody has a legal right to take it over, legitimate claim or no. And you are out."

Easterly further warned that claim jumping, theft, even murder were everyday occurrences in the Great Gold Hunt. And wandering Indians could be a problem.

"They never looked twice at any gold before last January when Sutter's carpenter, John Marshall, found it in the creek where he was putting up a sawmill," said Delvecchio. "You know the rest, the white horde came flocking here and overran the whole of central California. Now the Indians know what gold's worth and they hunt for it, too. And if they can't find it themselves they grab yours."

"As opposed to your fellow prospectors, who'll respect any legitimate claim," added Easterly. "Which most do."

Delvecchio patted his pistol. "It's simple, Noah, just be prepared at all times to protect what's yours."

They checked Noah's purchases of the day before and approved of his choice, although Delvecchio was all for throwing away the pan.

"Anything you're curious about before we move on out?" Easterly asked.

"What happens if we find gold, stake out the spot, run back here and file and return and somebody's . . ."

"Jumped the claim." Easterly nodded. "It could wind up

bloody. It *does* happen, which is why you pack a gun. Anything else?"

Noah grinned. "Later, when we find our lode."

"Only no panning, no fucking placer mining," said Delvecchio. "It's agreed, we're going out after a lode only. Jack here worked two whole days panning out his seven hundred bucks; shit, we can dig that much out of rock in ten minutes."

"He's right," said Easterly. "The trick is to find it. It's sure not here in town, so let's get out there and start looking."

Noah held up a finger. "I'm sorry, I'll need about half an hour. My wife's stuck in the house without any way of getting back and forth to town."

He hurried off to the nearest livery stable and purchased a fine, clear-eyed mare, a Columbia road buggy with a fancy trimmed and ornamented fringe canopy top, Evans leather upholstery, carpet, toe carpet, spring boot and antirattlers.

He dropped horse and buggy off with the boy selling coffee and hotcakes down near the river, handed him the munificent sum of two crisp dollars and gave him instructions on where it was to be delivered.

He was back at Tabor's in under thirty minutes; his impatient partners greeted him grouchily.

Off they rode.

FIFTY-ONE

Lucy's first night alone in the strange house in the strange valley was unnerving well beyond anticipation. She slept little, and when she did, she was beset by dreams of dying

oxen, attacking Indians and wagon after wagon tumbling
into ravines. By the fourth night she began to get used to
her surroundings and Noah's absence. For her part, Lynette
had little trouble adapting. She played by herself for hours.
In the late afternoon, Lucy sat reading to her, and they
talked before preparing supper together.

One afternoon, shortly after she'd finished reading to
Lynette, Lucy was taking a break from the kitchen, standing in the front room watching the sun slowly sink into the
unseen ocean, when she began wondering about her neighbors. From any window on all four sides she could not see a
single house. They were there, she knew, but a mile or more
distant, well hidden by trees.

Yielding to Lynette's pleas, she was baking a batch of
gingerbread men, with the requisite raisin features and but-
tons. At the same time, she was keeping an eye on a simmer
vegetable stew made earlier. She was at the stove listening
to Lynette singing in the bedroom when the front door
banged open loudly, startling Lucy so she dropped her spatula. She turned slowly. In tramped four Indians, slamming
the door.

"No, no, you can't come in here!"

She tried to stop them from coming into the kitchen but
they brushed by her and stood gawking. They looked not at
all like the Pawnees or the Sioux at Fort Laramie: no feathers, no war paint, no clothing other than simple loincloths.
Their hair was long, black, stringy and filthy; as were they.
They were barefoot and wore no ornaments of any sort.
They did carry weapons: knives, crude spears and one hefted a rusty-looking rifle.

"I said you can't come in!"

Which struck her as ridiculous since they already were
in and clearly didn't understand a word she'd said. Her

heart was pounding so it felt like it would break in the next instant. She had retrieved the spatula; she gestured as if to strike the first one who came any closer. Hearing the commotion, Lynette came to the doorway.

"Go back to your room! Shut the door and keep it shut!"

"But Mommy . . ."

"You heard me!"

Her shouting brought inane grins to all four faces.

"Heard me," repeated the tallest and oldest of the four.

To Lucy's surprise, her initial shock and fear gave way to anger. Whirling about, she snatched a knife from the drawer. Only it wasn't a knife, it was the potato masher. She was waving it threateningly before she realized her mistake. Sight of it puzzled the Indians. Lynette came back.

"I said into the bedroom! And stay there!"

"Stay there," mimicked another Indian, addressing not Lynette but her.

All four took a step closer to her. She backed away and into the edge of the stove, sidling off to the right toward the sink.

"You stay away. . . . Don't you dare touch me!"

The eldest one, who seemed to be their leader, kept coming, walking up to the stove. He lifted the ladle from the stew pot, smelled the stew and lifting his head poured it into his mouth.

Dropping the ladle, he screamed, hopping about on one foot and then the other and shaking his hands in front of his mouth without touching it, trying to fan away the pain.

Lucy snatched up the ladle. Dipping it into the stew, she stirred, raised the filled ladle and threatened to fling it at them. They shrank back. By now the taster had gotten control and turned to tentatively examining his lips with the tips of his filthy fingers.

"All of you stay where you are!"

She got down four bowls, filling each in turn. They stood watching. She set the filled bowls on the table in a row. One of the intruders hurried forward, but she stopped him as he reached for it, the ladle against his bare chest.

"Wait, you'll burn yourself, too. Watch me. All of you watch. . . ."

Picking up the bowl, she blew on it gently. In a few moments, satisfied that it had cooled sufficiently, she handed it to him.

"Blow on it." He eyed her stupidly. "Blow. . . ." She mimed blowing.

He blew too hard, raising a wave, sending a small portion sloshing to the floor.

"Gently. . . ." She demonstrated.

Staring fascinated at the stew, he lifted the bowl to his lips and drank. It trickled down either side of his jaw. The other three opened their mouths, widened their eyes and mimed drinking with him. Then one of them snatched the bowl from his grasp and finished it off. This was the signal for the other two to pick up their bowls while the first two drinkers began a tug-of-war over the fourth bowl. Lucy boldly stepped up and separated them. She then handed the bowl to the one she'd given it to originally and filled the empty first bowl for the other.

Within minutes the contents of the pot were reduced to two small bits of potato and a single limp carrot.

"That's all, now get out. . . ."

But the leader was eyeing the gingerbread men set out on a cookie sheet. Pushing past her he picked one up, burning his fingers slightly, tossing the man to his other hand and back. Then he bit off the head. The others oohed and ahed. He finished and rubbed his stomach. The remaining gingerbread men vanished in quick succession. The stew and the baking disposed of, the Indians looked about the kitchen. One began opening and closing cabinet doors.

"That's it, everybody out. Out!"

"Out!" echoed the leader. And to her surprise he started for the front door. His hand on the latch, he turned back to the others. "Out!"

They left. Lynette came running out, her eyes saucering, questioning.

"They're gone?"

Lucy leaned against the sink trying to catch her breath, her hand to her thumping heart. Lynette gasped.

"They ate the gingerbread men!"

"Please, I'll make another batch." She peered into the empty stew pot. "And something for supper while I'm at it."

"They were Indians."

"Miwoks, I think. Gordon Wirth said they're the tribe around here."

"Will they come back?"

Lucy stiffened; she hadn't thought about that. What was to prevent them now that they knew where they could get fed? And would they bring their friends? Their families? The whole tribe? Or were these just passing through?

Hopefully.

"Welcome to California, Lucy Scott Mitchum. . . ."

FIFTY-TWO

Nine days of prospecting brought Noah only discouragement and depression. Repeatedly he asked himself how it could be that so many prospectors had made and were making strikes all around them and all they could find was empty rock. He was saddle sore, tired, frustrated and angry. The three of them sat around their campfire in the shadow of a lofty hill under a million stars crowding the quarter moon. A breeze came down the hill to tease the fire and fling sand at them.

Delvecchio, too, was disgusted; Easterly was not, but his ability to maintain cheerfulness and optimism was beginning to get on both his partners' nerves. Failing to find so much as a speck of gold was bad enough for Noah, but riding back to Lucy after three weeks and admitting he'd come up empty would be the hardest part. They'd agreed the night before he left that he'd give it a try; but if he failed he wouldn't persist in looking. Three weeks struck Lucy as ample time to find it; he agreed, which in retrospect had been rash of him. Perhaps by next spring he'd be able to talk her into letting him try a second time. Only, what would he do to earn a living over the winter?

Arriving in Sacramento he'd wondered why there were so many able-bodied men about, why they weren't all out in the goldfields. Now he knew why.

Only it wasn't supposed to be like this; not that he'd believed all the gilded rumors about finding it lying about like hailstones. But others were finding it, some were striking bonanzas, leaping from poverty to riches in hours. Wasn't he as deserving as they?

"Deserving" had nothing to do with it he realized; it was luck, fate, some mechanism that governs people's destinies that had decided to draft him into the huge army of failures. It set him to wondering: was it the day he brought home the newspaper with the article on California that he was written off? Or sometime en route? Was it punishment for quitting a job he hated? Unemployment was high in Baltimore, was he an ingrate for quitting a job that any one of a hundred men would jump at?

What was he thinking? Why feel guilty? He had every right to try this; if it didn't work out it wasn't the end of the world.

"This fucking stinks," grumbled Delvecchio. "We can't find shit." He poked angrily at the embers and flung away the stick in disgust.

"I know why," said Easterly.

"Oh hell, what don't you know?"

"Don't go getting all riled up; this happens, we got to be patient."

"What do you mean 'you know why'?" Noah asked.

Delvecchio snorted. "He knows shit!"

Easterly fish-eyed him. "Can I speak? Up to now, Noah, we been following worn trails only. Oh, shooting off here and there, checking out ledge and outcropping, but I think what we've seen so far has been gone over a hundred times by others. There's even wheel tracks and hoofprints all around here." He raised his arm and pointed up the hill. "But what about up there?"

"Go on up and look why don't you?" snapped Delvecchio. "Look at that ground, there's no traffic going up there."

"That's my point, Abe."

"You're not making sense."

"Wait a minute," said Noah, "I know what you're saying, Jack, go on."

Easterly spat into the fire, hissing. "First light tomorrow I'm going up there; it's fairly steep. Maybe that's why nobody's bothered."

Delvecchio scoffed. "Nobody's bothered because there's

nothing up there but the top. The lower you go the better your chances of finding gold, everybody knows that."

"Who says?"

"It's a known fact."

Noah looked from one to the other, would they end up at each other's throats?

"Mines are up in the mountains," said Easterly.

The hill was high enough to qualify as a small mountain, Noah thought, a good twenty minutes up to the summit before they could see what lay behind it. Maybe it rose even higher. Still, Easterly had a point: from the base you could see there'd been no ascending traffic. It showed no ledge, no out-croppings of any sort. Only, what did it look like at the top?

"You coming with me, Noah?" Easterly asked.

Noah shrugged. "I guess."

"Don't get down, son, nobody said it was easy." Easterly chuckled. "If they did they got it outta the liar's book. You said you was from Baltimore; I never been there, never been east of Johnson City. Tennessee, that is, the Volunteer State. Born and raised. My people is all tobacco farmers. Hard-shell Baptists, too."

"My father-in-law is a minister."

"Is that a fact? What denomination?"

"Presbyterian."

"Where are you from, Abel?" Noah asked.

"St. Louis, originally."

"St. Louis. Say, is it true that Court House Rock on the Oregon Trail to Fort Laramie looks just like the Court House in St. Louis?"

"I wouldn't know, I didn't come out that way; I took the Santa Fe route from Westport. I came up here from Los Angeles."

"To hunt gold."

Delvecchio shook his head. "Not at the start; I came west ten years ago when all of California was Spanish. San Francisco was Yerba Buena, there weren't a hundred Norte Americanos in Los Angeles."

"Why did you leave?" Noah asked.

"He killed a man in a fair fight, beat the hangman by a whisker and got clapped in the *jusgado* for seven years."

"Why don't you shut up, Jack?"

"Hey, it's nothing to be 'shamed about. It was a fair fight."

"It *was*, it *is* none of your fucking business."

"He's got some stories to tell about being behind Spanish bars," muttered Easterly.

Delvecchio silenced him with a glare; then his features softened. "Maybe you're right, maybe while we're here we should at least take a look up top."

"That's the spirit!"

Noah slowly lifted his gaze up the hill to the summit; it had to be close to two thousand feet. His buttocks ached, his legs seemed permanently stiffened, he was sunburnt and his nose had been running for the past week with a cold that refused to go away. He was disgusted and soul-weary with the whole useless enterprise. Hunting gold took no education, no brains; no talent, no courage, no social graces; it was strong-back, weak-mind work, as Easterly repeatedly reminded them. It was dirty work, disappointing, demeaning. What was he doing here?

He lay awake that night long after the others slipped into snoring; he thought about Lucy and Lynette, home alone without even a pistol for protection. He thought of all the things coming west had taken away from Lucy: family, friends, home, dining room furniture, armoire, her roots, her security, her peace of mind. For what? What had he given her in exchange? What had he accomplished so far to repay her faith and loyalty?

They had to find gold; and if they did would that even matter? Did wealth make up for losses of the heart? Did a gold necklace make up for banishing her parents and her sister from their lives? He rolled over, pulling his blanket closer under his chin and looked up the hill. He listened to the night wind's mournful song. And suddenly wanted to jump up, gather up his belongings, mount up and race home to her. Kiss her a hundred times, hold her, never let her go.

No.

FIFTY-THREE

Jack Easterly fried eggs for breakfast and heated a pot of coffee. A lemon-colored sun was creeping above the ridge of the Sierra Nevadas when they finished packing and started up the hill. Easterly pointed at the ground.

"You can see nobody's come up here."

"They've got more fucking sense," growled Delvecchio. Noah noticed his skin was thinnest before his morning coffee took full effect. He wasn't hard to get along with otherwise—he did his share of the work without grumbling. He disagreed with Easterly on any number of things, but almost always ended up deferring to his judgment; as now. He did have a hard time containing his impatience at their failure, but for that matter so did Noah.

Noah did wonder about his killing the man "in a fair fight"; was it in self-defense? You don't get seven years in prison for self-defense—or was it that he couldn't prove it?

If it was out and out murder they would have hanged him, so it wasn't. So he was no Josiah Riley. And he didn't behave suspiciously like Josiah. But Delvecchio volunteered no explanation of what had happened and Noah did not feel he had any right to ask.

He wondered if Easterly knew the details?

Up the sagebrush-cluttered hill they trudged.

"I'm telling you boys we're onto something here. . . ."

Delvecchio grunted.

Noah turned, the Valley spread below all the way to the distant mountains; he recognized a dozen places where they'd already searched, finding not so much as a flake. At the current price in Denver, a single ounce was worth ten dollars. He turned back and hurried his step, catching up with the others. What was so wrong with panning? Or working a rocker? Most of the prospectors resorted to one or the other, why was Delvecchio so strongly against them? Many relied on panning exclusively, avoiding the back-breaking labor of excavating a mine; some found a fortune in the shallow creeks and streams that threaded the valley.

They were nearing the top now; as expected the wind blew more forcefully, catching the brim of Easterly's hat and tilting it back on his head, tightening the lanyard . . . reminding Noah of the scar on Delvecchio's throat.

Reaching the top, they paused to look down into an irregular cut. On the far side a large bird perched on a ledge, its back to them. It appeared to be staring at a rock no more than five feet away, transfixed by the sunlight bouncing off it.

Noah gasped. "It's huge, what is it?"

Easterly whispered. "A condor, biggest bird there is, maybe in the whole world. Wingspread o' twelve feet."

Delvecchio scoffed. "Not nearly that big."

It still had not moved. It's head was naked and egg-yoke yellow in color; around its red neck was a nearly black ruff. Its feathers were nearly black as well, with white wing linings.

"What's it staring at?" whispered Noah.

"That rock." Easterly started forward in a crouch, preparing to circle the cut. The condor heard, spread its great wings and took off. In seconds it was high above them, its wing-tip feathers reaching forth like fingers.

"Marvelous," whispered Noah.

Easterly led them to where the condor had perched and the rock it had been staring at. Delvecchio hefted it; Easterly ran a finger down it. Noah watched his eyes widen.

"It's galena, Abe," he murmured. Noah stared mystified. "Galena, part lead, part silver."

"Silver?"

"Don't look so," said Delvecchio. "It's goddamned good as gold, if there's enough of it. It's silver, all right, look there . . ."

"It's only worth about a tenth of what gold is when refined," said Easterly to Noah. "But like he says, if there's a load of it . . ."

"How much is it worth a ton?" Noah asked.

"It could be as much as six or seven thousand dollars."

Delvecchio nodded. "There's always more silver per square inch than gold ore."

They searched the ground. Easterly stood scratching his head. "There's a vein here, boys, I smell it; it could be wide as a barn door. We got to lug our tools up here. Let's get back down." He glanced overhead, the condor could no longer be seen. "I do believe we've found it: our fortune. All thanks to that bald-headed buzzard."

"Condor," corrected the ever-literal Delvecchio. "Which, if you think about it is a good name for the mine."

Noah's heart pounded. Silver! He'd never even thought about it; it was all gold, gold, gold, from the day he brought home the newspaper.

"Silver. . . ."

On the way back down he got a quick lesson in the differences in mining silver and gold.

"Silver's harder to recognize," said Easterly, "but it's in this rock, no mistake. And it didn't fall from the sky, it's part o' what's underfoot. O' course it could turn out to be combined with gold, we'll soon know."

"It's white," said Noah.

"Silver shows up all sorts o' colors: blue, black as tar, yellow, green, dark red, even brown. We got unbelievable lucky here, lightning striking. If we'd set out to look for it it would have been hard as hell to find. Much harder than gold. There's no simple test for it."

The only sure way was to test samples with hydrochloric acid and nitric acid, both dangerous to carry over rugged terrain. The question was would they find enough to make it profitable to mine?

"We'll damned well find out soon enough," said Delvecchio.

"If we do we've got a big decision to make," said Easterly. Noah questioned him with a glance. "Whether we keep it all for ourselves and dig it out, or bring in somebody with big money to do the digging and refining."

"Let's not get ahead of ourselves," said Delvecchio.

They dug all morning; it was nearing high noon when Easterly threw down his pick, mopped his brow and sat. "We got something good here, boys. Seven thousand dollars a ton if not more. There's no telling how wide it goes, how deep. Abe, what say we cover up here best as we can, put in our stakes and run back and file the claim?"

Delvecchio nodded emphatically. "You file, Noah and I'll get this to the assay office and get it analyzed. We'll sign the claim after you."

"I'll bet it'll assay out at fifty to seventy-five ounces per ton," said Easterly. He fisted the air and cheered loudly. The echo carried across the Valley.

"Damn it all, Jack, what are you trying to do, bring a crowd down on us?"

"Relax, partner, I'm happy; we all should be shouting and dancing. We're gonna be rich, rich, rich!"

FIFTY-FOUR

Otto Von Reitenberg was a stunted little man with a bowed back, thining, yellowing gray hair and eyes that magnified hugely behind lenses so thick their weight pulled his glasses far down his nose, obliging him to wind adhesive tape around the bows to prevent their cutting into his ears. He stood at a faded wall map at least eight feet long that broke the entire Valley down into half-inch squares. He quickly located the strike site. Delvecchio kept his finger on the top left corner of the square for him while he got out the detailed map of the area.

"First we check for prior claim," muttered Von Reitenberg.

Delvecchio snorted. "That's Moses Ascher's job, not yours."

"I always check. Why waste my time assaying rock that already belongs to somebody else?"

"There's no prior claim I tell you. There wasn't one stake up there."

"They could have fallen and been hidden behind vegetation, or whatever."

"Mister, if anybody staked up there they'd be working
the mine, they wouldn't just walk off and leave it."

"Patience, patience." Von Reitenberg laughed. "You
boys are all alike, you bring your rocks in here for me to
assay and can't wait two minutes to run through a few pre-
liminaries which are strictly for your protection."

"I have to go," said Noah to Delvecchio. "I've got to get
out to the house, my family's been alone almost two weeks."

Delvecchio called after him. "Don't stay too long, Jack's
waiting for us over at the district recorder's to sign the claim."

"An hour," called Noah over his shoulder.

He found Lucy in the backyard hoeing, preparing the soil
for her vegetable garden. Dropping the hoe she ran to him;
Lynette came flying out the back door.

"Daddy! Daddy! Daddy!"

The three of them hugged so tightly Lynette squealed.
Lucy held Noah at arm's length.

"Look at you, you need a bath."

"No time, I've got to get back." He explained hurriedly.
She listened openmouthed.

"I thought you were looking for gold."

"Gold, silver, what's the difference? It's all money, darling, our fortune! You see that house?" He faced her toward
it. "We're going to be using it for firewood in our new mansion!"

"How can you be so sure you've 'struck it rich'? You just
got through saying you've only dug into the surface."

"Jack Easterly says it's a bonanza. That's what they call

an exceptionally rich vein, gold or silver. Lucy, our troubles
are over!"

"What *troubles*?"

"I mean we really are going to be as rich as Croesus of
Lydia."

"Calm down. Come inside, take off those filthy clothes,
I'll wash them. And there's a leg of mutton on the stove."

"I can't, I really do have to get back; Abe and Jack are
waiting. If we don't get back there fast somebody is liable to
come along and jump the claim. God forbid that should
happen after all we've been through. I promised Abe I'd get
back." He checked his watch. "It's nearly half an hour
already. I can stay fifteen minutes, that's the limit."

"In the house, move!"

He stayed twenty-five minutes; he bathed but, despite
her insistence, passed up a meal, deciding that their brief
reunion would be better enjoyed in other activity. The two
of them stood in the doorway waving him away toward
Sacramento.

By God he'd done it, found his fortune! He heeled the
horse into a gallop; would the rock assay out at fifty ounces
a ton or seventy-five?

"A hundred?"

Was that possible?

FIFTY-FIVE

The certificate was bordered with fancy scrollwork and
marked with the registration: "No. 642." "O. Von
Reitenberg's Assay Office" floated across the top on a ban-

ner, under it "Sacramento, Ca." But it was the figures beneath that seized the partners' attention. "Silver, per ton of 2,000 lb. 42⁰⁰/₁₀₀ oz. Coin value $40⁰⁰/₁₀₀."

They reined their jubilation outside the assay office; nearby was Easterly's purchase, a high-sided box wagon capable of carrying forty-five hundred pounds on its tubular axles. It was drawn by four mules.

"We'll need at least one more," said Delvecchio.

"Never mind the wagon," said Easterly. "You two get over to Moses Ascher's office and sign the claim; he's waiting. And make it fast, we got to get back before dark."

They came in sight of the hill shortly after five and went to work moving tents, equipment, provisions, even mules and horses up to the top. Easterly ripped off the top of a crate of Sears, Roebuck June canned peas and using the burnt end of a stick wrote on it: CLAIM—DELV., MITCHUM, EASTERLY CLAIM THIS GROUND. JUMPERS WILL BE SHOT ON SIGHT.

Supper that night was beans, sourdough bread and coffee; Easterly got out a jug of whiskey and insisted that all three share in a libation. He poured a full inch into each of their tin cups.

"I propose a toast. To the biggest, the greatest bird in God's sky—the California condor. And to the silver mine of . . . of . . ."

"The Condor," said Noah.

"That's good. Bird, wherever you are, thank you from the bottom o' my heart. Drink up."

Noah gasped as flame struck the interior of his mouth and flared down his throat. Easterly guffawed and clapped him on the back.

"That's sipping whiskey, Noah, not for gulping. Boys,

we should hit the hay early, get up before the sun and get at it. Get out our first two tons!"

Two days after moving in, Lucy had written long letters to her parents and her sister. Now she was at work on an even longer letter to Marcia Talley. A thought had occurred to her shortly after arriving in Sacramento: contacting Marcia in the Willamette Valley might not be as difficult as the two of them had imagined back in Pacific Springs. They'd overlooked the fact that Herman Schwimmer would be taking a job with the Hudson's Bay Company at Fort Vancouver. He'd see to forwarding a letter to Marcia. Traveling all the way to Oregon with him he'd know where she was now.

> . . . *and now we're settled, at least Lynette and I are. Which brings me to my big news. Brace yourself, Noah went out with two men to search for gold and today they found silver! Absolute tons of it, he says; he stopped by just to tell me when he and his partners had to come back to town to file their claim. I assume it's all very legal now, all necessary paperwork taken care of. And as I write this they're back at work digging up their fortunes.*
>
> *So all my skepticism went for naught, he's found what we came all this way for, bless his heart.*
>
> *I've told you about the house, let me tell you about the neighborhood. Marcia, there is none, we're out here two miles from town all by our lonesome. But everybody in Sacramento says that by this time next year there'll be hundreds of families moved in, houses going up all over*

the landscape. The way the town is growing it's hard to dispute that.

We had a fairly easy time of it after we parted company with you and the others at Pacific Springs; the Wasatch Mountains didn't turn out as hard as they looked. We left Salt Lake City and headed out into the Great Basin and very soon it got so hot it made one long for the mountains, slave labor and all. By sheer luck we made it to the Carson River and got help from two men from the Relief Committee (the Government) getting over the Sierra Nevadas.

Enough of our travels, let's talk about you. I'm crossing my fingers you've all made it to the Willamette Valley by now and are at least somewhat settled. I know getting there takes longer than our getting here so all I can do is cross my fingers. I miss everyone, you especially. Lynette asks about you every day. She wants to know if she can go to your school. I tell her, of course, if she's willing to walk back and forth. Some mother. By the time this reaches you I'm sure you'll have found a school and are working. When you write you must tell me all about it, every detail: how many pupils, what you're teaching, the schoolhouse, how big it is, what it's like. And what about textbooks? I confess I think a great deal lately about taking a stab at teaching. And I mean "stab," not having the education or the training. But I've heard that the need is so great out here that anyone with the desire to teach and even minimal intelligence (that's me) is welcome. I know what I should do is get hold of some helpful books. There's no library in town, not yet, but there's a newspaper and magazine store down by the river that stocks some books. If I knew some titles I'm sure I could order them.

Lucy went on to tell of the Miwoks' visit and her apprehension that they might return. That she'd considered leaving food out for them, to keep them outside; only that would set a precedent and they'd expect to be fed daily.

For the most part, she asked questions about Oregon, teaching, the social situation, if Marcia had maintained contact with Abigail Havers and the others, if she'd made any new friends.

Not until she signed the letter and placed it in its envelope did she realize how terribly she missed Marcia; and how near-desperately she needed a friend. Just one neighbor, even somebody twice her age, another Abigail, would be welcome.

Even if Noah worked the Condor until it petered out and then returned home for good—as welcome as that would be—it wasn't the same as finding another Marcia. Who didn't need at least one close friend, an intimate to share secrets with, someone to help in times of stress or tragedy, someone to lean on or let lean on you? She needed someone to share a pot of tea or morning coffee; a laugh, long walks, holidays and birthdays . . .

Second only to love was friendship. A best friend brought a second sun into your life, a sun that neither cloud nor rain could keep from shining. Back East she'd never wanted for friends, never dreamed that one day she'd be without a single one.

A Marcia.

FIFTY-SIX

Delvecchio came up with a first-rate idea to load excavated ore into the wagon without having to lug it all the way down the hill. They dug a shallow trough down the southwest slope almost to the base. There the slope was dug out wide enough to permit them to back in the wagon. Chunks of ore were then rolled down the trough and thumped into the wagon. They took turns standing at the tailgate and rolling each arriving chunk forward in the bed to make room for the next one.

In roughly half an hour, they filled the wagon so full Easterly's brow crinkled with concern. "She may be over forty-five hundred pounds."

"We'll drive carefully," suggested Delvecchio.

"And when we get to Sacramento we'll get ourselves another wagon, same type and weight capacity."

Noah was examining the palms of his hands.

"Blisters?" Delvecchio asked him. "Look at mine. . . ."

Easterly scoffed good-naturedly. "They'll harden in no time. When you take a leak piss on your hands."

"What?" Noah asked.

"I'm serious. The acid'll harden your skin; fellows working with brick and stone do it all the time."

Delvecchio laughed. "Just remember to wash up before you eat supper."

Four straight days they worked until they were ready to collapse. They slept like stones, rose before the sun and went back at it. Around noon of the fifth day, the three of them were taking a break at the edge of the pit when Easterly put on a profoundly thoughtful expression and scratched his chin.

"We're getting down deep, boys; it's getting harder and harder to bring up the ore. Pretty soon we'll have to bust 'em up into the size o' doorknobs so's we can toss 'em up. We got to start thinking about changing how we get at it. An open pit isn't practical down so deep."

"We'll have to sink a shaft down at the base," said Delvecchio. "That'll take a week." He got out a cheroot and lit up.

Easterly edged out of the way of his smoke. "Maybe more, but I don't see no way around it."

"How about a Mexican dig?" asked Delvecchio. Noah looked his way. "A zigzag mine, we climb down and haul the ore up on our backs."

Easterly turned to Noah. "Any day now the sides'll begin slumping—risking a cave-in. Abe's right, a shaft down at the base is the only way." Delvecchio groaned. "You knew we'd have to sooner or later," Easterly went on. "We'll need a load o' timbers for posting and capping, we'll need tools. We could . . ."

He stopped suddenly, setting his finger to his lips. Noah strained his ears, he could hear the faint rattle of loose stone descending the slope behind them. Easterly had gotten slowly to his feet. Delvecchio drew his pistol as the older man started toward his gear, his rifle and pistol. He froze as faces appeared. Indians!

Delvecchio fired instantly, killing a brave preparing to let fly an arrow. At once the air was filled with whooping and arrows and gunfire.

"Down into the cut!" shouted Easterly, and in they jumped. Indians came swarming into view, all of them crowded on one side. Noah raised his already loaded Hawken; Delvecchio was shooting like a madman, emptying his pistol into attackers who made it over the edge, fum-

bling cartridges into the cylinder, shouting. Noah got off a
shot, driving a young brave backward as if he'd hit him full
in the chest with a shovel. Down he went, kicking.

Fear gripped Noah by the throat. No protection of a
stockade here, this was wide open. He lay prone, then risked
a peek over the edge of the cut. He counted four dead, three
others badly wounded, out of the fight; the rest now charg-
ing forward. Again he fired. The distance was less than five
yards but he missed. Delvecchio killed the man with a bullet to the face.

Smoke whitened the air, the whooping and the steady
crack of pistol and rifle fire went on. Delvecchio was curs-
ing Easterly for leaving his weapons where they were now
out of reach. Noah swallowed, sweat came furiously, his
heart pounded so it tugged at its moorings, as if trying to
get free of his chest, on he fought . . .

FIFTY-SEVEN

Lynette was in her room, as usual playing with her imagi-
nary friends—Lucy was becoming increasingly concerned.
Not since Baltimore did she have a child her own age as a
playmate; only, where would she find one out here in the
middle of nowhere? In time families would arrive and build;
gradually the neighborhood would develop. But that could
be months. In the meantime Lynette's bedroom continued
to be crowded with friends only she could see.

Lucy was in the barn grooming the chestnut mare Noah
had bought for her to pull the buggy. She brushed the poll
and was working down her neck to her forelegs when

through the partially opened door she saw two men approaching the side gate. They were leading their horses, which resembled Wirth's and Bellows' horses, only these were dusty all over, not just their upper halves. One man's arm was in a sling; his older companion barely came up to his shoulder and walked as if his feet hurt. Both looked travel-weary. As they came closer she could see their somber expressions. Then the one wearing the sling tossed away a cheroot butt.

She went out, leaving the barn door open.

"Can I help you?"

"Mrs. Mitchum?" asked the man with the sling.

They came forward; the rear fence was between them and her. She leaned on the gate. They took off their hats, holding them against their chests, both so solemn-looking she had to consciously force herself to keep from smiling. They introduced themselves.

"You're Noah's partners, where is he?"

"Ma'am," said Easterly, "can we please go inside so's you can sit?"

"I asked you where Noah is. Why isn't he with you?" Her hand flew to her mouth as the significance of Delvecchio's sling registered. "My God, he's not hurt . . ."

"Mrs. . . ." began Delvecchio.

"Noah's dead," said Easterly, and hung his head.

The brush slipped from her hand, both hands flew to her breast, her knees unhinged, Delvecchio caught her.

"I'm all right, I'm all right. . . ."

Lynette came out. "Mommy, I'm tired of playing . . ."

"Come here, sweetheart." Lucy retrieved the brush and handed it to her. "Go into the barn and brush down Dolly for mother."

"Mommy . . ."

"Please, just do it. Use the stool. I'll be there in a few minutes." Lynette left muttering. "Let's go inside."

She gazed unseeing out the window as one then the other recounted what had happened. Their tones were subdued, neither was able to look straight at her.

"It was all so suddenlike," muttered Easterly, revolving his hat between his hands. "We was sitting resting when up they popped and it started. Caught me without a weapon, but Abe here and Noah was getting the upper hand when one of the buggers shot at Noah and missed, but the bullet hit a chunk o' ore lying at the side of the pit, it ricocheted off and . . ."

"Straight into his heart," murmured Delvecchio. "Killed him instantly; he felt no pain, he felt nothing."

Easterly slapped his knee with his hat; dust lifted and found a sunbeam slanting into the room. "It was crazy. I never seen anything like it. That shot never came close till it ricocheted. A superstitious soul would figure the way it hit the silver ore, bounced off and killed him, in that split second his good luck turned into . . ."

Delvecchio's hand on his knee stopped him. Lucy only half-heard. Her cheeks felt as if pins, their points dulled, were poking, leaving little stinging sensations. A burst of heat filled her upper body. What they were saying hadn't happened . . . they weren't even there . . . only their voices. . . . She wouldn't listen, they'd give it up, leave. What was she thinking? How could they? They weren't there. Delvecchio stopped circling his hat; his voice dropped lower, his words were fewer. He said something about the hilltop possibly being sacred to the Indians, which was why they attacked, not because they knew there was silver up there. He stopped abruptly.

"We're so very sorry," said Easterly. "We'd gotten close to Noah . . ."

Delvecchio nodded. Easterly went on, reaching into his pocket, bringing out what looked to be a bank check.

"We didn't bring back his horse and mule," said the older man. "Figuring they could wait, I mean the shock o' you seeing 'em . . . We didn't bring his . . . the remains neither on account o' your little one. Took him straight to Basset's Funeral Parlor. Paid for everything in advance— even the headstone. If you wouldn't mind, when you feel up to it, you could tell Basset what you want carved on it."

Easterly waved the check. "This is for about seventy-one hundred. Noah's share of the profits up to day before yesterday. More will be coming, you'll get every cent of his. The Kinsolving brothers, the company extracting our silver, keep the records to the penny."

He was *not* dead. They weren't there—voices only, her mind playing tricks. That's what came of living alone day and night for so long with no adult to talk to for an extended time. One's brain could slip a cog and wander into fantasy. This couldn't be, what they were saying was impossible—he was off working the mine, the Condor, after the bird they'd seen there. There were no Indians in the gold-fields; too many prospectors. If the Indians had an ounce of sense they'd stay away just as they stayed away from town.

"Your check, Mrs. Mitchum," said Easterly, laying it in her lap when she didn't reach for it.

She read the figure; tried to. Was it slightly more than seventy-one hundred dollars? She couldn't see it clearly; it seemed to float upward, clear of the pink paper, and shift about. Then the paper itself began to swim. It angled sharply as she started to fall. Easterly jumped up and caught her; he sat beside her, holding her.

"Are you okay?"

"A little dizzy."

"Of course."

"You need a shot o' whiskey," said Delvecchio. "Jack, go out in the kitchen, make her a cup of tea."

"That's all right," she said. "I will."

"Are you sure you're okay?" Delvecchio asked.

She went into the kitchen, they followed, their expressions continuing self-conscious, somber.

They had their tea in the kitchen. For some reason, the air was suffocatingly close, the pump dripped, a brown towhee landed on the windowsill, cocked its head, watched them, decided they were of little interest and left. Neither man had much to say, now that they'd gotten out their horror story. To dwell on it would have been sadistic. Or could it be that in hearing their own words they realized what a terrible lie it was and now were ashamed of themselves? They looked ashamed.

They drank their tea, wished her well in awkward tones and were gone. As she closed the door she could imagine their relief in getting outside, away from her.

It wasn't until she moved to the window to watch them disappear behind their dust that she realized all this time she'd been holding the check. And still held it. *Pay to the order of Mrs. Noah Mitchum, $7,100 and 43⁰⁰/₁₀₀.* In the upper left corner were the words: Condor Mine Account. She couldn't make out the signature. The pink was the pink of a lovely billowing gown her mother had taken four months to make for her. One more luxury they didn't have room for in the wagon.

Mrs. Noah Mitchum.

She didn't hear Lynette come in. She stood with her feet

together, hands folded in front of her. Where was the brush? Why were her hands so red? Lucy could never remember her looking so sober.

"Who were those men? Why did they come? What's happened to Daddy?"

"Come, sweetheart, sit. Let's hug. Then we'll talk. I'll make another pot of tea."

FIFTY-EIGHT

Lucy had a hard time trying to explain Noah's death to Lynette. There was just no way to ease the blow, and her own tears didn't help. To Lynette's credit she managed to get down some supper, and when Lucy tucked her in she fell asleep right away.

Mercifully. Lucy sat at the kitchen table, the check within reach. She wished, despite the lateness of the hour, that she might drive into town and see Noah at Basset's. But that would mean taking Lynette with her, and she couldn't subject her to the sight of her father's corpse this soon. She stared at the check: a great sum of money, with more to come. She could put the house up for sale, furnishings and all—a combination of the furniture they'd brought with them and what Elvira Brady sold or gave them that she couldn't fit in her wagon.

She would go to San Francisco, arrange passage on a ship around Cape Horn to the East Coast. Bring Noah's remains home with them.

A long trip, thirteen thousand miles; six months, she'd heard. And no pleasure trip. Her ticket would be three hundred dollars, what would Lynette's be? Did it matter? The food on board ships was notoriously bad. So many months at sea; what if one of them took ill? Back to Baltimore to pick up their lives where they'd left off. Back to family and friends and all that was familiar, predictable, comfortable, safe. The spirit of adventure satisfied, the whole experience would be relegated to memory.

What was here for either of them? No friends, for one thing. If this had happened in Baltimore, friends would flock around; here, the only people she knew were his partners in the mine. They were just easing their consciences. No, that was unfair, it wasn't their fault, they'd been sincere. And were being honest with her.

"The Widow Mitchum."

She hated the two words combined, the label suddenly stuck on. Permanently. It was true, though, there was nothing here for her. There had been for Noah, and he never tired of reminding her. He'd come here with a definite goal in mind and by God he'd achieved it. Gambled and won. Most commendable of all, he'd kept his faith intact through the worst of it. It never flagged, and hadn't it rubbed off on her? Hadn't he infected her with a trace of his fever? In him it raged, in her it was beginning to show signs of at least developing. Not for gold, for California.

An office clerk and an aspiring schoolteacher; together they'd seized on his dream, together they'd brought it to realization. Was she to throw away all this potential? Sacramento was growing daily; one could see the gradual changes taking place even in the brief time they'd been there. She had a house and land, she was a true pioneer here; others would be coming. By spring Lynette would have children her own age to play with, and Lucy would make friends, too.

Money was no problem as long as the Condor kept producing. His partners had given her this check and other checks would follow, Delvecchio had said. Abel Delvecchio and Jack Easterly—honest men, ethical, responsible partners of Noah Mitchum.

It would be difficult returning to Baltimore; hard getting there, but an easy decision to make. It would also be giving up; Noah would be more than disappointed, he'd be appalled. Here was potential, indeed; Baltimore and the East had run out of it long ago. If she and Noah agreed, as they had, that there was good reason to pick up stakes and move west, there was equally good reason to stay.

And no real reason to go running back.

Noah was buried in the little cemetery at the edge of town in the shadow of Sutter's Fort. No minister to eulogize his virtues and accomplishments, to promise a better life in heaven, to offer her condolence. Mr. Basset came and directed the gravediggers. Delvecchio and Easterly came in Sunday clothes, not a mote of dust, shining faces masked with sympathy. Lynette was left with Mrs. Tabor at the store; why put her through it, what was the point? Daddy would approve, Mother would not.

Mother was three thousand miles away.

The casket lowered, the gravediggers began filling in the grave. Delvecchio turned Lucy away from the sight and proffered a second check. It was for nearly fifty-three hundred dollars.

"One of us'll come to the house every week if you want," he said quietly. "Or if you rather, just deposit it in the bank for you and when you come into town . . ."

"That's the best way, and thank you. Both of you. For being so fair and honorable."

"What's right is right," said Easterly, coming up.

They had even sold his horse and mule for her; Easterly had given her the cash before Basset and the gravediggers arrived with the casket. Easterly and Delvecchio said good-bye. She watched them walk back to the grave, pick up a handful of dirt and toss it on the casket. The gravediggers continued their shoveling without breaking their rhythm.

Lucy sighed to herself. Couldn't they at least wait until everybody left? She placed the bouquet given her by Ernest Basset against the headstone and walked with him toward the funeral parlor, making a mental note to bring Lynette back later, after the workers were done. Basset had been elected mayor back in June. He was considered the prime mover behind the effort to get Sacramento named the state capital. He was tall, at least six-foot-six, white-haired, dignified-looking; he reminded her of Daddy. Basset was also warm and caring.

"If I may be so bold, Mrs. Mitchum, what are your plans? I mean, will you be leaving us?"

"I'm leaning strongly toward staying."

"Wonderful!" He seemed both pleased and relieved, as if they knew each other much better than they did. His reaction surprised her.

"You're doing the right thing, Mrs. . . ."

"Lucy."

"And I'm Ernest, just not Mayor Basset. Not that I mind being mayor, I just don't go in for titles and ceremony."

"I'm the same."

"Did you know that just this week four families moved in." He pointed in the direction opposite from Lucy's house. "Others are coming; come spring you'll see droves. By the end of next summer I'll wager you'll see so many houses around you you'll have a hard time keeping count."

"The weather's wonderful, there's plenty of land, there's the goldfields, but what's the really big attraction?"

His grin showed a single gold tooth surrounded by white. "The weather, the land, the gold."

They had come within sight of the funeral parlor. She stopped, stopping him.

"Tell me something, Ernest. How do people educate their children here? Does one woman convert her parlor into a schoolroom?"

"Not that I know of; every mother teaches her own." He smiled. "Which makes for fairly loose standards."

"There's no schoolhouse anywhere near here?"

"The nearest one I know of is in Stockton; that's close to a hundred miles round-trip. Say . . ." His eyes lit up. "Are you a teacher?"

"I planned to be before I was married."

"By George that's what we need around here! A school-house, teaching the little ones. To help give us a sense of community." He brought his hands together into a basket of fingers, giving Sacramento unity. "That's what I want to do more than anything else, Lucy; right now we're a glorified trading post. We've got to tighten as we grow, and for that we need schools, churches, a fire department. . . . Make us into a real community."

He repeated the word frequently as he rambled on. In his eyes was the glow of yearning, in his voice appeal for agreement; he wanted a municipal and social cohesiveness, where government would be shared, where people could develop a cultural and historic heritage they could pass on

to their heirs. They stood sharing ideas near the doorway
to the funeral parlor for half an hour before Lucy suddenly caught herself.

"I left Lynette at Tabor's; she'll think I've deserted her!"

"Go," said Basset, "we'll talk again. It's been wonderful.
Bless you for your interest. By all means a schoolhouse.
With a bell up top to tell everybody who hears it that
Sacramentoans take seriously their obligation to educate
their children. A bell, yes, that's the kind of school I attended back in Michigan. One bare board room, a potbellied
stove, one teacher teaching every subject and all the grades.
Miss Hampton . . . Millicent. I can still see that woman: big
as a house, pinch glasses with a black ribbon trailing down,
you talk about strict . . ."

Lucy waved and ran.

FIFTY-NINE

Dearest Lucy,

*Your letter arrived less than an hour ago. I read it five
times; it was like a delicious dinner after not eating in
days. I savored every syllable. Herman Schwimmer rode
all the way down from Fort Vancouver to deliver it,
wasn't that sweet of him? He insisted he had business in
Oregon City, but who knows?*

*I'm delighted at your wonderful news. To think Noah
struck it rich that soon! Others search for months and
some don't even find enough to keep looking. But the
Condor is a bonanza and you two will be rich! Hurray! I
can see it now: your enormous mansion surrounded by*

lovely gardens, distinguished and famous people coming to call, servants running around, you sending off to Paris for the very latest fashions, Noah sitting in his easy chair with a glass of outrageously expensive Scotch and a ten-dollar cigar. It couldn't happen to two nicer people.

Now to poor, dull, downtrodden me. I shouldn't say downtrodden, everything's working out fine, if slowly. Yes, I'm teaching, which is what I came out here to do. The schoolhouse is a glorified shack, but it serves, although the roof leaks in one corner and nobody seems able to fix it. At least snow doesn't blow in through any cracks. I have nineteen pupils, but I'm getting ahead of myself.

When we finally got here—all wagons intact, miraculously, and no more additions to the graves by the wayside—Abby insisted I move in with her and Maynard, bless her heart. Just until I'm established and money's coming in. I checked first thing with our esteemed mayor and found out that the teacher they had was eighty-six and thinking about retiring. Can you imagine? My credentials and letters of recommendation apparently did the trick, because they offered me the job. Although I got the distinct impression that Mrs. Dunwoodie (the octogenarian) was on pins and needles waiting for someone to come along so she could step down.

Actually, taking over proved a bit complicated. First I had to pass a series of tests on various subjects given by the mayor's wife. I passed them all and was awarded my certificate. By that time everyone evidently agreed that I showed "good moral character." Very important in Oregon City. And I thought Boston was puritanical!

I teach Mental Arithmetic, Written Arithmetic, Civil Government, Blackboard Drawing, English

Composition, English Grammar, Geography, U.S. History, Orthography, Penmanship and Reading. For which I receive the generous sum of twenty-five dollars a month and Mrs. Buchanan (the mayor's wife) has promised that the school will be kept in good repair and there'll always be plenty of wood for the stove. (Good repair evidently doesn't extend to the corner of the roof.)

Marcia went on to describe the schoolhouse in detail and talked about some of her pupils, including her prize and the school bully and an eleven-year-old girl "so pretty she takes your breath away." Then she got onto the subject of Lucy's interest in teaching.

Good for you, dear, I knew the bug would bite you, and there's plenty of room in the club. You asked about books. I recommend two in particular: Granby's Principles of Teaching, published by the Burrows Company of Milwaukee, Wisconsin, and Grade School Instruction (excellent), by Lincoln W. Wilmott, published by Howard & Fisk Publishers, New Haven, Connecticut. There are lots of books on teaching, but most aren't worth the glue that binds the pages they're printed on. Stick to Granby and Wilmott.

I got the impression from your letter that in Sacramento education is buried under all the gold, that everybody gives it their left hand. Get busy, Lucy, get parents organized, get them to build a school. Build ten! Shame them into doing it, you'll end up their first teacher. And Lucy Scott Mitchum will be a great one! You've the fire, I can tell. Not something you get out of a book, you've got to be born with it in your breast.

I never told you this, but Noah and I once talked about

you teaching. Lucy, he's all for it, just ask him. (I'm sure you already have.) He's such a good soul, so good-hearted; when I think of how he came to Olin Coombs' rescue. So caring and so sincere; sincerity is such a rare quality. In men it is! When he said he'd be behind you 100 percent I could see in his eyes that he wasn't just talking to impress me.

Most husbands just have to compete with their wives. Not him, he's the sort we women need on our side in the battle for equality. Which, I should add, I see little of around Oregon City. Abby and I will have to do something about that!

Give Noah a big hug for me and a hug and kisses for Lynette from Aunt Marcia. All hail the wealthy Mitchums, America's next great dynasty!

Abby and Maynard send their best and Herman Schwimmer asked to be remembered to you both. He's doing fine with the Hudson's Bay Company. No one seems to know where Olin and his children finally landed, but the Willoughbys are in the area.

Oregon City is on the east bank of the Willamette River; we're growing, new shops and stores and churches going up. There's talk of building a library next spring after the ice breaks in the river. I'm crossing my fingers that by then they'll be building a bigger schoolhouse as well. The way the population is growing they'll also have to hire more teachers. When the time comes I plan to set my cap for the principal's job. They'll no doubt give it to a man, but I won't be shy about my willingness to take it if offered.

Lucy paused, the writing was beginning to blur; she daubed at her eyes with the corner of her hanky. Such a charming, chatty letter, so warm and newsy, so welcome. It was like fresh air blowing into a stuffy room. She'd answer her right away. Tell her everything.

Or should she? Did one automatically rope one's dearest friend into sharing one's tragedy and heartache? Was it necessary? She thought about it. Marcia was entitled to know. Sooner or later she'd have to tell her, if she delayed too long every letter would come with some reference to Noah, to his goodness, his capacity for caring, his sincerity.

Again she used her hanky.

1851

Class dismissed, Lucy looked about the schoolroom and congratulated herself for having the foresight to insist on installing desk-chair combinations that were permanently fixed to the floor in every room. Otherwise it would fall to the teachers to straighten up their rooms every day after class. She erased the long division examples from the blackboard, straightened her desk top and sat in her little-used chair. Outside, the liberated pupils, including her own class, carried on loudly: the boys showing off for the disinterested girls.

The last two years had brought near-remarkable change to Sacramento. As former mayor Basset predicted, emigrants descended on the area in droves; Lucy's house was now surrounded by neighbors, many with children Lynette's age, many of their mothers becoming Lucy's friends. Sacramento itself now boasted a population of ten thousand souls, thanks in large measure to the extraordinary richness of the nearby placer mines. Trouble with land squatters had almost led to hostilities the year before, and that same year California was admitted to the Union. Sacramento was still waiting for the honor of being designated state capital.

The first schoolhouse, built in December two years

before, was speedily replaced by a building housing no
fewer than ten classrooms. As the population grew two
more schools went up. The school board had voted to make
Lucy principal of the first school, and later superintendent
of the three schools; she declined both appointments to
stick with teaching. The salary was a fraction of what the
superintendent's job would have paid, but money wasn't a
factor. The Condor produced for nearly eighteen months
before the lode eventually petered out.

Abel Delvecchio and Jack Easterly were still around.
Both had become wealthy gentlemen of leisure, and Abel
had given up his cheap cheroots in favor of expensive
imported cigars.

She got her drawstring handbag out of the desk and got
out the latest letter from Marcia. The school year ended in
June, less than three weeks from now. Marcia had invited
her to come with Lynette and visit; she was seriously considering it. Regular stagecoaches now ran back and forth
to San Francisco, and from there packets ran up the coast
to Cape Lookout, where she could get a public coach to
Oregon City. Marcia would come visit them, only on her
salary she couldn't afford it.

There was nothing to prevent their going other than a
speaking engagement, the evening of June 29, a Saturday.
The week of the twenty-third was Sacramento Valley
Suffrage Week, and the association would need her to direct
all sorts of events leading up to Saturday night's open meeting. Men in Sacramento outnumbered women by almost
three to one, the result of so many failed prospectors who'd
returned from the diggings to settle there permanently. The
small group of women Lucy had assembled shared her views
of equal suffrage and were willing to work as tirelessly as did
she to achieve the vote and other equal rights. They had

been the target of widespread ridicule when they first banded together and announced their objectives in the newspapers. Now, nearly two years later, even the men who refused to share their views—the majority—at least took them seriously.

She couldn't possibly desert the cause at such a critical time; she was dying to see Marcia, as Lynette was, but they couldn't leave until July.

She would write her tonight and explain. Marcia would understand; considering the reason for the delay she'd be pleased if not overjoyed. Lucy read her letter once more before restoring it to her bag.

Marcia had met a man, a lawyer, and although she was purposefully vague about her feelings for him, from the tone of her writing it was obvious it was serious. Lucy was delighted, no one she had ever known deserved a happy marriage more than Marcia, if for no other reason but that she had survived an unhappy one unscathed by bitterness or cynicism.

Drawing the strings of her bag tight she went out, pausing at the door for one last look around the room. Lynette, her timing perfect, had come in from the schoolyard and was walking toward her from the far end of the corridor. Seeing her mother, she ran. Lucy caught her, swung her three times around and set her down.

Lynette erupted in a flurry of words about playing outside. Lucy gazed into the wise and marvelous eyes of her child, into the source and sanctuary of her contentment.

EPILOGUE

On a rainy Monday, January 24, 1848, John Marshall, a carpenter from New Jersey employed by John Augustus Sutter to build a sawmill on his property fifty miles north of Sutter's Fort, discovered gold in the mud in the tailrace of the mill. Ironically, the land where the mill was situated actually belonged to the Coloma Indians, but, since the days of the Spaniards' arrival in California, the various tribes' rights to the land were conveniently ignored.

Marshall immediately informed Sutter of his discovery; the secret was kept by the two men and the sawmill workers for a few days and then was let out. The news quickly spread about the area. On March 15, the *Californian* reported GOLD MINE FOUND. The gold rush was on; in the next eleven months nearly a quarter million dollars in gold was panned and mined by squatters invading Sutter's vast properties. By 1849, argonauts from all over the world were en route to California, overland from the East and around Cape Horn to San Francisco by ship.

Noah and Lucy Mitchum were a rarity: husband, wife and child, setting out for the goldfields of the Sacramento Valley. Most forty-niners left wives and families home. While the rush for gold persisted and fortunes were made, lost and stolen, more practical-minded emigrants from the

South and East continued loading wagon trains and heading westward, attracted not by the promise of great wealth but by land: opportunity to build a new life on the rubble of failure, to exchange disillusion with their lot for promise. Emigrant families able to reach the east bank of the Missouri River at various points, from Westport and St. Joseph in Missouri and north as far as Council Bluffs in Iowa, were confronted with a choice of trails to new homes in the West.

The principal artery was the fabled Oregon Trail, which started in Independence, Missouri, and ended in the Northwest. An offshoot of the Oregon Trail, the California Trail, ascended the Sierra Nevadas and ended in the Sacramento Valley. The main trail to the Southwest was the Sante Fe Trail, which linked two routes to southern California, the Old Spanish Trail and the Gila River Trail. Eighteen fifty saw the peak of emigration, with some fifty-five thousand pioneers in wagon trains heading westward.

The thrust to the Pacific actually began in the spring of 1841, when sixty-nine people banded together, loaded their wagons, hitched up their oxen and left Missouri. The following year saw two hundred pioneers headed west. By 1844, five thousand emigrants were in wagon trains rolling toward the Pacific. Eighteen forty-nine—the year the Mitchums started west—Noah and Lucy were two in an army of thirty thousand souls.

By 1869, the year the first transcontinental railroad was completed, approximately 350,000 emigrants had rolled and walked westward. What exactly inspired the Great Emigration? There were a number of reasons. For one, many Americans (in the middle South especially) strenuously objected to the slavery they saw all around them. Their belief in freedom for all men took them to new and

sparsely populated territory in the West. The lingering
effects of the financial collapse of 1837, which sent Noah
Mitchum westward, was another reason. The chance to
exchange an unhealthy environment for a healthy one
prompted many to head west, for in the East more people
died of yellow fever, malaria, typhoid, cholera, dysentery
and tuberculosis than from any other cause.

The Mormons trekked westward to escape religious
persecution; more than anything else they wanted to be
left alone, and left alone they were in the Salt Lake Valley
of Utah. Lastly, the Civil War infected thousands of
Americans with wanderlust.

Some imaginative souls concluded that many traveled
west for no other reason but that it was there. There were
the loftiest mountains on the continent and people's curiosity about what lay beyond set their wagons and their feet on
the two-thousand-mile trek. They willingly sacrificed most
of what they owned to cram what was left into a ten-by-four
foot wagonbed in hopes of finding fertile, uncrowded land
where they could build homes.

It cost up to fifteen hundred dollars to outfit a family for
the trip, not counting the expense of getting to the selected
jumping-off place on the east bank of the Missouri. Lured
by exaggerated promise, heady with eager anticipation,
most emigrants were ill prepared for the rigors and dangers
of the wilderness, the severe extremes of weather, the burning heat, the freezing cold. Thousands perished en route,
but thousands more made it to settle and become western-
ers. The attraction of living beyond the mountains must
have fulfilled expectations, for once arrived few emigrants
gave up and returned home. Possibly because they had put
themselves through such travail, such suffering in getting
there, and had, in the process, become so toughened and so

resolute that their pride would not allow them to give it all up.

By the time Noah and Lucy Mitchum reached the Sacramento Valley, the United States had taken possession of the highly desired province of California. By August 15, 1846, all of California had fallen into American hands without bloodshed. Troops under the command of Commodore Robert Stockton and the redoubtable Major John C. Frémont were not, however, able to hold the region. The crisis lasted until Colonel Stephen W. Kearny, marching across the deserts of the Southwest, arrived with support troops. California was speedily conquered.

The year before the Mitchums arrived, the United States had acquired from Mexico all of California, Nevada, Utah, Arizona and parts of Colorado, New Mexico and Texas under the Treaty of Guadalupe Hidalgo, which ended the Mexican War. For a payment of $15,000,000 the United States received more than 525,000 square miles of territory and in return agreed to settle the more than $3,000,000 in claims made by U.S. citizens against Mexico.

The urge of the era is exemplified in the sentiments of one farmer from Missouri who decided to pick up stakes and move his family to Oregon. One evening shortly before Farmer Morrison and his family planned to leave, a friend came to the door of their log cabin. He was deeply disappointed by Morrison's decision to leave Missouri. In very certain terms he told him that journeying to Oregon was "just plain foolishness," and an "unnecessary search for toil and danger."

"Why go?"

"Well," said Morrison, "I allow the United States has the best right to that country, and I'm going to help make that right good. Then I suppose it is true, there are a great many Indians there that will have to be civilized; and though I'm no missionary, I have no objection to helping in that. Then, I am not satisfied here. There is little we raise that pays shipment to market; a little hemp and a little tobacco. And unless a man keeps niggers, and I won't, he has no even chance. There is Dick Owens, my neighbor; he has a few field hands and a few house niggers. They raise and make all that the family and themselves eat and wear, and some hemp and tobacco besides. If markets are good, Dick will sell; if not, he can hold over, while I am compelled to sell all I can make every year in order to make ends meet. I'm going to Oregon where there'll be no slaves, and we'll start even."

Like Noah and Lucy Mitchum, every individual who trekked westward did so for personal reasons; but as much as the fulfillment of wants and needs was the satisfaction, the joy and relief at accomplishing what so many had failed to achieve, actually reaching their destination. Prepared to start a new life. Families were more successful in completing the trek than were individuals, mainly because the family had a wife-mother at the tiller. From departure to arrival, she was the heart and soul of the effort. It was she who held the family together; in the most trying circumstances, against daunting odds, in the presence of danger and despair, during illness, during tragedy, she maintained a unity.

And when they got there, it was she who settled them into their new surroundings, who founded and organized and stabilized their new home, bringing to it all the attributes, the comforts, the warmth they had sacrificed upon leaving the East.